SATURDAY NIGHT AT THE TRAILER PARK

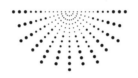

KAE G. WAGNER

Saturday Night at the Trailer Park
A Story of Love and Redemption

Inspired by my dad,
because he drove the school bus for Sunday Morning Church.

In honor of the many women whose #MeToo moment happened in the 1980's but stayed buried way too long. I share Frankie Girl's story with hope for healing, justice, and redemption. I fervently wish for a future where redemption and justice are not just ideals but realities for all those who have suffered.

CONTENTS

CHAPTER ONE

SECRETS IN THE TRAILER PARK

Frankie settled in on the bottom step at the back side of the trailer that housed *Buck's Bar and Grill*. She was taking a break in the only spot in the trailer park with a clear view of the lush, surrounding fields of corn and hay. These fields stood in stark contrast to the four run-down, rusty metal trailers in the rural trailer park the Taylor family called home.

As she kicked her feet back and forth, little clouds of dirt bounced in the air onto her dirty Doc Martens. She glanced over her shoulder at her older sister, Debbie, who sat one step up, staring down at Frankie with her dark, flinty eyes.

"Daddy loves me more than he loves you," Debbie accused, breathing shallow breaths through her slack jaw. She glared at her younger sister as she waited for a rebuttal.

Frankie kicked up another cloud of dust and stared at her sister. She hated how Debbie never closed her mouth when she breathed. The sound was obnoxious and noisy and grated on her nerves.

Debbie had a traumatic birth, requiring her to be surgically removed with a forceps. As a result, she suffered a brain bleed, which ultimately hindered her intellectual development. Frankie learned early on to be her sister's protector and to pay special attention to Debbie's words and actions. Even now, in her late teens, she was the one to lead the way for her older sister.

She took a long, measured breath. "Debbie, do we have to have this conversation again? You know Daddy doesn't love you more than me. He loves Butch more than the two of us put together."

She slid up a step and sat beside her sister. She pushed against her until they were thigh to thigh, and she wrapped her arm around Debbie's shoulders. "Daddy loves Butch more, and here's why. Because he's a boy, and Daddy says he will run this joint one day." She made a grand gesture to include the trailer behind them. "Boys rule the world, Debbie. Good thing to know."

Four trailers occupied the property. The one closest to the road was *Buck's Bar and Grill*, with its greasy kitchen. The trailer closest to it housed her daddy's bedroom and the family living room. Frankie motioned toward the third trailer, where the three kids slept. A fourth trailer was located off to the side but had remained deserted since Daddy booted out old "Eagle Eye Joe" years ago for trashing the place one night in a drunken rage.

"Daddy says he has great plans for me," Debbie interrupted while jutting out her jaw in defiance. "He says he will do something special for me in the empty trailer."

Her eyes widened, and she grimaced when she realized she shouldn't have told her younger sister.

"No, no, Frankie, promise me you won't say nothin," she begged with desperation. "Please, please, please, Frankie. Daddy told me not to say anything to you."

Frankie stared at her intensely. Debbie didn't always catch on to what was going on, but lately, she'd been hinting at things that Frankie thought were nonsense. The bullies at school sometimes called Debbie slow, and Frankie had gotten into a few scraps when that happened. She even got sent home one day when she punched a red-headed kid named Rusty. Frankie was Debbie's protector, and no one was going to push her around.

But this time, Debbie's comment caught Frankie's attention. She leaned into Debbie. "Daddy told you not to tell me what?" she questioned her.

Debbie shook her head and jumped off the steps, starting toward the trailer where Daddy slept. "I'm not telling, and you can't make me."

Frankie smiled. She'd find out soon enough as Debbie had never been able to keep anything from her.

She drew in another deep breath. Today would be another long, dull day, just like the last string of days that summer. Every day was the same; making breakfast for Daddy when he finally got up, helping Debbie clean the bar, and keeping an eye on her bratty little brother Butch.

Mama, she whispered as sadness settled in her bones. *Why'd you have to leave me?*

---

*I*n the early 1980s, the Eastern Shore of Maryland was a picturesque region located on the eastern side of the Chesapeake Bay and was known for its natural beauty, rich history, and unique culture.

The region's landscape was dotted with marshes, forests, and beaches that provided a haven for wildlife and offered ample opportunities for outdoor activities such as hiking, bird watching, and hunting. The Eastern Shore was also home to numerous rivers, creeks, and bays which drew many visitors who loved fishing, boating, and water sports.

And, while Buck Taylor and his family loved the occasional trip to Betterton Beach, it was the five-acre trailer park that kept his attention daily.

Buck's Bar was at the center of a small trailer park on the corner of MD Route 314, intersecting a country road called Lowery Lane. A rural location with hay and corn fields surrounding it, half the year it wasn't visible from the main road. A dilapidated sign on Lowery Lane signaled an arrow into the Bar.

All the locals easily found it, whether the corn was harvested or not. But tourists headed South on 314 looking for seafood, beaches, and boating, would pass by and never notice four trailers haphazardly clustered together.

Buck liked it that way. He wanted to stay under the radar and avoid trouble showing up at his front door. He'd had plenty of it when he was a kid, and his only solution was to sign up for the military the day he turned eighteen.

Now, troubles were afoot every day. His sixteen-year-old daughter, Frankie, worked in the bar, and that would certainly be a problem for the authorities. He'd taught her how to disappear in less than a second, if need be, but they were both always on the lookout.

His older daughter, Debbie, missed too much school, potentially raising suspicion, but his only goal was to provide for his family and take care of his kids. He didn't think he was asking for much, just what the everyday man would want.

Lately, things had deteriorated from bad to worse for Buck, and he felt more anger and resentment than ever. His plan for a meaningful life was shredded, and he knew he would never be the man he was a few years ago.

He was shattered. The love of his life, his anchor, was gone, and the hole in his heart would never be fixed. She was gone. Cold, dead, and buried. He had no idea how the family would survive. Mama had been the oxygen they all breathed to survive.

Buck was slumped on a bar stool when Frankie walked into the bar with an inquisitive look on her face. She swung up onto a bar stool and glanced over at her dad.

Daddy's troubled, she thought. *He's in a foul mood. I'll ask him later about Debbie's secret.*

"Whatcha doing, Daddy?" she called down to the far end of the Bar where Buck was lining up beer glasses for the night's crowd.

He glanced her way and then stared at her. "What the hell did you do to your hair?" he asked as he nodded toward her braids. "You always gave your Mama a hard time when she braided your hair, so what made you do that now?"

He winced inwardly at the thought of his wife braiding Frankie's hair. If only she were here to do that now.

"All the girls at school had braids in their hair today, and I was the only one who didn't, so I braided it after I got home from school." Frankie twirled around on the barstool and her braids whirled into the air. "No one cares about telling me anything. I didn't get the memo that braids were the *thing* to do today." She air-quoted the word 'thing', scrunching up her nose at the same time.

Frankie didn't care much for the girls at school. They were too prissy for her, and they always stopped talking and stared at her when she walked by. Most days were like that, but today was different. She was the only girl with no braids, and everyone noticed. Even the boys noticed, nudging each other at lunch and pointing at her.

Buck went back to lining up the bar glasses, thinking Frankie normally didn't care about the other girls. "Was somethin' special goin' on? Is it National Hair Braids Day? It sounds stupid to me. Why would you care?"

Frankie stopped the movement of the bar stool and walked down to where Buck was.

"Daddy," she asked quietly. "Do you think I'm a stupid girl, or do you think I'm an airhead?"

"I can't tell you," Buck said, not understanding the question. "Aren't they kind-of the same thing?"

Frankie started taking her braids apart and fluffing out her hair. "No, Daddy, they're two different things. You can change stupid, but being an airhead is forever." She laughed loudly at that thought. "I'm not stupid, and I'm not an airhead, and I'm going to stay away from those girls at school. They aren't any better than me, even if they think I'm poor and ugly."

Buck stopped what he was doing and let out a long sigh. "Frankie, you are not ugly, and no one can call us poor either." He lifted his arms and motioned to the rest of the bar space. "I have a business, and I pay the mortgage. Have you ever gone hungry or needed clothes to wear? If we don't have food and you don't have anything to wear, then they can call us poor."

Buck was a proud man. He would never admit to being poor, even though money was tight right now.

"Go on and get your 'poor self' out of my bar. Find your brother and sister and give them their chores. None of my kids are going to grow up lazy." He opened the back door and pointed toward the porch. "Go now and make sure Butch is doing some-thing productive to keep himself occupied."

Frankie gave her dad a half-smile before walking out the door. He was very moody and preoccupied these days, and she felt his sadness deep inside her heart.

Today was not the day she would dig for more details about what Daddy had in mind for Debbie in the empty trailer. She decided to do her homework and would wait for an opportunity after the weekend.

What was Daddy scheming now and why was it a secret? Whatever it was, Frankie knew they couldn't keep it from her much longer. She knew Debbie wouldn't be able to hide anything from her for long.

*S*aturday nights at *Buck's Bar* started around four in the afternoon. Most of the bar's patrons were tradesmen working in masonry, carpentry, and roofing. They started work early and finished mid-afternoon since Saturday was the end of the work week for them. They were hungry and thirsty by four o'clock and ready to get off the job site.

The bar went from empty to standing room in only a matter of thirty minutes. Buck and Frankie were pulling draft beers, popping tops off cold Millers and Rolling Rocks, and taking orders for burgers and fries. The menu was limited, offering grilled and fried foods only, which often required Frankie to sidestep grease splattering off the hot, sizzling grill.

Someday there's going to be a fire, she thought, eyeing the piles of napkins and paper plates cluttering the countertop on either side of the grill as her arm burned from another greasy splat.

The hungry crowd pressed up to the bar for their orders. They were impatient and noisy and yelled out their orders while Buck and Frankie slammed burgers on the grill and passed out drink orders. Soon the crowd quieted down and dug into their messy meals.

The smell of fried food and the feel of cold beer on the back of their throats settled the guys down as they relaxed from the hard week of work. Conversation, jokes, and barbs were flowing loudly as the bar got noisier.

Frankie took a moment to survey the crowd. The regulars were here, and mixed in were several new faces. One caught her attention, and she made a mental note to keep track of him. He was too slick to be from around here.

The food and beer orders kept coming in, and Frankie managed to keep up the pace in the crowded bar. She was flipping burgers, and Buck was pulling beer out of the cooler when a guy at the end of the bar started getting noisy.

He was feeling the three beers he'd guzzled since he sat down, and now he was getting raucous and loud.

"Hey, Buck," he yelled after slugging down the rest of his beer. "How about another beer and another hamburger? I'm hungry."

"You got it, George," Buck nodded to the guy as he reached back into the cooler. "You might want to slow down, though. Don't wanna hav'ta cut you off so early in the night."

"No, sir, I ain't slowin' down," grunted the scrawny kid. "It's Saturday night, and I come here to let off some steam."

Buck slid him a beer, "No worries, bud, you just relax, and everything will be fine. Just don't get stupid." Buck laughed at George, and the rest of the crowd turned away.

"Hey, Buck," George added in a quieter tone of voice. "I'd like to talk to your daughter someday. Maybe learn more about her. Be her friend, you get my drift?" And he winked at Buck.

Frankie froze, pausing while the burger she had been taking off the grill was still in mid-air. Buck ignored George and walked out of the back of the bar to get more beer.

"What the hell do you mean?" Frankie turned toward George and asked in disbelief. "What would you possibly want to talk to me about?"

George laughed in her face. "Not you, Frankie. I don't want to talk to you. What would I want to talk to you about?" He shook his head and scoffed. "I got nothing to chat with you about. Besides, you're too skinny and got nothin' too exciting goin' on." He reached over and gestured toward her chest.

Frankie was livid now. Not only did George insult her, but he was hinting at some sort of nastiness.

Oh my God, Frankie thought, *he wants Debbie.* She scanned the room for her father, but he was bringing in beer from the far side of the room.

She moved swiftly to where George was sitting and lowered her face to his. "You'd better watch what you say, George, or I will have Daddy kick you out of here."

George sneered and reached up to touch her hair. Frankie jerked back and moved away from him. "We'll see what happens when I ask your Daddy about your sister." George laughed again and turned away when he saw Buck stacking the cases of beer he'd just brought in.

Frankie moved back to the grill. A chill crept up her spine and her fight-or-flight instincts were on high alert. Her mind was flooded with so many scenarios of Debbie's vulnerabilities.

Daddy would never let anything bad happen to Debbie...would he?

What did George have in mind...exactly?

Would George do anything to Debbie...something terrible?

Frankie's mind raced, and she was a jumbled mess inside. Her stomach rolled at the thought of Debbie being on George's radar. Even though Frankie was the younger sister, she was the one in charge. She was the protector.

Frankie wondered if Daddy overheard George's comment. She glanced over at him, but he had turned away and was putting more beer in the cooler. From his reaction, Frankie couldn't tell if her father caught the insinuation George made or not. Daddy ignored her and kept working.

Debbie wasn't in the bar often because she couldn't keep up with the work. Her body had developed at an early age, and at 18, she had a Marilyn Monroe body with shapely curves and an hour-glass figure. She was used to boys staring at her and whistling when she came by.

The occasional times she visited the bar, Mama had always shushed the guys and told Debbie to never mind those silly men. But since Mama was gone, Frankie was working in the bar with Buck, and she didn't like George's sudden interest in Debbie.

Drinking at Buck's Bar and Grill on a Saturday night was the highlight of the week for these guys, but just under the surface, it seemed like trouble could easily erupt.

George had moved from the bar to a table and was doing shots with his buddies when Frankie finally had a chance to talk with Daddy.

"Did you hear what George said to me?" she asked in a low voice. "I think he's up to something, and I'm nervous about what he might do to Debbie." She leaned closer to Buck as he threw more burgers on the grill.

Buck glanced at Frankie, motioning for her to move back from the grill as he flipped some of the burgers.

"Don't you worry about George," he told her dismissively. "I have him under control. He's not going to do anything except drink shots and beer. Besides, he always pays his bar bill and doesn't cause any trouble."

Buck turned his back to the grill and moved closer to Frankie. "Frankie Girl," he said as he slouched against the counter, "I'll always take care of you kids. But cash is tight right now, and we need to keep these guys happy. We all have a job to do here to keep a roof over our heads. Do your job, and it'll all work out somehow."

Frankie stared at Daddy with a question on her face. She wasn't sure what he meant about money being tight and her doing her job, but it didn't sound promising. She'd never noticed her dad talk about money problems much before, but lately, he'd mentioned it a few times. Frankie wondered if she should be concerned.

"Hey Frankie," George shouted from across the room, "I'm going to take your sister on a date! What do you think of that?"

The whole room erupted in laughter, and George was slapping his thigh repeatedly like he had just said the funniest thing ever. She threw him a wicked glance and turned her back on him.

A few moments later, she was in a cold sweat as a freaky thought crossed her mind. She turned George's comment and Daddy's words over in her head. Was this related to the secret Debbie and Daddy had?

Her brain buzzed with an idea so horrible it had her stomach rolling with nausea, and the bile rose in her throat. She sat down on an overturned milk crate and hung her head between her legs as she sucked in a deep breath.

Buck peered over at her and shook his head in disapproval. "You can't sit down on the job, Frankie. You've got to take these plates over to table fourteen. They're waiting for their burgers and fries."

Frankie lifted her head and shot him an angry look. The nausea lingered, but she shrugged her shoulders and grabbed the plates as she attempted to shove the thoughts from her mind. "Sure, Daddy, I've got this."

As she walked the plates over to table fourteen, she surveyed the bar, looking for George. She couldn't see him anywhere but thought it was too early for him to have gone home. Feeling suspicious of his absence and wondering what the rest of the night would be like, she slipped into the bathroom and took a deep breath.

Whatever is going on here at the trailer park is creeping me out, she thought. *I wish I had someone to talk to.*

CHAPTER TWO

MAMA, IS THAT YOU?

*M*ama was walking down the corridor of light toward Frankie, calling her name.

"Come join me, Frankie Girl," she said with a softness in her tone. "Come to Mama. Take my hand."

Tiny purple flowers were braided into Mama's blonde hair, her blue eyes sparkled brightly, and she held out her hands to Frankie, beckoning her to take her hand.

The glow framed Mama's body, giving her an angelic radiance. Frankie ached to reach out and touch her, to feel her Mama's arms around her and to bask in the sweet love her mother always showered on her.

The air in the corridor of light was cool and as Frankie watched Mama coming closer, the light behind her grew brighter and changed colors from bright white to an azure blue and then a vibrant purple. Frankie was mesmerized by the changing hues and watched intensely as Mama came to the end of the corridor and started down the stairs toward Frankie.

Mama pushed off the stairs and floated down to where Frankie sat on a small bench in a wooded area lush with flowers and singing birds. The scene was ethereal and surreal; pink and purple flowers blossomed on vines around the bench and the fragrance was heavenly.

Frankie reached out as Mama's feet touched the luscious green grass and she settled down beside Frankie on the bench. Mama seemed alive, her bright eyes were focused on Frankie and her cheeks were a delicate pink. Her skin was milky white, and her hair glowed with a silky sheen. She seemed so real, so vibrant, and so full of life.

Frankie stretched out her arms toward Mama, wanting to hug her closely, bury her head in her shoulder, and smell her sweet perfume, just like in old times.

Are you dead, Mama? she asked, her voice floating around them as the words fell from her lips in slow motion.

Mama put her arms around Frankie and gave her a warm hug and whispered in her ear. *Frankie Girl, I love you.*

Mama, I miss you so much. Frankie clung to her mother and tried to hold her down on the bench, but Mama was rising, flying back to the stairs and the corridor of light. Frankie tried to run after Mama, but her feet felt like they were trapped in heavy mud, and she could barely move. She reached the bottom of the stairs and tried to grab the hem of Mama's dress. Just as she touched the shimmering gown and her mother floated back to the light, Frankie's body twitched, and she jerked awake.

Another Mama dream. She cried softly into her pillow and pulled the covers over her head. *I miss you so much, Mama.*

*O*ne Year Earlier...

Mama was asleep on the sofa when Frankie got home from school and cracked open the door to her parents' trailer. It was the smallest trailer on the lot with one tiny bedroom, bathroom, small kitchen, and combined dining area and living room.

Years ago, Buck and his new bride, Eloise French Taylor of Philadelphia, had moved to the Eastern Shore of Maryland and purchased a small trailer park. Buck had recently been discharged from the Army and the newlyweds dreamt of opening a bar to make a life together and prepare for their future family. They remodeled the largest trailer into Buck's Bar & Grill and took the smallest trailer for themselves. The other two trailers were rented out until Ellie found herself pregnant with one daughter, and shortly after, another one.

Over time Buck's Bar became a modest success and Buck and Ellie were happy in their trailer park. Buck loved his free-spirited soulmate wife who grew vegetables, sewed dresses for her daughters and couldn't contain her delight when they had a son several years later. She was the light of his life and made him laugh.

Mama obsessed over mail-order seed catalogs that were filled with colorful pictures of exotic flowers with shades of deep purples, pale pinks, and sienna oranges. She planned extravagant gardens, carefully cutting out her favorite botanicals and arranging them into gardens on graph paper, showing the kids how someday soon she'd liven up the trailer park with her creative garden designs.

Buck's love for Eloise was fierce and he felt he was born to be her protector. Mama often said he rescued her from dirty money, but Buck knew he was just lucky to have won her love.

He still couldn't believe what she gave up for him. To her wealthy family, he was a nobody, a good-for-nothing con man. But to Ellie, he was the world. She was sure her mother and father were dead wrong about Buck, so she walked away from everything to elope in Elkton, Maryland. With the stroke of the District Justice's pen, she left behind a life of status and ease.

The Taylor kids didn't have many details about their Mama's past. She seldom talked of her parents, except to say that Buck and the kids were more important than anything else in her life. She'd squeeze the kids tight and pull them into her for a hug and swear that she'd be the best Mama a kid ever had. Way better than her mother, who was strict and never played with her daughter or paid any attention to her at all.

Frankie thought Mama was the sweetest mother ever. She didn't care about money or working or fancy things; she was content to stay put in the trailer park and care for her family's needs. It seemed like whatever she touched could be made into a work of art; a small stone suddenly came alive with Mama's paint-brush revealing a pretty flower or she'd weave a leftover piece of fabric to hide a torn sleeve and bring new life to an old dress. Mama had a knack for taking everyday objects and turning them into little collector's works of art like she was a master craftsman.

And then, after years of working hard and putting her family first, she was ill. She'd been sick longer than anyone knew. Even Buck wasn't aware when she first discovered a lump in her breast and dismissed it as nothing. Then, later on, she discovered another. And by the time she faced the fact that something was deadly wrong, the Doctor's diagnosis gave them little hope.

The doctor didn't even glance at Mama when he described to Buck what would happen next as the cancer progressed. He detailed how Mama would get sicker, she wouldn't be able to care for herself and the prescription he was writing out would alleviate the pain but only delay the inevitable. He explained they were out of options, there was no treatment to help her get better, and the disease was too far gone, but the medicine would keep her from suffering too badly.

"I'm sorry I can't do more, Mrs. Taylor," he said, with a sideways glance at the pale woman as he left the room.

When Buck and Eloise got home after the doctor's appointment, he made a bed for her on the sofa and held her close. She clung to him, but he couldn't bear to look her in the eyes. Eventually, she faded off to sleep. He went over to the trailer housing Buck's Bar, poured himself a drink and put his fist through the bathroom door.

Anger at his helplessness raged in him and he swallowed his drink in one long draw, then poured another. Anything to stop the dark rage in his heart.

The kids went to school every day to keep life as normal as possible. They never talked about Mama at school, but on the bus ride home, knowing glances would be exchanged between them as they neared the trailer park. After the bus dropped them off, they'd head over to their trailer to drop off their backpacks and get started on homework. Debbie and Frankie were in several high school classes together because Debbie had been held back due to her developmental issues. Frankie would assist her sister and together they would get their assignments done.

One day, Daddy and Mama were sitting in the big trailer when the kids got off the bus and went to start their homework. Their parents were sitting on the sofa, holding hands, and waiting for them.

Mama motioned for the kids to sit on the floor in front of them and then explained that she was very sick and would be in bed for a long time.

"Don't you kids worry about me," she said and held out her hands to them. They all scooted closer to her and watched her intently as she gazed from one to the other. "Daddy and I have a plan for me to get better, but it's going to take some time."

The room was quiet, and no one breathed until Butch fidgeted with his shoelaces and then jumped up beside Mama and hugged her. Debbie followed and sobbed as she repeatedly questioned Mama about whether she was going to die.

"Shhh, hush now," Mama kept saying to calm Debbie down.

Frankie stood up and glanced at her father. She already knew her job would be to take care of Mama, whatever that would end up being. Daddy nodded and motioned toward the counter where colored pill bottles were stored in a plastic bag. The pills would be her job now.

She looked at Mama and her throat was constricted with a large sob. She pushed Debbie and Butch aside and knelt beside Mama and hugged her tight. "I love you, Mama, and I'm not going to let you die." She whispered as Mama clung to her tightly.

As the days passed, Frankie became the most efficient adult in the family. Daddy was heartbroken and stayed in the bar as soon as the kids came home from school. Butch was bouncing off the walls with anxiety and tension he couldn't handle. Debbie was exhausted from sobbing without relief. Frankie oversaw Mama's medicine in the morning and after she got home from school.

Frankie was cautious as she neared the trailer when she got off the bus. She was never sure what she would discover when she stepped in to check on Mama after school. Frankie couldn't fight the fear that crept into the corners of her mind.

She was fearful that one day she would walk in and it would have been Mama's last. She was afraid she would be the one to find her in eternal sleep, peaceful as ever on the couch.

The past days Mama had been crying with pain and Frankie knew that meant things were getting worse. The end was nearing with each passing day.

Today, she stood at the door watching her sleeping mother and her stomach clenched with fear and sadness. She held her breath and counted two heartbeats as she waited for her mother's chest to rise. Mama's breathing was much slower and as she inhaled a shallow, ragged breath, Frankie sighed in relief.

Her mother looked like an angel, with her blonde hair curled around her face, eyes closed, and a peaceful look that masked her continual pain. Frankie took in the scene for a long time before she moved across the room.

It seemed like an eternity since this cycle of Mama's sickness began. Medicine, homeopathic treatments, long low talks with Daddy that stopped when the kids walked in the room. Mama was exhausted most of the time and Frankie was afraid. She was, in fact, terrified.

After Daddy and Mama initially told them about Mama's sickness, they didn't mention it again. No one gave Frankie any more information, not even their neighbor Tesh, and that made her even more anxious. She was old enough and had a right to know what was going on.

She didn't dare ask Daddy because he was in bad shape, too. He seemed preoccupied, sad, angry, and frightened, all at the same time. His emotions seemed all tangled up. Frankie stayed quiet when she was around him and didn't want to upset him any more than he already was.

She hesitated to wake Mama, but the evening dose of pills was due. Daddy said the doctor was adamant about giving her the medicine at the same time every day. Waking her seemed like a cruel thing to do because of the constant pain causing Mama so much suffering.

Frankie found the bag of pill bottles in the cupboard and began counting out the many medicines, very carefully palming them into piles on the coffee table so there was no mix-up on the dosage.

"Mama," she said quietly as she gently shook her mother's shoulder. "Can you wake up? I need to give you your meds." Her mother didn't move.

"Mama," she said again with a little more force. "You have to wake up so you can take your pills."

"Frankie, my baby girl," Mama murmured as she stirred from her sleep. "I was dreaming the most beautiful dream. Sit here beside me and I'll tell you about it."

Mama's dreams were always about flowers and gardens and the beauty of nature. She tenderly described her dream and softly spoke of the same dream that seemed to be on repeat. Flowers, gardens, blue skies, and walks with her father. The dream was always the same.

Mama was talking more than she had for days and Frankie was relieved that she was feeling better. She wanted to ask a question she'd never dared to pose before.

"Mama, when you were a little girl did you have lots of gardens at your house?" Frankie held her breath. Would her mother share any childhood memories with her? Mama always brushed off any questions about her past life, but Frankie hungered for information about her grandparents and what Mama's childhood was like. A hazy memory of a mansion with beautiful gardens passed through Frankie's mind from time to time. But she was never sure if it was an actual memory or an image she had pieced together from the few fragments Mama shared.

Her mother shifted her position on the sofa and took a deep breath to ease her discomfort. "Frankie, I grew up in a big house with beautiful gardens. The flowers were my friends because no one was allowed to come and play with me."

She turned to her daughter and motioned for her to sit on the edge of the sofa. "Kids at school called me names and said my Daddy was a bad man. I never knew why they thought he was a bad man. He was nice to me. He said I was his beautiful little lily. He loved flowers, too. We used to walk in the gardens together."

Mama closed her eyes as memories flashed through her mind. A wave of pain swept over her, and Frankie watched her wince beside her on the sofa. Talking was becoming more difficult for Mama, but she wanted Frankie to understand a few things about the grandparents Frankie had never met. "Your grandmother and grandfather were good people, but they never understood me. They never knew I was a lonely child and that little girls should have more than flowers for friends."

Frankie helped her mother sit up as she began the long process of helping Mama swallow all her pills. "Do you want me to call your parents about your cancer?" She sucked in her breath waiting for Mama's answer as she handed her several pills at a time.

"No ma'am," Mama said immediately as she grabbed Frankie's arm. "You are never to call them, do you understand, Frankie? They said if I married Daddy, I would be dead to them, but I married him anyway and you want to understand why I would leave a rich family for a poor soldier?"

Frankie nodded, hoping her mother would continue. Mama paused as she took small sips of water to wash down the pills. Her lungs spasmed with a phlegmy cough between the medications as she choked them down.

"I married your father because he loved me more than anyone else ever did. He said he would protect me and take care of me, and he has. You three kids and Daddy are the only family I ever needed. You are all the love I've ever had."

Frankie's interest in her grandparents was even greater now that Mama had given her a glimpse into her childhood. Even more, questions arose about how bad her grandfather could have been and why sweet Mama didn't have any friends. She was determined to find answers and made a vow to locate these mysterious people and make them understand the truth about their daughter and her family. Mama and Daddy had a good life together, with three great kids and the French grandparents deserved that information.

We might not live in a mansion with lush gardens, Frankie thought to herself, *but we have love in this trailer park. As long as we have Mama, we have love.*

The thought of losing Mama ripped through her heart and her tears dripped onto the remaining pills in her palm, tinting the lines of her hand a delicate pink.

---

*B*uck closed the trailer door softly, not wanting to wake Mama as she slept. She seldom woke up when he entered the small trailer lately and he was grateful for every moment she didn't feel the pain that made her restless and delusional.

Frankie was in charge of Mama's medicine procedure, and she had divided out the appropriate pills for Daddy to give Mama during the school day. Buck hated the pill routine because Mama had resisted the medicine in the past few days and would flail about, pushing the pills and water away from her mouth. He had called the doctor and was waiting for a new liquid medication to keep Mama as comfortable as possible in her declining condition.

Buck's feeling of helplessness was foreign to him, and he countered it with anger and booze. It was noon, Mama was still sleeping and he already had his first drink. He hated himself.

Back in the tiny bedroom he fished through the closet and found his one white shirt. He replaced his stained tee shirt and put on a nicer pair of trousers than his jeans. Glancing in the mirror and seeing his image made him stop cold.

Looking back at him was an aging, exhausted man, in ill-fitting clothes with messy hair. He tried to flatten his hair with water from the bathroom, but he only managed to slick it back and his cowlick was not behaving. He shrugged. *It's only the minister,* he thought to himself. *He's seen worse.*

Buck moved through the small hallway into the living area and tiptoed toward the door.

"Where are you going, Buck, all dressed up like that?" Mama was staring at him with a glazed look in her eyes.

Her voice caught him by surprise, and he stopped just as his hand was reaching for the door handle. "Nowhere, Ellie, just going to clean up the bar." He turned to see if she believed him and saw that she had closed her eyes again and was breathing shallow sleeping breaths.

He waited for what seemed a lifetime and then reached for the door handle again, quietly turned it and silently left the small trailer. A long, slow exhale made him realize he had been holding his breath to make sure Ellie was asleep before he carried out his plan to visit the minister at the nearby church.

He drove the short distance to the small country church by the side of a lake and parked in the gravel driveway. One car was in the parking lot and there man on the far side was mowing the spacious churchyard on a tractor with an attached mower.

Buck had never met the minister, he wasn't the church going type, and this was by far the worst reason to go to a place of worship. But it had to be done and Mama didn't have much time left. Her skin color was changing, and the doctor had indicated in his last visit that Mama only had a few more days or a week at the most.

The man on the tractor was driving over to where Buck was

parked, and he cut the engine when he neared Buck's pickup truck. "How can I help you?" he asked politely after the tractor motor shut down.

Buck hesitated for a moment to control his emotions before he spoke. "I'm here to see the minister. Are you the minister here?"

"The minister is out of town this week, that's why I'm mowing the lawn today." The man wiped the sweat from his forehead with his sleeve and stepped down from the tractor. "Can I give him a message when he returns?"

Buck's shoulders slumped at the news. He wasn't sure Mama could hold on that long.

"I'm Buck Taylor, from up the road." He motioned in the direction of the trailer park which was out of view from the church. "We're right on the corner of Lowery Lane and I'm here to talk to the minister about my wife."

"Great to meet you, Buck, I'm one of the church members here and I help with the building and mowing when the minister needs me. I'm Charles Bailer, but everyone calls me Chuck."

Buck smiled briefly. "I'm Buck and you're Chuck. Nice to meet you." The two men shook hands.

Mr. Bailer smiled at the small joke, studied him for a moment, and noted that Buck was familiar to him.

"Buck, are you Mr. Taylor from up the road, at the trailer park?" Mr. Bailer vaguely remembered him, but the faces of the Taylor children flashed through his mind. They had occasionally been passengers on the church's Sunday Morning school bus.

"If I remember correctly, you have two girls and a boy," he continued. "I used to drive the bus on Sunday morning and your children would come to Sunday School here at the church. Do I have that right?"

Buck nodded, remembering how grateful he had been to sleep in on Sunday mornings. The kids loved going to Sunday School, too, but they especially loved the Peppermint Patties Mr. Bailer doled out on the trip home. After a couple of years, they seemed to lose interest and stopped going.

Chuck glanced his way. "How can I help you today, Buck?"

"I'm here to see the minister because..." Buck couldn't bring himself to say the words. He hadn't said the words to anyone. He didn't ever want to say the words: *my wife is dying*, but he had to say them today. He had to tell Chuck his wife was dying and suddenly he found tears flowing down his cheeks.

He fought hard to keep his composure and bit down on the inside of his lip to stop the tears.

"I'm here to see the minister because my wife is dying, and she wants us to have her funeral here in your church. She would like a proper service."

He looked up to see Chuck's reaction and continued. "She and I have never been to church here, but she always comments about it when we drive by. When the doctor told us how sick she was on our last trip to his office, she mentioned your church on the way back home. We stopped and drove in, and she pointed to your graveyard and said, 'Bury me at that church, so I'm close to home.'

Buck leaned against his truck and weariness engulfed him as his denial of Mama's death was stripped away. The fear and anger on his face were evident to Chuck who also noted the slight hint of whiskey on his breath.

"How long does she have to live?" he asked.

"Maybe a few days, maybe a week."

Chuck looked out toward the small cemetery where five grave-stones were visible. He had dug every one of those graves, and the ground held the tragedy of a family killed in a fiery car crash.

"Are you asking for a funeral and a cemetery plot?" He turned back to Buck as he leaned against the front of his tractor. "I'm sure we can help you, Buck. I'll need information from you. Can you take a moment and come inside the church?"

The two men walked silently into the quiet church and Buck paused at the doorway. It had been decades since he'd seen the inside of a church and he was immediately uncomfortable, even a little afraid. He didn't spend much time thinking about God, but Mama always said God loved everyone so maybe he had a chance.

Chuck went through the few pages of paperwork and had Buck sign a request for a funeral service and a burial plot. "You rest easy now and tell your wife what you've done. It will help her in her final days to know that her wishes are granted, and God has a spot waiting for her in heaven."

He reached out to shake Buck's hand and asked if he could say a prayer for Buck's wife.

Buck gripped the back of a pew and his tears spilled onto the bench as he leaned over for the short prayer Chuck offered up. At the sound of Amen, and without a goodbye to Mr. Bailer, he headed to his truck before his sobs could be heard by the kind man inside the country church.

He held Mama tightly when he got back to the small trailer. "The church is yours for a service and burial," he whispered in her ear.

Her eyes flickered briefly, and she kissed him sweetly on the cheek. "You're a good man, Buck Taylor," she murmured. "I love you forever."

CHAPTER THREE

NOTHING LEFT IN HER

*M*ama died on the stained sofa in the little trailer two days after Buck went to the small country church to ask permission for her funeral service and burial. As she passed, he clutched her hand and breathed every last shallow breath in rhythm with her. The moment she stopped breathing, Buck was sure he did, too.

He sat on the floor, next to the sofa where Mama's lifeless body lay and sobbed. He cried out, pleading for God to bring her back to him. He was completely devastated. His heart had been ripped out of his chest and was torn to pieces. Buck had no idea what he was supposed to do now. He wasn't prepared for her to be gone.

He was confused and utterly broken. Was he supposed to put a sheet over her head? Should he call 911? He didn't know what he was expected to do with Mama's lifeless body. The kids were at school, and it was eerily quiet in the little trailer where he and Mama had spent so many years together.

He stared at her body, willing her to wake up. He so badly yearned for her to sit up and glare at him while saying "Just kidding, Buck, I'm not dead after all." He waited for her to take one more breath, make one more movement, or let out one last sigh. He was scaring himself with crazy thoughts of whether she was dead or just pretending.

Finally, he reached out to touch her face and gasped at how soon the coldness was settling into her soft skin. He kissed her forehead and his tears dropped on her chin. He tenderly wiped them off with his sleeve.

He hadn't cried like this or been so utterly confused and abandoned since he got out of the Army. Back then, he was completely lost and alone. He came back to the States after Vietnam, feeling so afraid.

He had been numb for a long time, drinking too much and getting into fights at the slightest passing comment from another drunk. He was jumpy for a fight. His nerves were always on high alert until he drank himself into a stupor and passed out. Only then did he get some reprieve from the thoughts that plagued his mind.

But when he met Mama, things changed. After meeting Eloise French at a Servicemen's picnic in Philadelphia, his heart filled with a reason to continue living. With Eloise French, he felt like a man instead of a useless failure with ugly scars and a bad tattoo.

At night, when they lay in each other's arms, she would trace his scars with her lingering touch and call them his hero's badge of courage and honor. He could have slain an army with how proud she made him feel.

But when his terrifying, war-filled nightmares got the best of him and he lost his way, she bore the brunt of his rage. And when the damage was done and he was exhausted, she tried to soothe his hollow apologies with her damnation of war, declaring that no man should ever have to fight or die for peace.

"What's the point of killing each other, anyway?" she'd whispered when he'd calmed down. "Why can't we all get along and love each other."

She'd lay beside him until he fell asleep, and then with a frozen bag of peas on her swelling cheek, she'd cry until nothing was left in her.

***

*F*rankie's nerves had been on edge for the last several days and when she got off the bus that afternoon, her stomach fell to the floor. She saw their neighbor Tesh's car at the trailer park and her throat was constricted with a lump the size of a walnut. She couldn't breathe anymore. Her gut clenched and tears stung her eyes as she fought back the thought that Mama might have died today or would die soon. *Very soon.*

She rushed off the bus, tossed her backpack outside the little trailer and rushed in the door. Mama wasn't on the sofa, and she called for her as she rushed to the back of the trailer. No one was in the back bedroom either.

Her mind raced with the horror that perhaps Mama was dead. Frankie was fearful they had taken her body away and she'd never see her again. Tears were streaming down her cheeks as she ran toward the bar. Breathless and scared, she burst into the bar and saw Tesh and Daddy sitting on bar stools.

"Where's Mama?" Frankie's voice was frantic.

"Frankie Girl, she's gone." Daddy looked at Frankie with glistening eyes, and Tesh stood up, reaching her arms out to Frankie.

"I'm so sorry," whispered Tesh. Her dark eyes were filled with sympathy and sorrow. "Your Mama loved you so much, but today was her day to go to heaven." Tesh knew this wasn't an easy message for Frankie to absorb, and she hugged the young girl tightly as the tears spilled and turned into sobs.

Buck moved over to them and put his hand on Frankie's arm. "Your Mama died peacefully, and now she's not in pain anymore." With a gentle pat on her arm, he moved behind the bar to pour himself another drink.

"Where is she?" Frankie looked his way as another deep sob escaped her throat. "Where is her body?"

Buck sighed as the memory was ingrained in his mind. "The funeral director took her this afternoon. We'll go to the funeral home tonight and make arrangements." Buck's weary voice quivered with the weight of what needed to be done. "We'll have a service at the church by the lake and bury her on Monday."

Frankie couldn't contain her grief and she sobbed harder as Tesh lowered her onto a bar stool. They went silent as the sadness swept them into memories of Mama.

Butch popped into the bar with Debbie following behind. They realized what had happened, and anguish overtook the family. Tesh hugged Debbie and Frankie and soothed their grief as best she could. Tears flowed, as the older daughter grew agitated and restless and moaned with low guttural groans. Tesh motioned to Frankie that she was taking Debbie to the big trailer and to come along with them.

Butch was wide-eyed, bewildered, and fighting to be a man like his father. He sat at the bar, close to his dad, who was staring at his glass of whiskey.

"Daddy, where do you think Mama is now? Can she see us? Did she go to heaven?" Butch wanted to ask his Mama these questions; she would have known the answers and wouldn't have made fun of him for crying. She always had the right thing to say to make things better. He peered up at his dad and saw pain and sadness in his father's eyes.

Buck was silent as another tear slid down his cheek. "I'm not sure where your Mama is, son. But, if there's a heaven, I know she's there looking out for us."

Butch thought if a God would do this to them, he wasn't much of a God, and heaven was probably a made-up story anyway.

Life is hard, Buck thought to himself. *This kid will have to learn that sooner or later.*

"Go find Frankie," he said to his scared son. "She's with Tesh, and they'll answer your questions."

Butch scooted out of the bar in search of his older sister. As he crossed the parking lot, he reached down, picked up a stone, and hurled it at the small trailer, missing the living room window and putting a dent in the trailer wall. Twenty stones later, he had successfully hit two windows and left more marks on the trailer walls.

His mother had just died, leaving him with a mean dad and two stupid sisters. He had no idea what to do with himself.

"Dammit," he said, looking around to make sure no one heard him. *I'm going to have to take care of myself,* he thought. *Frankie will care, but no one else will even notice me.* He was damn sure about that.

Nine people attended Mama's funeral: the Minister, Buck, Debbie, Frankie, Butch, their neighbor Tesh, and her husband Alfred, and two ladies from the church who'd brought lunch. The funeral director and his helpers were at the back of the church, but when Frankie made a count of the small group who came because they cared about Mama, she didn't include them.

No one from the Philadelphia French family showed because Daddy wouldn't let Frankie call them. And Mama had insisted the same before she died. Even so, Frankie thought her grandparents should have known she was gone.

Mama lay in a pine box coffin, dressed in her wedding gown, with white flowers in her hair. Tesh didn't think the wedding outfit was appropriate for a funeral. Still, Daddy had insisted that Mama would have wanted to look nice to go to heaven. The minister said kind words about Mama and gave a short sermon about how wonderful heaven was and now Mama was happy and had no more pain.

Frankie couldn't focus on what the minister said as she stared at the box where Mama was lying. *Mama is dead*. Frankie struggled to wrap her mind around the thought.

The church lunch ladies and the minister sang *Amazing Grace*. They might not have known it was Mama's favorite song, but Frankie knew, and the simple hymn ripped through her heart, spilling tears down her cheeks. Butch reached over and grabbed her hand and squeezed it tight. She pulled him into a hug as he leaned into her and sobbed into the only black dress she owned.

At the graveside on the far side of the church property, the funeral director motioned for the family to gather around. Butch couldn't bear to look at Mama up close and buried his head in Frankie's shoulder as they stood silently, looking at Mama one last time. Debbie stroked her hair, took out the flowers one by one, and made a little bouquet in her hand. The coffin was closed, and Mama was lowered into the ground. Buck gathered his children in his arms and hugged them tightly. "Let's go," he said, his deep voice breaking. "We have to open the bar."

Frankie pulled away from her father and wiped away her tears. She knew their world had changed forever.

CHAPTER FOUR

THE COLOR PURPLE

"hat will you do after you graduate high school this year?" Frankie's guidance counselor questioned her. She looked up at Frankie with a softness in her expression.

Frankie shrugged her shoulders. "I don't know," she said, rubbing her hands on her jeans. It felt like the walls of Mrs. Davis' office were closing in on her. "I guess I'll work at the restaurant and take care of my brother and sister."

At school, she always referred to Buck's Bar as a restaurant. It seemed safer that way. It didn't leave as much room for judgment from her peers and teachers at school.

Mrs. Davis took a deep breath and picked up Frankie's file. She had watched Frankie's progress for several years and saw a bright girl capable of much more. She only wanted the best for Frankie and knew if she could just see past her current situation, she'd one day be able to move on.

"You are brilliant, Frankie," she told her as she pulled a paper from the file and handed it to the high school senior.

"Straight A's in everything for four years. I've checked with your teachers to verify these grades, and they all say the same thing—you're a quick learner and retain things with an almost photographic mind." She stared at Frankie intensely. "Do you see that you have an intelligence most others don't?"

Frankie fidgeted in her chair, not knowing how to respond. She'd always felt like she was one step ahead of Daddy and the rest of the family. The kids in school meant nothing to her, so it didn't matter to her whether she was smarter than them or not.

She knew teachers were eager to hear her answers to the questions they posed in class, but she didn't think it was that big of a deal when she was the only one to fully understand algebraic equations or chemistry formulas.

She wasn't sure what to do with what the plump, pleasant guidance counselor was pushing on her.

"Being smart is probably not that important in my life or my future," Frankie said softly. "I don't see how I will use this intelligence you're telling me about. I'm planning to run the restaurant with my father and take care of my brother and sister. That's my future."

She looked at Mrs. Davis with a sad smile. No *other choices exist for Frankie Taylor*, she thought.

The older woman carefully watched the young girl processing the information before pressing her again to consider a new idea. "I've gathered these brochures for you," she said as she handed an envelope across the desk. "Would you go through them and seriously consider going to college when you're out of high school? I can work with you for an academic scholarship, and you would be accepted into any of these colleges for free—a full ride. No cost to you."

"But what about my family?" Frankie asked sharply. "I'm responsible for them, and I can't leave them now. And I'm not sure what good college would do for me if I'm running the restaurant."

"It's a big step to consider," Mrs. Davis responded with a look of reassurance. "You have a lot to consider, and I promise to help you in whatever way I can. You are an amazing young lady, and I want only the best for you and your brother and sister."

This girl should not be allowed to waste her intelligence and talents, Mrs. Davis thought to herself. *We cannot let that happen.*

"Why don't you look at the brochures and we can talk next week. Will you do that?"

Frankie fell silent and nodded in response before she shoved the envelope in her backpack and stood up to leave.

She stopped and turned back to look at Mrs. Davis once more. "I can't make any promises about this idea," she said with a declaration. "It's scary and makes me nervous, but I do appreciate what you've done. No one has ever said those things to me, and I think I know what you're thinking. That I need to leave this town. But it's not as simple as all that."

Frankie walked to the office door and opened it to leave. "I promise I will look at these brochures, and we will talk next week," she disappeared from Mrs. Davis' office. Without looking back, she walked down the hall in the direction of her next class. Rounding the corner, she reached into her backpack, pulled out the envelope and dropped it into the nearest trash can.

At the end of the hall, she abruptly stopped. *What an idiot,* she thought to herself. *I have an opportunity to dump this hell hole, and I just trashed it.* She spun on her heel and returned to the trash can to fish out the envelope. She slid it back into her backpack. *Wow,* she thought, *sometimes I'm more stupid than smart.*

*B*uck was wiping down the far end of the bar counter when Debbie slipped in through the back door at the bar.

She hesitated before she spoke, knowing Daddy wanted to tell her something very special since he'd told her to come by the bar. She coughed so he'd notice her. He lifted his gaze to her and chewed on the toothpick in his mouth for a moment as he gave her a long look.

"Debbie, come on over here." He gestured for her to take a seat and poured some whiskey into a small glass. He held it up in her direction. "Cheers to Debbie," he said with a fake smile. "It seems like you've gotten very popular."

A shy smile spread across Debbie's face. "What do you mean by popular, Daddy?

"All the boys are asking about you, lately, and that's a good thing." Daddy paused as he took a long swig of the whiskey. "I've been putting them off as long as possible, but they like you and I'm not sure what else to tell you."

Debbie looked at Daddy expectantly. She had no idea what he was up to, and she wasn't sure what he meant. The boys were always whistling at her when she went into the bar, but that wasn't anything new. They were just boys, and their whistles weren't anything threatening.

"Remember several weeks ago I told you I was going to do something special for you?" Daddy turned and poured himself another shot of whiskey. "Well, I've given it a lot of thought and I'm ready to let you in on the big secret." He took another sip of whiskey and turned back to her.

"You haven't told anybody about the secret, have you?" Debbie vigorously shook her head and dropped her eyes. She hoped

Frankie had forgotten about the comment she'd let slip, but Frankie hadn't mentioned it again so maybe the secret was safe. Debbie looked back up at Daddy and shook her head again, with conviction this time.

"Okay, Debbie, that's good," he nodded at her with assurance "We're going to keep this a secret between us. Frankie will find out about it soon enough. I want to do something special for you since you're getting more mature." Daddy had shifted away from her to lean against the grill and Debbie thought he was acting odd, but she was excited to know the secret.

"Tell me, Daddy." She tilted her head and flashed a big smile at him. "Come on, tell me."

"The first step, Debbie, is something I'm going to show you, not tell you." He held out his hand to her and led her out the side door of Buck's Bar.

"We're going to the empty trailer," he whispered. "I want to show you something."

Debbie was puzzled. Nobody ever went in the beat-up trailer, and she hadn't been in it since her little brother, Butch, said rats lived there.

"I'm scared, Daddy, I don't want to go. Butch said rats are there." She hung back but Daddy pulled her forward.

"It's ok. I'll keep you safe." He held her hand firmly as they crossed the parking lot where he led her up two steps onto a small porch. "I just cleaned it out last week, so it's clean now."

He unlocked the door and swung it open. Debbie laughed out loud and squealed with delight. The trailer hadn't been rented for years but now it was clean and a purple chair in the corner caught her attention.

"Oh, Daddy, you know I love the color purple. Is this chair for me?" Debbie was super excited now and ran over to the chair and

37

sat down. It was a rocker, so she slowly rocked the chair back and forth, smiling and telling her father how much she loved it.

"Why'd you do all this for me, Daddy?" She rocked and smiled some more. "It's not my birthday for another two months."

"I know it's early for your special day. But when I saw it in the store downtown, I thought I had to buy it for you." He grinned at her and then he suddenly got serious.

"You know I told you about how popular you are now with the boys?" Daddy stared at her, gauging her reaction.

Debbie stopped rocking. She looked at Daddy and saw how solemn he was. "You did, Daddy. But they don't like *me*. They just whistle because I'm a girl." She blushed a little thinking about the one guy whose whistle really got her attention.

"You know I think you're too young to go on dates, right?" He leaned against the wall and turned to look out the window. Debbie nodded; she knew. He'd told her many times she wasn't old enough to date. She was older than anyone at school because she'd been held back twice and was now in the same grade as Frankie. Even so, Daddy had laid down the law about no dating.

Debbie believed Daddy when he said he was protecting her by not letting her date. Protecting her from what, she wasn't sure, but she couldn't go against Daddy, so it didn't matter what she thought.

As he gazed out the window, Buck was thinking about his oldest daughter and the challenges she'd had with the kids at school. They often made fun of her, called her slow, and often pushed her aside when they were close to her. He'd heard some catcalling himself when she got off the bus and knew her mind did not comprehend what her body did to guys her age and even older.

"Because you're so popular," he sighed, and made an exaggerated air quote gesture to show that it was a good thing, "I've been thinking maybe one or two of the guys who like you could have a date with you here in the empty trailer." He didn't pause long enough for her to respond.

"What do you think of that, Debbie? Would you like to have a date here?" He couldn't bring himself to look at her, but it didn't matter. She jumped off the chair and hugged him so hard she almost knocked him over.

"A date? Here in this trailer? Of course, I want to have a date!" Debbie was thrilled and immediately thought of who she wanted to have the first date with. "Do I get to pick the first date?" she said breathlessly.

"Hmm, I don't know," Daddy teased, but his face went solemn. "As your father, I say who comes in this trailer. Do you understand?" He looked down at her. Buck's stomach rolled with a wave of nausea, and he fought to swallow back the bile that rose in his throat.

"Come on, Debbie, I have to go back to work in the bar." He pulled her close and squeezed her. "You still can't tell anyone about this, ok?" He looked at her sternly, grabbed her chin and looked straight into her eyes. His eyes were dark and earnest, and she wriggled to loosen his grip.

"Ok, ok, Daddy. I get it. My date room is a secret." She sighed and glanced at the purple chair. She felt so happy, but Daddy wanted her to be serious. "Thanks, Daddy, for my early birthday present. You sure surprised me."

He opened the door for her and then said hesitantly. "Debbie, this is our secret. If you tell anyone, I'm going to take the purple chair back to the furniture store." He lowered his voice and whispered, "I'll tell you when it's time for the first date night. Until then, don't tell a soul."

At the bottom of the steps, he pushed her toward the family trailer. "Now, go and hang out with Butch and Frankie and do your homework. And wipe that silly grin off your face." He grabbed her arm, and she twisted out of his grip. "I'm serious about this, Debbie."

He watched her walk over toward the big trailer where the kids' bedrooms were. She turned and waved to him at the door and made a zipper motion across her lips. He shook his head and turned to cross the parking lot and start his evening routine at Buck's Bar & Grill.

Thoughts raced through his mind of what he was about to do to his innocent daughter. He had thought of a hundred ways to avoid this wicked path. But once he signaled to the guys at the bar that if they met his price, he'd let it happen, it was too late to go back. The money would make a big difference in his cash flow and maybe he'd finally have some financial relief.

But no matter how much justification he used to convince himself of why this would save Buck's Bar & Grill, he knew Mama up in heaven was disappointed in him. And, when Frankie found out, she would be so furious she might turn him in to the authorities. No matter, he was the boss of Buck's Bar & Grill and he had made the call.

Good Lord, what have I done? he thought. *Surely, I will go to hell for this.*

It was a light evening crowd at Buck's Bar later that night and Frankie was relieved. She still had homework to do and was in a cranky mood. She didn't want to be bothered by the bar guys and took their orders without saying too much.

"What's the matter, hon?" said the guy who seemed a little too slick for Frankie's liking. "Something on your mind, pretty girl?"

"What do you want to eat?" Frankie did not want to have a conversation with this slimeball. "Just give me your order and we can have a heart-to-heart talk later on," she said sarcastically.

"Ok, if that's how you want to be, fine with me," he snarled. "Just so you know that me, the famous Larry O, tried to be your friend and you weren't having it. I'll take a hamburger, a beer, and a shot of whiskey. And I'll have the whiskey first to heal my broken heart." He laughed and put his hands on his chest as if he were dying. He lit up a cigarette and blew the smoke at Frankie as she coughed in his face and glared at him.

It's going to be a great night, she thought to herself. *I can't wait to get out of this place.*

Later that night after she showered off the grease and grime from her shift at the bar, she remembered the college brochures. She reached for THE ENVELOPE, buried in her bedstand drawer, and pulled out the brochures she'd fished out of the trash can. A university, a liberal arts college, and a community college–all three brochures showed very happy students in the library, gym, cafeteria and walking in the courtyard areas of stately stone buildings.

She tossed the brochures in the drawer of her nightstand. *Not my kind of people*, she thought.

She was putting on her pajamas when Debbie knocked on the door. "Frankie, are you still awake?" Debbie cracked the door open and stuck her head in.

"Sure, Debbie, what's up?" Frankie was tired from working at the bar and didn't want to have a conversation with her sister, but she could tell Debbie wanted to talk. She was probably lonely from being in the trailer by herself all evening.

"Do you ever dream about Mama?" she asked sadly, looking

straight at Frankie. "I had a dream about her last night. Do you remember what her favorite color was?"

"Mama loved bright colors, didn't she, Debbie? Remember all the pretty colors of the gardens she wanted to plant one day?" Frankie thought of Mama in her many shades of yellows, blues, pinks and purples; her clothes always flowing in the casual hippy style that Daddy loved.

"Was it a good dream, Debbie?" Frankie took a few steps to hug her sister. Debbie had weekly dreams about Mama, and it usually took her a few days to recover. "Are you sad?"

Debbie sniffled and remained silent. She hugged Frankie tighter, almost as if she were afraid she would vanish in thin air.

"Easy, Debbie, you'll be ok. I'll take care of you. Remember, I'll always take care of you." Frankie grabbed her shoulders and gently turned her toward the hallway to her bedroom.

Debbie turned to leave but stopped in the doorway. "Frankie, do you have dreams of Mama, too? You never tell me when you have dreams about Mama."

Frankie smiled sadly. "I used to, but not as much anymore. I will never stop loving Mama, though. She was the best Mama ever." She turned back to her bed. "She loved you, Debbie, don't ever forget that. It's time for both of us to get to bed. I'm exhausted." She waited until she heard Debbie's bedroom door close, and her room went dark.

Before getting back in bed Frankie tiptoed down the hall and stopped outside Butch's bedroom. She could hear his heavy breathing through the crack in the door and knew he was out for the night. She pulled the doorknob to close it tightly and returned to her bedroom at the other end of the big trailer.

As Frankie got in bed, she had a flashback of watching Mama, wearing a flowing purple and yellow skirt, gracefully dancing in the bar with Daddy. They were dancing to an old love song and

Daddy twirled Mama around as her skirt flared and filled the air with a burst of colors.

It was the color purple, Debbie, she thought. *Purple was Mama's favorite color. She loved purple the most.* Frankie pulled the covers over her head and drifted off to sleep.

CHAPTER FIVE

FIRST GLANCE AND A COLLEGE CRUSH

Frankie was frustrated with how Daddy ran the bar. She worked almost every evening and saw easy ways to make the work run more smoothly. Simple things like having the inventory organized, the beer stock in order, and a simpler menu. But Daddy didn't want to change anything because his ambition had dried up after Mama died.

Frankie knew her father would be of no help to her and realized little would alter her future unless she did something about it.

Despite her best intentions, if things kept going the way they were, she might end up flipping burgers at Buck's Bar for the rest of her life. She almost threw up at the thought.

That night she pulled the college brochures out of her nightstand drawer again and took a more thorough look at the materials. It had been several weeks since she'd last leafed through the brochures, and she noticed some interesting items she had missed. The local community college had a series of business courses that interested her and one course in computer science.

Frankie had a few opportunities in high school to use a

computer and she was fascinated with the latent power of the machine's capabilities. She'd also checked out several library books on computers and was amazed to learn that computers have a language called code. She decided she'd check out the community college and take a look for herself.

The next day she asked Tesh if she would take her to a meeting with an admissions officer to investigate the college scene. Tesh was happy to oblige and several days later they were headed to the appointment.

Frankie sat silently in the car, her palms sweaty and her heart racing. She repeatedly traced the college's logo on the brochure cover, wishing the car door would fly open and she'd get thrown out.

"You're very quiet," observed Tesh as she pulled into the college's main gate. "Maybe a little nervous?" Frankie nodded and pointed to a building at the far end of the parking lot, indicating their destination.

"I think this might be a bad idea." Frankie was clutching the brochure and looking at the quad of four buildings that made up the campus. "It's not a very big college, is it Tesh?"

"I've never been on a college campus before, but the buildings are nice here." Tesh didn't know what to expect either.

Frankie pointed to a building numbered 1905 as Tesh parked the car in the parking lot. "That's where I'm headed. I should be out in an hour." And she headed off to her appointment with Ms. Abbott in the admissions department.

Frankie was amazed to find that Ms. Abbott wasn't much older than her. The young, blond admissions counselor was in her fifth year in her career as the college's admissions director, and she loved the surprised look on students' faces when they noted that she was almost a peer.

Ms. Abbott stood up to shake Frankie's hand and greeted her

with a pleasant smile and a friendly manner. Both women sat down, and Ms. Abbott started the conversation.

"Tell me about your interest in going to college, Francine," she said.

"Nobody calls me Francine anymore," noted Frankie with a shy smile. "It's been ages since I heard that name. That's my given name, but it's fine to call me Frankie."

Their conversation continued, and Frankie explained her interest in business and computer science. She didn't mention anything about the trailer park and her wish to leave the Eastern Shore.

Ms. Abbott listened carefully to Frankie's guarded comments and when Frankie was finally finished, she opened the file on the desk that had Francine Taylor written across the top.

"I noticed that you have very high SAT scores. They're the highest I've seen in the five years I've been in this job." She looked at Frankie as though she was looking for an explanation.

"I have a letter at home with my SAT scores, but I don't have anything to compare them with," said Frankie as she took the document Ms. Abbott was handing to her. She scanned the document and then handed it back. "What does it mean in terms of studying business and computer science?"

Ms. Abbott smiled at Frankie. She liked this young lady and it was evident that while she was nervous and a bit naive, she had smarts. Ms. Abbott was a champion for any kid who was street-smart, highly intelligent and had inner motivation. She believed these three factors were the trifecta for college success and Frankie appeared to have all three.

Frankie was the kind of student Ms. Abbott loved to enroll in community college because the education there was pragmatic and realistic. No hoity-toity, Ivy League school for this girl. With Frankie's intelligence and evident ambition, she would blow through these classes so fast she'd finish early and be out of town in no time.

She took a long look at the young lady who was squirming in her seat. "Your SAT scores would indicate that you'd do well in business and computer science. But first, we should talk about your goals for college. Do you plan on staying here on the Eastern Shore?"

She sensed this appointment was a big step for Frankie who hadn't brought anyone else with her to the meeting. Ms. Abbott guessed she was motivated by much more than getting a business degree.

"It's not so bad here, I guess. My family is here, and I need to help them for a while," Frankie smiled, knowing the admissions counselor had picked up on her mission to move on.

"I'll need a year or two before I'm ready to leave. My Mama always said a good education was the ticket to success, so I figure I should follow her advice." The thought of her mother and of leaving the Eastern Shore of Maryland gave her an unsettled feeling.

Ms. Abbott went through the materials and paperwork required to make the admissions date for the next semester. Frankie knew the paperwork wouldn't be difficult, but the issue was how she was going to pay the college tuition. Her brow furrowed as she looked at the cost for the fall semester.

"I'm not sure I'll be able to find the money for this." She pointed to the tuition amount on the paper. "How do people afford college? Does everything have to be paid upfront?"

Frankie was worried now that her dream was going to be shattered and she'd be stuck here forever.

Ms. Abbott noticed the worried look on Frankie's face and moved to hand her some additional documents she had collected for her, ever since she'd looked at Frankie's file.

"I wouldn't worry about that, Frankie. Look at these documents and you'll notice that you are eligible for an academic scholarship. After I saw your SAT scores, I did some research and I'm certain your tuition will be covered. College tuition, books, and other incidentals are normally around five hundred dollars a semester, but you'll be completely covered, for sure."

Frankie studied Ms. Abbott as though she didn't comprehend what the admissions counselor just said. She wasn't sure if going to college for free was a joke or if she had heard Ms. Abbott correctly.

Five hundred dollars was a lot of money in Frankie's world. "You mean I won't have to pay anything? Who will pay for it?"

Ms. Abbott smiled at the puzzled look on Frankie's face and explained how academic scholarships worked, where the money came from, and why Frankie was more than qualified for a free ride.

Frankie couldn't let herself feel too excited, but the thought of free college was making her giddy. She didn't trust the admissions counselor yet and hoped she was fully understanding this conversation. She regretted not bringing Tesh in with her so they could recount the conversation together. But a white girl with a black neighbor at the appointment might have raised an eyebrow or two on the local college campus.

"OK, let me get this straight." The shy Frankie disappeared as she realized the impact of what she had just learned. "I can go to college for free and not have to pay anything at all. I can study business and computer science without any cost?"

Frankie couldn't believe the joy that was welling up inside of her. She wanted to jump up and hug Ms. Abbott, but she restrained herself and allowed a small smile to flash across her face.

She couldn't wait to tell Tesh, and she was hit with sudden

emotions of joy and happiness that she hadn't known for years. *I'm going to college,* she thought. *Me, I'm going to graduate from college.*

Ms. Abbott was as thrilled as Frankie and gave her a big grin. "Girl, you are going to be a star student here at Community College. I can't wait for you to take this place by storm.

"Not many girls want to study business, let alone have an interest in computer science. Can you come back next week so we can complete the paperwork? I'll send it with you so you can look it over, but I'd love to help you with it and spend some time together. I am so excited for you."

Frankie nodded, laughed and high-fived Ms. Abbott. "It's the beginning of a new journey, Frankie Taylor. I'm happy to be on it with you." The admissions counselor was having an equally good day and was excited to enroll this bright girl as a student in the community college she had grown so fond of in the five years she'd been here.

Frankie floated out of the admissions office and ran out the front door of the building looking for Tesh. She scanned the parking lot and couldn't find Tesh's car anywhere, so she took a seat on the stairs outside the building.

This would be her future college life and she couldn't stop smiling as she looked around the campus and then at the documents in her hands.

"Hello, young lady, you look very happy." Frankie turned her head toward a deep voice and saw a tall, young man smiling down at her. "What's up with the big grin you can't keep off your face?"

She shaded her eyes with her hand for a better look at the face behind the voice. His sharp jawline, high cheekbones, dark curly hair, and bright eyes caught her attention. The handsome stranger looked too old to be a student and not old enough to be a teacher. Frankie caught herself. *Not old enough to be a professor.*

"What's up with the big grin?" he repeated with a friendly smile.

Frankie suddenly felt foolish for acting like a naïve high school student and her grin disappeared. She realized Ms. Abbott's good news had gone to her head and nothing real had happened yet.

The reality of college could vaporize at any moment. She sucked in a breath and considered ignoring the question, but then reminded herself that she might need a new friend at this community college.

She returned his smile, and he dropped down to sit on the steps beside her. "I just learned that I'll be able to come to college and take the courses I'm most interested in. And I may be eligible for an academic scholarship." She smiled again at the news she was sharing.

"That is wonderful news. Congrats. I'm Todd Burton by the way. What's your name, future student?" He laughed, and Frankie giggled, too. This guy was flight-hearted, and all of her good news put her in the mood for some fun.

"I'm Frankie Taylor," she said as she shifted to scan the parking lot for Tesh's car. "My friend dropped me off to meet with Ms. Abbott in the admissions office. I think my friend, Tesh, went to the grocery store so I'll just wait here for her."

Frankie was curious about Todd but wasn't sure how to keep the conversation going.

She looked down and paused as her stomach tightened and she became anxious. This was the second person she met on campus, and she wasn't sure she'd be accepted by college students. Ms. Abbott had been nice and helpful, but she wasn't a peer.

She took another look at Todd and couldn't stop herself from asking, "Are you a student here?"

He laughed out loud and shook his finger at Frankie. "You're trying to butter me up, aren't you?" His laughter continued to ripple out of him, and Frankie couldn't help but laugh along. "That's the nicest thing anyone has said to me all semester. I thank you very much for that." He grinned at her and pulled a card out of his backpack.

"Here you go, Frankie. Look at what this old guy does." He looked at his ID card before handing it over to her.

"Here's the deal on me. I'm a professor here at the college. I'm on a two-year stint to test a new concept in computer science and code development. We have a government grant for a pilot program to expand our work into the community college level."

Frankie's mouth dropped open, and she knew she was dreaming now. So much good luck in one day was unreal!

"Wow, that's cool," she gushed, "Computer science is one of the courses I plan on taking, although I don't understand computers. So, you'll be my professor! What a lucky break and it is my lucky day!"

She was flabbergasted at the coincidence of meeting Todd and Ms. Abbott all on the same day.

College is going to be great, she thought to herself and looked over at Todd with another broad smile on her face.

He glanced her way and saw utter joy on her face and smiled to himself. Student interactions were the best part of being a professor, and he was inspired by seeing fresh, innocent faces who weren't jaded by the work world or the politics of academia.

Todd was three years into his academic career and had seen enough to realize that if you wanted a tenured professor position you had to be distinctive early on. And, he had his eye on the highest level possible.

Two years ago, when the higher-ups at MIT approached him about managing a pilot program at a little community college on the Eastern Shore of Maryland, he thought he was doomed.

It looked like a career move indicating he was stalled and going nowhere. He had been dead wrong about his initial reaction, though, as the first year proved to be extremely productive and was getting noticed by the right people at MIT.

"Hey Frankie, want a coffee while you wait for your friend?" He glanced at her casually, taking in the green eyes and slender build. 'A coffee?' Frankie had never had 'a coffee' before but it seemed like *No* would be a naive answer.

She wanted to impress this friendly professor. She nodded and Professor Burton headed off in the direction of the campus coffee shop. "Be right back," Todd called over his shoulder.

Frankie hoped Tesh was getting lost in the grocery store so she and her newfound friend could chat about his course and college in general. She had so many questions to ask and was so happy he had stopped to talk with her. The events of the day were making her heart swell, and her mind was in high gear. So many possibilities were flying through her brain she could barely sit still.

Todd's backpack was on the stair step, so she took another look at his ID card and then stuck it in a front pocket. If what he said was true, she would be in his class and be part of the pilot program.

Frankie wasn't sure what a pilot program was, but it sounded important, and Todd's description made it seem of great interest to the MIT guys, whoever they were. She'd never heard of MIT before and made a note to check it in the library.

She saw the coffee shop door open, and Todd walked out with a young student around Frankie's age. The female student was looking at the professor as though he was a god, and she was giggling and smiling up at him in an openly flirtatious way.

Frankie was shocked to feel a wave of jealousy pass through her, and her face flushed before she could switch her thoughts. She looked away and wished the earth would open and swallow her whole.

She'd never experienced this feeling before, and she was confused and embarrassed. Once again, she felt out of place and thought she might never be comfortable in a place like a community college.

"Here you go, Frankie," the professor said moments later as he sat down and handed her a coffee, followed by two little creams. "Some people like cream in their coffee, so I picked these up for you." Todd looked at her carefully.

Immediately he perceived a shift in her energy and wondered what had happened. She mumbled "Thanks," but didn't look up at him.

"So, you're interested in computers?" He wanted to bring her happy, glowing face back, but she suddenly seemed distant.

Maybe he had been too friendly, he thought. She seemed a little young for college, even a bit naive, and had been so excited but now it seemed like she was shutting him out.

Frankie acknowledged his question with a nod but didn't make eye contact. As she looked out across the parking lot her face brightened.

"There's Tesh," she exclaimed, jumping up and flashing him a strained smile. "Sorry, I have to go. Thanks so much for the coffee, Professor, let's hope all this good luck lasts." She turned abruptly and headed to the parking lot, waving her friend over to the curb.

Todd stood up and watched Frankie disappear into the car with her friend, a black woman in her mid-thirties. He waited until they were out of the parking lot before grabbing his computer bag and backpack and heading back to his classroom.

He was puzzled, *what just happened here?* he thought. All afternoon his mind was drawn back to Frankie, the beautiful girl on campus who caught his eye and then vanished into thin air.

*T*esh pulled out of the college parking lot eager to hear what happened in Frankie's college admissions appointment. She looked over at the young girl slouched in her seat and thought she might be in for bad news. Frankie did not look happy, in fact, she seemed very anxious.

"What happened? How'd it go?" Whether the news was good or bad, Tesh wanted to hear everything.

Frankie looked over at her friend and sighed. "I had a great meeting with the admissions counselor, and she thinks I can go to college on a full scholarship. She doesn't think there will be any problem getting the business and computer science courses I want." Frankie's tone was neutral, but it didn't fit with the good news she shared with Tesh.

"That's great news, Frankie, but I can tell you aren't happy about it. What's up?" Tesh knew she would have to pry the information out of the now-silent girl. She kept her eyes on the road and waited as the silence grew heavy.

Frankie turned and Tesh saw that she was teary-eyed and struggling with her emotions. "Oh, Frankie, what's going on? Are you afraid to go to college?" Tesh was concerned. Frankie was a tough kid and never showed her feelings and now she just got the best news of her life and was upset.

Then it dawned on Tesh that something else must have happened after the admissions appointment. She remembered seeing Frankie sitting on the steps with a guy as she drove into the parking lot. "Who was the guy you were talking to back there? Was he a student? Did you make a friend?"

Frankie's face flushed and she cringed. She couldn't keep her thoughts to herself, and she knew Tesh would hear her out as the words gushed out of her. "I met a professor who will be my teacher in computer science, and he was so nice to me. I like him. He was so friendly and funny, and I think he's really super cool.

"I guess I fell for him a little bit. He offered to get a coffee for me and when he came back out of the coffee shop he was talking with a girl, and it looked like it was his girlfriend or someone who had a crush on him. I felt jealous and then I felt stupid because I had no reason to feel jealous. I just met the guy. I don't know if he likes that girl or not, but she wants to be his girlfriend. That wasn't hard to tell. He's a professor anyway, so I just felt stupid at the end."

Tesh laughed out loud. She realized this was the first time Frankie had feelings for the opposite sex and the feelings were confusing. "What a day you've had!"

She reached over and nudged Frankie's shoulder. "Look at you - getting into college and having your first crush all in one day. I'd say that makes for a super day! We should celebrate. I'm so proud of you, Frankie Taylor. You are going to college and after that, there's no limit to what you can do."

Frankie eased up as she listened to Tesh's light-hearted explanation of what Frankie was feeling. She didn't feel so embarrassed anymore as Tesh continued laughing and chatting about how wonderful college was going to be for Frankie and the great opportunities coming her way.

Frankie filled Tesh in about the pilot program and what the professor was doing here on the Eastern Shore. She remembered she wanted to go to the library and look up MIT and find more books about computer science. She mentioned it to Tesh, and they decided to stop at the library on the way back to the trailer park.

"Are you coming in with me?" Frankie asked as she opened the car door.

"Nah, I'll just stay here in the car, and you go on in. Take your time and find what you want." Tesh sat quietly in the driver's seat and gave Frankie a stern look. "You go in there and find some books that will make you even smarter. I'm going to use the public restroom over there on the edge of the park." She motioned across the street to a park in the town center.

"OK, I won't be long. I've been in that book section before." Frankie slammed the door shut and sprinted into the library building, leaving Tesh in the car.

Tesh watched the restroom for a few minutes, gauging if there was any activity in the park. She saw a door open, and a mother and her child exited the ladies' room.

There was no other activity in the park, so she opened her door to go over to the bathroom, but she stopped and quickly got back in the car when she saw a man enter the bathroom adjacent to the ladies' room.

Her pause quickened and her heart beat faster as she quietly closed the car door. Something about that man just didn't look right.

Just stay in the car, Tesh thought to herself. *No need to use the restroom right now.*

When Frankie returned to the car, she was surprised to see Tesh in the driver's seat. "Oh, you're back already."

"I decided I'd just wait until I'm home," said Tesh trying to sound calm, hoping Frankie wouldn't notice a quiver in her voice.

"I thought you'd be pretty quick to sign out those books and start reading immediately." She smiled weakly but Frankie didn't notice. She was already scanning the latest book on computer science and was in her own world.

What an amazing young woman, Tesh thought. *This child has her whole life in front of her and doesn't even realize how unusual and bright she is.*

Tesh drove home without saying a word as Frankie read her

book. Neither of them realized the full impact of the decisions they each had made that day.

———

*E*ven though Todd Burton busied himself with the current semester's workload and tweaked the pilot program to maximize the outcomes and ensure his pilot program was noticed at MIT, he couldn't get Frankie Taylor out of his mind. He hoped he'd run into the beautiful girl with the gorgeous chestnut-colored hair and striking green eyes, but she hadn't enrolled yet, so that wasn't likely.

She seemed a little young for first-year students, but maybe it was her interest in business and computer science that made her seem more mature. He hated the professor-student stereotype, but he realized she had crawled into his head and his thoughts came back to her more often than he expected.

He decided to take action and dropped in to visit Ms. Abbott who was flustered to see him at her door. Professor Burton was the current darling of the campus and most of the female students openly flirted with him, while the older women on staff had secret crushes on him that would never materialize. Wherever he went, he was noticed, and he was used to women being flighty when he was around.

Professor Burton was in his mid-twenties, tall and lean, with thick, dark, curly hair that made him look like he had just docked a sailboat from a morning sail on the Chesapeake Bay.

His star as a computer science expert had risen rapidly at MIT, as he was not only brilliant but also handsome and popular.

Now, on the Eastern Shore of Maryland, his computer science pilot program at the community college was going well. His confidence after getting noticed at MIT was enhancing his presence wherever he went.

Ms. Abbott chatted him up, settling herself down while she wondered why he was stopping by her office. Finally, he mentioned the young student who had been at her office a week or so ago who was interested in computer science. He noted that he'd never had a female student show any interest in computers and wondered if she knew about the young lady.

Ms. Abbott paused, and a few thoughts crossed her mind. Why was the Professor so interested in a future student who wasn't even registered yet? She sensed his interest wasn't just curiosity about Frankie as a student.

She'd seen them talking on the steps outside the building and thought there might be something else behind his interest. She'd seen them laughing and chatting in more than a friendly manner.

She'd watched as the Professor brought coffee to Frankie and then Frankie had abruptly left. Ms. Abbott sensed there was chemistry between the two and she was curious about his interest in Frankie.

Now that the Professor was directly asking her for information, she was suspicious. "I can't give you any personal information about the student if that's what you're asking," she said, surprised at how harsh her voice sounded. She didn't want to alienate the Professor, but she didn't want to give any of Frankie's info to him either.

"She hasn't registered yet, and even if she had, I can't give out that kind of info. Sorry." She moved several files around her desk, hinting that she was finished with their conversation.

"Sure, I understand," Todd noticed her brusque manner as soon as Frankie's name came up. "She was very excited after meeting with you, and I wanted to encourage her interest in business and computer science. I have a few books to recommend to her."

His tone showed no hint of interest other than genuine professorial care for a student learning and growing in knowledge. Ms. Abbott immediately regretted her reaction. Her tone softened and she told the Professor if Frankie came back, she'd tell her the Professor had some book recommendations for her.

Todd seemed satisfied with her response and turned to leave. "Is there a library in town?" It looked like he'd need to circumvent the hesitant college admissions woman to find the info he wanted on Frankie.

"I'd like to check out what's available in their computer science section. The college has a few textbooks, but maybe the local library has what I'm looking for."

Ms. Abbott chuckled and commented that there wouldn't be very much info there and then gave him directions. She watched him head for the parking lot and drive off in the direction of downtown.

He's headed for the library, she realized, *and he'll charm the librarian into giving him all the information he wants.*

CHAPTER SIX

DATE NIGHT REVEALED

*D*ebbie's special room in the empty trailer was decorated in shades of pink and purples, which she adored.

In addition to the purple chair, a pull-out sofa and a white side table with a lamp that had a purple shade decorated with shiny silver glitter had been added to the room.

Her 'dates' hated it, although they usually came in the dark and left in the dark.

The pinks and purples helped Debbie ignore what was happening and how she felt when she was grabbed and abused below the fluorescent cloud stickers on the ceiling.

An entire sky glowed above her and she focused on the way the stars shimmered in the darkness.

But she knew what was going on. She didn't fight date night because now Daddy loved her more than Butch, since she was helping to save the bar. He told her how special she was and how date nights were helping to keep them afloat. The last thing she wanted to do was let him down.

Debbie wanted Daddy's love more than anything in the world. Except now she thought she liked Larry O's love almost as much.

She heard the door close softly and felt the cold end of a pistol at her ankle. She froze for a minute and then chuckled. "Larry O," she said. "Is that you?"

"How did you guess, baby?" It was Larry O, and Debbie loved that he called her baby. He didn't treat her like all the other guys who just came in, did their thing, and never talked with her.

Larry O liked to chat and tell her jokes and stories about the other guys. It was their secret to talk trash about the dumb rednecks that Larry O said were hanging out in the bar.

Debbie laughed at every joke, even the ones she didn't understand. She smiled when he trash-talked the other guys. But if he ever said anything about Daddy, she would smack him on the head.

"Don't ever talk bad about my Daddy," she would always say to him. Larry O never argued with her. He never put her down or made her feel like she was any less than him. He simply agreed and listened to her instead.

Lately, though, Larry O had been saying some things that excited Debbie. Last week, Larry O called her baby and asked her to be his girlfriend.

She had looked him in the eye, smiled a big smile, and said, "Larry O, yes, I'll be your girlfriend, but you can't tell my Daddy. Or Frankie, because she would freak out."

The week had dragged on forever for Debbie, and she was excited to see Larry O again. It was worth it to Debbie for all the other guys to come visit her first because, at the end of the night, she and Larry O had more time together. Larry O liked to chat with Debbie before he said he was ready for the "good stuff."

She didn't care what the other guys did to her because now she was Larry O's girlfriend, and that mattered more than anything else to her. The thought had never crossed her mind that she would ever have a boyfriend.

"Debbie, you're so beautiful," Larry O said, interrupting her thoughts. "I've had a lot of time to think this week while I've been on the road. I wonder if you want out of this hell hole."

Debbie's eyes widened, and she felt a slight twinge in her stomach. "What do you mean?" she asked. "This is my home. This is where I live. I can't go anywhere else. Daddy wouldn't let me, and I wouldn't want to live anywhere else."

She was panicking now as she thought about leaving the trailer park and not being with her family.

"Calm down, Debbie," Larry O told her as he noticed her sudden agitation. "I'm thinking of the future and maybe you and me being together. You know, like more than girlfriend and boyfriend someday. You'd like that, wouldn't you? To have a home together and have kids someday. Don't you want that?"

Larry O rolled onto his side and propped his hand under his chin. He smiled at Debbie and raised his eyebrows. "Don't you think you deserve the things other people have? Like a husband and a family?"

Debbie thought about his question for a moment and started feeling better. *Would that even be possible?* She thought to herself. She wasn't anything like Frankie, who was strong and smart and determined to make something of herself.

The kids at school called Debbie slow; although she never knew exactly what that meant. She knew it wasn't a compliment.

"But I like it here in my pink and purple room," she said after a long pause. "Don't you like it here, Larry O?" The thought of leaving the trailer park had never occurred to her, and it was beyond her comprehension.

Debbie was nervous again, and she wanted Larry O to leave. She pushed him away, but Larry O wouldn't budge.

"Just think about it," he said. "But don't go tell your Daddy or Frankie anything. They would kick my butt out of here so fast, and I'd never be able to be with you again. You don't want that, do you?"

He reached over and pulled her into his arms. He pressed the tip of his pistol on her stomach and started making bigger and bigger circles. "You want me to show you how much I love you?" he asked Debbie.

Debbie reached out to him and put her arms around his neck. "Anything for my boyfriend," she said shyly. "But put that gun away first. It makes me nervous. And don't forget about Daddy's rule."

Larry O laughed and hugged her tightly. "We don't need to follow that rule now, Debbie, because we're boyfriend and girl-friend. That's just for the other guys. I'm the only one who cares about you."

Larry O was her last date for the night and after he left, Debbie stayed in bed to think through what had just happened. *Did he mean what he said?* She questioned whether he was sincere or not.

No one had ever treated her nicely. It wasn't making sense, even though she liked the thought of it. It was confusing for Debbie, and she didn't do well with confusion.

How could anyone love me like he says he does. A tear slid down her cheek. *Mama,"* she whispered, *"Where are you when I need you?*

A soft knock on the door caught Debbie's attention, just as she was getting out of bed in the pink and purple date night room.

"Hey, Tesh," she said when she saw her neighbor quietly opening the door. "Come on in. Are you going to help me clean up?"

Tesh helped the Taylor family with cleaning and other small chores since Mama was gone. She kept an eye on the trailer park traffic on Saturday nights and she hated what was happening in the trailer on "date night".

"Honey, I'm here to help you," Tesh whispered to Debbie as she sat down on the bed. "How are you doing? I noticed you had a busy night."

Debbie looked up at Tesh, her eyes glistening. "Tesh, I have a boyfriend. I think he loves me, but Daddy is going to be very mad at me."

She started crying as Tesh wrapped a robe around her and hugged her. "Why do you think your dad will be mad at you?"

Tesh was furious about the whole situation but had no solutions to change what was happening at the trailer park. She only wanted to do her Christian duty and help Debbie in whatever way possible.

Discussing the matter with Buck wasn't an option as he would go into a rage and immediately deny it and ban her from seeing Debbie and Frankie.

"Larry O told me tonight he loves me so he doesn't need to follow the rules for date night." Her sobs continued as Tesh stroked her hair and continued to soothe her.

"You need to be careful, Debbie, just like you promised your dad. No need for Larry O to be excused from the rules. Now you calm down and let me clean up this place."

The word was getting around about Debbie's new career and it made Tesh very nervous for the Taylor family. Trouble would be brewing as soon as the local police found out, and the townspeople would be horrified about Buck pimping out his daughter.

Tesh also knew the local police were as likely to take advantage of Debbie as they were to arrest her or her father, Buck. Small-town corruption was nothing new to Tesh, as she'd seen her fair share of what a cop gone bad was capable of.

The small block building on the edge of town was familiar territory to Sheriff Allen. As he walked in the back door of the Sheriff's station, he noticed his usual cup of coffee waiting for him on his desk. He could always count on his assistant, Doris, to be one step ahead of him.

Sometimes though, he thought she was too many steps ahead of him, and she got on his nerves when she tried to be too helpful. He didn't need or want her help with his duty reports and other paperwork, especially when it felt like she was fishing for info under the guise of being helpful.

Also, how she looked at him from time to time was starting to creep him out. Sometimes she'd hold his gaze for a little too long after he thought he had concluded a discussion. He saw the way her eyes would travel up and down his body. It was like she was waiting for him to slip up and say something she could use to trap him.

Doris never did anything to make him angry or warrant dismissal, but he was always more relaxed when she left at the end of her shift.

Back home in Tennessee, folks would have called her nosy and a busybody, he mused. But maybe women were the same every-where. He knew all too well how fast gossip traveled around a small town and became a tangled mess. Doris seemed like some of the folks back home.

Like someone who seemed to know just enough to be dangerous.

Allen often thought Doris might be the reason for some of the rumors around town because he often overheard her chatting with the local women who occasionally dropped off donuts for the Sheriff. Like the latest rumor about the Taylor girl at Buck's Bar.

He was especially troubled by the implications of what he had been hearing lately.

Doris had been on the phone the other day when he got to the station, and he overheard her chatting about Buck's Bar and the Taylor family's troubles. At first, Allen thought a brawl had broken out at the bar. But, as he continued to eavesdrop, he heard a different story altogether.

What he gathered from Doris' side of the conversation indicated something going on with the Taylor children. The oldest girl, specifically. Allen wasn't familiar with the family, just that their mother had died a few years ago, and the father hadn't been the same since.

The townspeople talked about Buck drinking too much and recently the kids were missing some school days.

He continued listening as Doris chatted away, seemingly oblivious to Allen listening in on the conversation. He waited until the talk turned to other matters, took a sip of coffee, picked up a stack of papers, and started filling out reports.

Investigating the Taylor situation was on his checklist for later in the week. In the meantime, he thought he'd keep a closer eye on Doris. He didn't want the town gossip to start from inside his station house.

Doris glanced back at Allen, hard at work at his desk. He seemingly wasn't paying attention anymore to her conversation, so she said, "Gotta go. Talk to you later." and hung up the phone.

With another quick look at Allen, she turned slightly in her chair, reached down beside her desk, and plugged her phone line back in.

She got up and headed down the hall to the lady's room, passing Allen on the way. "Let me know if you need anything," she said, holding his gaze as he looked up, nodded, and said, "No, I'm good. Thanks for the coffee."

Allen had been staring at his paperwork and thinking about the implications of what he'd just heard about Buck's Bar.

Booze, he thought. *Nothing good ever comes of that.*

He'd had that thought pounded into him by his father, who was proud to say he'd never had a drink in his life. All the church people smiled behind his back when he said that.

They knew who did the drinking in the family; it was his mother secretly passing out in the rectory reading room and occasionally stumbling into the Wednesday Ladies' Bible Study.

Allen hated that his father wouldn't acknowledge what was happening in his own home even as he poured his heart and ambition into saving souls for the kingdom.

Every Sunday morning, his dad preached hellfire and brimstone to his small congregation in the Tennessee hills, but Allen knew God wasn't enough to keep his mother from stumbling around in the dark when it was time to put him to bed.

As a child, he learned not to expect much from her, and as a young man, he'd smile politely when the church ladies dropped off another casserole and asked him how she was doing.

"Such a sweet lady," they'd say. "So sorry she has the sickness. She'll be better soon." They often wanted to pray with him, but he would just shrug off the request and walk away.

He decided in his teens that he would do what God and his father had not been able to accomplish. He would use the power of the law to stop people from destroying themselves and their families.

To hell with waiting for eternity, he often thought. *I'll do good right now, here on earth, to make things right for folks.*

After high school graduation, he was on the first bus out of town, headed for the police academy. He might not save souls for the kingdom, but he was committed to protecting people from themselves.

Allen sighed and went back to his paperwork.

---

*F*rankie was washing dishes in the bar when she heard a car pull into the gravel parking lot. She waited to hear a door slam, but there was no noise other than the car engine which hadn't been shut off.

It was early afternoon; she was the only one at the trailer park and she wasn't supposed to be here.

She was playing hooky on a school day. She'd told her dad she wasn't feeling good because 'it was that time of the month.' He never questioned her and so she pulled this trick on him every month. Mama wasn't there to call her out on it and no one at school noticed when she brought her excuse slip the next day.

She went to the front door of Buck's Bar and saw the Sheriff's vehicle. *Great,* she thought, *this is not going to go well.* She watched as Allen got out and started walking toward the bar.

She stepped out of the trailer and said, "Good morning, Sheriff, how can I help you?" She paused, attempting to calm her nerves. "Are you looking for my dad? He's not here. He went to town for some supplies."

Allen looked Frankie up and down. She appeared to be around 16 or 17, slight in build, with chestnut-colored hair. As he got closer, he saw her piercing green eyes giving him a hard once-over and he saw a slight flash of fear cross her face.

"What do you need? The bar is closed until 4 o'clock. We won't serve food until then." Frankie was hoping he would leave as soon as possible.

"What's your name?" asked Allen. He took a good long look at her, from head to toe, searching for bruises or any other signs of abuse. She didn't appear to be neglected in terms of being too thin.

"I'm Francine, but everyone calls me Frankie," she replied, drawing herself up into her best imitation of an adult. "I was sick this morning with…" Her cheeks turned pink as she didn't want to say anything about her period. "I wasn't feeling well, and my dad said I ought to stay home today. He should be back soon."

Allen noticed she was trying to hide her nervousness. She didn't look sick to him, just scared that a lawman was in the parking lot. Frankie fought her anxiety and flashed him a smile. She noted the slight shift in his body as he relaxed a bit.

Daddy had told the kids many times to be nice to the law and to be friendly, but not too friendly.

Frankie did not want the Sheriff to be here when Daddy got back from town, so she stepped down from the trailer porch and walked over to the Sheriff.

"Is anything wrong?" she asked.

"No, ma'am," Allen told her as he shook his head. "I was just driving by and thought I'd stop in and do my regular check-in with your father. I like to chat with him now and then to make sure everything is ok. We usually have a cup of coffee, and he clues me in if there are any strangers in town or other new people passing through."

Allen rarely stopped to visit Buck, but he wanted to learn more about Francine and see if there was any truth behind the rumors going around town.

Frankie paused for a moment. Daddy had never mentioned the Sheriff stopping by and it seemed a bit odd to Frankie that Daddy would buddy up to the local law. She was unsettled by this information but thought she'd play along and learn more about the Sheriff.

"I'm sure my dad would want me to be helpful," she said. "I'm not feeling well today but I'll brew you a cup of coffee to take with you if you'd like." She wasn't interested in spending any more time with the Sheriff than she needed, and she certainly did not want him to come into the bar.

"Wait right here and I'll be back with some coffee."

Allen nodded and took the time to take a long look at Buck's Bar and the trailers around it. Although the trailers were old and some needed repair, the place was neat and orderly.

Buck liked to keep a low profile and rarely reported any trouble to the Sheriff's office, but the latest rumors were disturbing to Allen.

He noticed that one of the trailers had a small sign in the window, handwritten in purple ink, that read "NO." Other than that, everything seemed in order, and nothing else struck Allen's attention.

Frankie walked over with a steaming cup of coffee for him. "Thanks for stopping by Sheriff. I'll tell Daddy you stopped and asked for him." She handed him the coffee, hesitated, then turned to go back to the trailer.

"Thanks, Francine," Allen said. He didn't want to leave yet. There seemed to be something hanging in the air between them, but she didn't seem interested in talking with him. "I hope you feel better soon. You need to go to school and get an education."

"Yes, sir," she said as she turned to look at him. "Education is the only way out of here," my Mama always said. "I'm not staying here forever."

She looked at him intently. "You're young to be a Sheriff, aren't you?" With that, she turned on her heels, disappeared into Buck's Bar and closed the door. Allen thought he heard the quiet sound of the door being locked.

As he left the trailer park, he looked back in his rearview mirror and made a mental note of a car pulling in toward Buck's Bar. *Strange*, he thought, *who was that?* He slowed down and kept watching until he saw a black woman slip behind Buck's Bar and disappear.

Throughout the day the interaction with Frankie played through his mind. His Sheriff sense told him something was going on at the trailer park, but even more so, he felt himself drawn to Frankie.

There was something fierce in those green eyes, the slight shiver in her shoulders when she said she was sick, the way her face darkened when she mentioned her Mama, and her willingness to give him coffee that intrigued him.

He decided he'd pay a visit another day and check for any other clues waiting to be discovered at the trailer park.

esh happened to see the Sheriff's car pass her house earlier in the afternoon and wondered if he was headed to Buck's Bar. That could spell trouble for the Taylor's, and she didn't want anyone getting hurt, especially Frankie.

If the Sheriff was sniffing around for trouble, it was a signal the rumors had intensified, and the townspeople were putting pressure on the Sheriff to investigate Buck's Bar.

Tesh thought she'd better check out the visit and headed over toward the trailer park. She'd noticed that Frankie hadn't been in line for the bus this morning and that was on her mind, as well.

She was curious about the Sheriff's visit and why Frankie was skipping school.

As she approached the trailer park, she saw the Sheriff's car pulling out. She pulled in behind Buck's Bar and hoped she hadn't been spotted.

When she knocked on the door, Frankie opened it and was surprised that it was Tesh.

"Hey Tesh, come on in," Frankie motioned toward the bar and Tesh took a seat. "Want something to drink? I just made fresh coffee for the Sheriff." Tesh nodded and Frankie poured a cup for her.

"Why was the Sheriff visiting today? I just saw him leaving." Tesh nodded towards the front yard where Frankie and the Sheriff had their conversation.

"Oddly enough, he said he comes to visit Daddy regularly, but I'm sure that's not true." Frankie was certain Daddy would have mentioned it to her and she intended to check with him later.

On second thought, she decided she might not mention the Sheriff's visit at all to her father. Not for now, anyway.

"I agree with you, I don't think that's true, either" noted Tesh. She wanted to talk with Frankie about the rumors swirling around town about Debbie, but she didn't know how to bring up the subject.

The town folk are very cruel, she thought, *they will bring this place down with righteous anger, if possible.*

The Eastern Shore of Maryland was a conservative area, and the upper echelon of townspeople were from families who had farmed and fished the area for generations.

There was a strong sense of pride in the area and a belief that bad things like pimping out your daughter didn't happen here. And, if that kind of thing happened, you had to get rid of it immediately.

Tesh shivered at the thought. Frankie noticed and hopped up on a bar stool beside Tesh. "What's wrong?" she asked with concern.

"I have a bad feeling about what's going on." Tesh wrapped her fingers around her coffee cup, feeling the warmth on her hands.

Frankie arched an eyebrow. "What do you think is going on?"

She and Tesh hadn't talked about this before, and Frankie wasn't prepared to share the dirt on Debbie just yet.

"I think we're both well aware of what's going on," Tesh wasn't about to let Frankie play innocent. "We're not stupid about what Debbie means by 'dates' in the small trailer. I know she's mentioned it to you. She loves to brag about how she's helping to save the bar from going under. Have you taken a good look at her lately? She's lost some weight, and she looks a little haggard."

Frankie had to admit that Tesh's observations were true. Debbie wasn't looking too healthy these days and she was spending most of her time in her bedroom when she wasn't in school.

"Ok, I agree with you, Tesh, we both know what's going on." Frankie felt a wave of sadness come over her and she put her head down on her arms on the bar. "Daddy and I have been fighting about this ever since I found out what's going on. I hate Daddy for this. I've been so mad at him, and he won't listen to me."

Frankie and her dad had fought for days when she found out several months ago about his date night scheme.

Debbie hadn't kept her secret from Frankie for very long and when Frankie discovered what 'date night' meant, she was livid. She and Daddy had huge blow-ups and when he slapped her face one night, she turned against him.

That night, Frankie accused Daddy of being a pimp of the worst kind, not caring about Debbie and her fragile state at all but using his own daughter to make money.

She called him despicable, disgusting and a string of other names that made him furious.

They argued for hours about Debbie and date night and finally, when Frankie asked him what Mama would think of him now, he slapped her face, threw her down on the bar floor, and pinned her arms down with his knees.

She wriggled and squirmed, but his grip wouldn't loosen as he tried to slap her again.

He screamed at Frankie as she thrashed about under his weight. "You stay out of my business and leave Mama out of this." He kept trying to slap her as she frantically twisted and jerked under him.

He was out of his mind that night and Frankie's blood went cold when he finally got up, gave her a nudge with his foot, and said, "You best behave yourself, Frankie Girl, because you might be next in line for date night."

"I'll kill you first!" she screamed at the top of her lungs before he kicked her one more time and slammed the door as he left the bar.

Frankie curled up in a ball on the bar floor and cried for hours until she finally went to sleep.

As the sun was coming up, she groggily came to and saw her younger brother Butch sitting beside her on the floor, gazing at her with an intense look of concern on his face.

He slid over closer to her as her eyes flickered and she grimaced with pain. He picked up a bag of frozen peas from the floor beside him.

"Frankie," he whispered, "Put this on your face. Mama used to use a bag of peas when she got hurt." He handed her the peas and then a glass of water with a bendy straw in it.

He sighed as he stared at her with a knowing look. "You look really bad."

Frankie groaned as she tried to sit up and take a sip of water. "Were you here with me all night?" He nodded and she was touched that her little brother was taking care of her.

How does he know about the bag of frozen peas, she thought to herself.

She was roughed up and wouldn't be able to go to school for a week. In her mind, she ranted and raged against her father, but they never spoke about what happened and he ignored her for weeks. Her heart hardened against him, and she started locking her bedroom door at night.

She didn't tell a soul about the incident, but the damage was done, and their relationship was damaged beyond belief. She swore revenge on him and determined she would run away or even kill him if he ever tried to pimp her out like he had Debbie.

She was fierce about her intentions and knew she had to protect herself as well as take care of Debbie and Butch. She never thought Daddy would turn against her, but now he was a monster, and it didn't bode well for any of them.

As Frankie pushed away memories of the fight with Daddy, she looked up at Tesh and a tear slid down her cheek. Frankie found it hard to keep from breaking down now that Tesh had opened the conversation and she had someone who cared enough to listen.

Frankie knew Tesh was trustworthy, and she felt a gush of emotion coming over her.

"It's ok, Frankie, let your feelings out," Tesh moved to put her arm around Frankie who was about to start sobbing. "You've been holding this in for way too long. Let it out, honey, let it go."

At that, Frankie's shoulders began to shake, and sobs came out of her, slowly at first and then from deep within. She was angry and sad, all at the same time, and Tesh's kindness broke down the walls around her heart.

Tesh held her until her sobbing subsided and Frankie got up to wipe her face and blow her nose. She was exhausted.

There had been too many nights of bar work and acting like she didn't see what was happening right in front of her.

But what kicked her in the gut most was when she had to wash Debbie's date night sheets. She felt so dirty when she did the laundry, but Debbie wouldn't do it and that had caused the two sisters to fight like they never had before. Frankie hurt all over and had a constant headache.

"When did you start suspecting something?" Frankie returned to the bar stool and turned toward Tesh. "Did Debbie tell you?"

"She told me Daddy had a secret for her - that was a while back. Then several months ago, she told me about the purple chair and how Daddy had cleaned everything up in the empty trailer. She was so excited. I felt sorry for her immediately, but then I lost my mind when Debbie told me about the bed."

Tesh looked away. She couldn't look at Frankie as she thought of what 'date night' really meant.

Frankie's mind raced back over the last months as the date night situation had taken over her life. She was furious at Daddy, sad for Debbie and just sick to her stomach about all of it.

Daddy had invited a dangerous element into their lives when he hatched the 'date night' scheme as a way to cover their living expenses.

The worst of it was that Debbie thought she was doing a good thing - helping Daddy save the bar, making money for them, having 'dates' with guys who liked her - just thinking about it made Frankie want to puke.

Tesh broke into her thoughts. "What was Sheriff Allen doing here at the bar? Did you talk with him?"

Tesh had witnessed the Sheriff and Frankie's exchange in the parking lot and Frankie kindly giving him coffee. She was curious and afraid of what the Sheriff knew or heard from the town's gossip circuit.

"Like I said, Sheriff Allen said he stops in to visit Daddy regularly." Frankie still found that hard to believe. "We chatted briefly, and I gave him a cup of coffee. He didn't come into the bar, and I hope he didn't notice anything unusual about the place." Frankie's hands were shaking as she lifted her coffee cup to her lips.

"I'm sure the rumor mill is going crazy with this one." Tesh's face was very sober.

"I'm sure the bar jerks won't be able to keep their mouths shut about what's happening at Buck's Bar. It won't be long until some self-righteous woman or man takes it on themselves to make this a cause to clean out the trash in this town."

Tesh was no stranger to the danger of righteous anger. She'd seen its ugly face before.

"What do we do now?" Frankie's face was white with fear of the unknown.

This was the ugliest situation she'd ever seen, and she felt like the whole world would be against them if the town's people found out. The Sheriff had to have an inkling of some mischief going on for him to call on Daddy.

Frankie had turned on Daddy but not enough to drop her loyalty to her father and alert the Sheriff, even though she knew if nothing changed, the law would eventually step in.

This path would not have a good ending.

Frankie continued. "I've got to find a way to convince Daddy to stop date night, otherwise he'll end up in jail and we'll end up in foster care." Frankie shivered at the thought.

She knew kids in school who were in foster care, and she didn't like the way they tried to stay invisible just to make it through each day.

"I'll try to talk with him before the weekend and threaten him if he doesn't come to his senses." Frankie was doubtful that would work.

"There is no way this can go on."

Frankie and Tesh discussed different ways to approach Daddy and what to do if he didn't listen.

Frankie's mind was so distracted by the memory of Daddy hitting her that she didn't remember much of what they said. Her heart was so heavy with mixed emotions and grief that she started to cry again.

"Baby girl," Tesh moved over to hug her again, "just let it out. Don't hold it back." She stroked Frankie's hair and hugged her tightly.

Just as Frankie was about to let out another sob, they heard the crunch of tires in the parking lot outside of Buck's Bar.

A door slammed shut, and they heard Buck yell out, "Frankie, come out here and help me with this crap. I have a ton of stuff to do and need some help. Come out here now."

Frankie got up and her face went dark. "Go out the back door so Daddy doesn't yell at you, too," she pushed Tesh toward the back door. "Hurry. Don't let the door slam."

"Coming, Daddy," She yelled in her dad's direction. "I'm on my way."

"What's Tesh's car doing out back?" Buck was struggling with the bags and in a foul mood. "What were y'all talking about anyway?"

Deep down in Frankie's soul, a fire lit up. She knew there was a way out of this situation and had thought about where the solution might come from. *Mama, you've got to help me figure this out,* she thought to herself. *We've got to save Debbie and Daddy...we have to save all of us.*

CHAPTER SEVEN

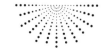

A SECRET ALLIANCE

*F*rankie groaned when she heard Debbie getting sick again in the bathroom. It was only six in the morning, and this was the third day she heard the sickening sound before dawn.

"Debbie, are you ok?" Frankie waited in bed for a response. The only sound was Debbie slumping to the floor and sighing loudly. Frankie couldn't stay in bed while her sister was having such a hard time. *What's wrong with Debbie?* She thought to herself.

Debbie's face was pale, and the bathroom smelled bad. Frankie held her nose as she helped her sister to the sink to wash her face. She soaked a washcloth with cold water and patted Debbie's face as she leaned against Frankie.

"I feel so sick this morning. What's wrong with me?" Debbie had dark circles under her eyes and she was exhausted. "I've been sick all week and I don't think I can go to school again today."

Frankie tucked Debbie back in bed and patted her on the head. "I'll grab some crackers for you and let Daddy know you can't go to school."

Both sisters knew their father wouldn't be happy if Debbie missed school three days in a row.

It would raise suspicion from the administration office, and someone might come sniffing around the trailer park to check things out. Daddy did not want that to happen.

He was always on edge when a stranger, especially someone with authority, pulled into the parking lot to look around.

Frankie grabbed crackers and a Coke from Buck's Bar and left a note on the bar top letting Daddy know that Debbie was sick and wasn't going to school.

Daddy usually slept until around 9:30 so Debbie would have an hour or two of sleep before he'd come over and yell at her for being lazy and pretending she was sick.

Debbie would end up crying and Daddy would leave in a huff. He would always come back and try to make up to her as soon as he realized how harsh he'd been.

He wanted Debbie to feel like he needed her and that she was a big help in keeping the bar afloat.

By 7:30 in the morning, Frankie and her younger brother Butch had eaten breakfast, made lunch for school, and cleaned up just like Mama always insisted they do before school.

The bus picked them up at 7:40, followed by a 20-minute ride to middle school, and then high school.

Butch was a squirrely kid who often got in trouble at school for not listening to his teacher or for a scuffle on the playground.

Frankie loved her brother, but she often wondered if he had much sense at all. But what he lacked in brains, he made up for in personality. He was a funny, likable kid and always seemed to be leading a group of boys into fun games that went too far.

He had street smarts and used his charm and good looks to talk his way out of getting detention or other punishment.

As for Frankie and high school, she was always ahead of her

classmates in grade level and was bored most of the time. She had a knack for math and science and a deep curiosity about everything.

Most of all, she loved the library, and the kind, sweet librarian, Mrs. Balmer.

"Frankie Girl," Mrs. Balmer, would say to her, "you are the smartest kid in this school. I swear you've read every book I have in this library." Frankie would nod because it was true. She'd read every book on the shelves, or at least leafed through them.

When Mrs. Balmer noticed Frankie's voracious reading appetite, she'd introduced her to the county library in town.

Frankie was proud of her library card and loved the feel of the heavy paper stock with her name and library number at the top. Frankie Taylor, 062255. Every book had a card in the back on which the librarian wrote the due date. With every book, she'd pull out the due date card and use it as her bookmark.

The smell of library books, with their plastic-covered book jackets and Dewey Decimal numbers, welcomed her as she walked through the book stacks trailing her fingers on the backs of the books, randomly stopping to pull one out.

Her favorite time of the week was Saturday morning when Tesh would occasionally offer to take her to the county library in town. Frankie was in awe of the huge number of stacks in the big library, which had two floors.

Books were her ticket to new worlds, scenes, characters and places to transport her out of this boring, stifling town. She'd be swallowed up within minutes by the wonder of what else was in the big, wide world, in places miles from the dismal life of the trailer park.

While Frankie loved school for the learning it provided, she didn't love the social aspect.

Like every high school in America, Kennedy High had the jocks and the jerks, the popular girls and the nerds, and every awkward iteration in between. Frankie was keenly aware that she didn't fit in, so she laid low and didn't draw any attention to herself.

She'd be out of school before long and, in the meantime, she'd take advantage of every book available to her.

Mrs. Balmer looked up when Frankie walked into the library during lunchtime. "Aren't you eating lunch today, Frankie?"

Holding up her peanut butter and jelly sandwich, Frankie smiled broadly at the librarian. Frankie walked over to her, her voice dropping to a whisper. "Mrs. Balmer, I'm looking for a specific book today."

Mrs. Balmer gave her a questioning look as Frankie checked to make sure no one was listening in. "I need a health book or maybe a medical book. I was hoping you'd point me in the right direction."

Frankie leaned in a little more closely towards the librarian. "I need to understand my period. It comes for longer than a week and at different times during the month. I'm not sure, but I don't think that's normal."

Frankie trusted Mrs. Balmer to understand this was a private matter and to guide her in the right direction. The librarian flashed a knowing look at Frankie and held her finger to her lips indicating she'd keep their secret.

She led the way to a shelf of thick books that looked like textbooks and studied them for a minute before pulling out the *Current Medical Diagnosis and Treatment* textbook.

"You can find anything you need in this book." She handed it over to Frankie and took a long look at the young girl whom she'd known for many years as a bright student eager to learn.

She hoped Frankie wasn't having a medical problem, but she would help her if that was the case. Her heart broke for the girl who didn't have a motherly figure to turn to in moments like this.

"Let me know if you don't find answers to your questions." She smiled gently at Frankie as they walked back to check out the book. After she stamped the library card, she put her hand on Frankie's arm.

"I hope everything is ok, but if you need help you can come to me with anything. You know that, right?" Frankie nodded, thanked her, and left with the heavy medical tome.

Mrs. Balmer watched Frankie walk out the door and felt sad for everything the girl had been through recently. She didn't have a mother to ask private questions to and no known relatives to take her under their wing and look out for her future.

The librarian knew Frankie was a tough kid, but she wished someone would be doing something to help her use her bright mind. She made a note to talk to the guidance counselor about it.

Later that night, after homework and bar work, Frankie hefted the book out of her backpack and looked through the Table of Contents searching for anything related to menstrual cycles and pregnancy.

She found what she was looking for on page 597 and stopped short as she read the section on signs of pregnancy.

Dread filled her and her eyes welled up with tears. She was terrified and excited all at the same time, but soon complete anxiety overwhelmed her when she thought of Daddy and his certain reaction. It wouldn't be good.

We are in for some trouble now, she thought to herself as she climbed into bed and drifted off to sleep.

---

*E*very morning when the young, newly hired Sheriff looked in the mirror, shaved his chiseled face, combed his coal black hair and put on his hat, he'd pose and think, *There's a new Sheriff in town.*

He'd smile a broad smile, breathe some heat on his badge and shine it up with his sleeve.

Sheriff Allen was happy to be in this small town at the start of his career and took his oath of office very seriously. He had sworn to protect the townspeople and he meant to keep his word.

Every morning, he also thought of Frankie with her chestnut-colored hair, intense green eyes, and the way she held his gaze the day he stopped by the trailer park. She had caught his eye, unlike the other girls in this small town.

He was new to the Eastern Shore, and he didn't have much of a social life. And he wanted one.

Maybe it was time to take the law into his own hands and use the power he had. He decided to head over to the high school and do a safety check with the principal.

It was close to lunch time and maybe he'd run into Frankie in the cafeteria.

Lou Harris had been the principal at Kennedy High for several decades and he was at his desk planning his retirement when Sheriff Allen knocked on his door. Out of habit he checked the clock and noted the time before he called out to say the door was unlocked.

Sheriff Allen opened the door and nodded to Mr. Harris. "Do you have a minute?" The two men had a mutually respectful relationship and Mr. Harris motioned him to sit across the desk from him.

"Nice to have a visit from you, Sheriff. What can I do to help you today?" Mr. Harris was always happy to have the Sheriff visit the school. He liked having the presence of a lawman in his building and saw from the Sheriff's demeanor that his visit was not because of a crisis.

"I'm just dropping by to check in on security here in the school. I heard about several fights on the edge of the schoolyard, back by the wooded area, and wanted to hear about it from you." Sheriff Allen knew the fights were a minor, ongoing issue and something the principal would want to discuss.

Mr. Harris rose from his chair and motioned to the Sheriff to do the same. "Let's go take a look at where these fights take place. I think you'll understand the problem a little better if you see where they start."

The two men left the principal's office and headed toward the back of the school building. As they rounded the corner of the corridor the library door flew open and out walked Frankie Taylor with a huge book in her arms.

Sheriff Allen almost bumped into her, and he caught her arm as she brushed against him.

Frankie was shocked to see the Sheriff at school, and she clutched the book to her chest, hiding the cover from the two men.

"So sorry," she muttered under her breath. The hall was empty, and Frankie kept walking in the direction of the cafeteria.

The principal motioned Sheriff Allen to follow him and glanced back as Frankie rounded the corner and disappeared.

"That's the Taylor girl. Frankie's her name. One of the brightest students we have here at Kennedy High. Always reads books and keeps to herself. Her SAT scores are off the charts. I wish our school system was better prepared for a bright girl like Frankie and that we'd have better opportunities for her."

Mr. Harris was concerned about Frankie's future, as he was for all the students who spent time in his school. His care for students was legendary in the community and the townspeople counted on him to prepare their children for life in a small town where jobs were not plentiful.

Not many people wanted to leave the area, but like most small towns, the economy wasn't strong, and many students left the area for college and never returned.

Sheriff Allen's head was replaying the unexpected run-in with Frankie, and he was wondering about the huge book she had just checked out of the library. His curiosity was getting the best of him, and he lost all interest in the principal and the report he was giving about the school fights.

Mr. Harris had switched the subject from Frankie back to the fights and he was droning on about having tried so many different ways to stop the fights, all to no effect.

But Sheriff Allen wasn't listening anymore. His mind was racing with thoughts of Frankie and how to break through the fear that flashed across her face every time he showed up.

He needed someone to break the ice for him and suddenly the path became clear to him.

He humored Mr. Harris and his concern about the school fights by carefully evaluating the site and nodding at each point the principal made.

"Yes, this seems like a good place to start a fight." The Sheriff nodded when Mr. Harris noted the site was not visible from the school. Perhaps that was the biggest problem. The Sheriff also noted it was a grassy spot, which would reduce brush burns or other impacts from falls.

The conversation continued with Mr. Harris pacing around the site and the Sheriff not paying attention.

Finally, Sheriff Allen interrupted the principal with a recommendation to remove some of the trees and open visibility to the spot. At that, Mr. Harris nodded vigorously.

"Well done, Sheriff, what a great idea. I think the Board will appreciate your insight." H motioned toward the school building and they started back to the principal's office.

As they approached the library, Sheriff Allen stopped. "I'll be in your office in a minute or two. I'd like to stop here for a second." Mr. Harris nodded and continued on his way.

The librarian was nowhere to be seen and Sheriff Allen was hesitant to ring the bell at the desk, so he checked the library stacks for Mrs. Balmer.

The previous year he had met the librarian when he was called in to develop a security drill to make the library a safe space.

Just as he thought she was not to be found, she appeared from the far side of the shelves, and she greeted him with a delighted smile. "Sheriff Allen, how wonderful for you to stop by. What brings you to our school today?"

"Just checking in with Mr. Harris about those nasty fights that are happening too frequently. I thought I'd stop in and check on the plan we put together. Have you had any drills to try out our safety plan?" He couldn't believe how easily the lie rolled off his tongue.

"We've only had one drill since we put the plan together and it worked fine." The middle-aged librarian pushed her reading glasses up on her head and gave him a good look.

She was pleased to see the Sheriff again but wondered if there was something more behind his interest in the security plan. Was he checking up on the school for a report of some kind?

"Happy to hear that," noted the Sheriff as he leaned against the librarian's check-out desk. "I'm certain you would catch anything we might have overlooked." He was searching for a way to transition to Frankie, but nothing was coming to him.

There was an awkward pause, so he decided to move the conversation along. "Mrs. Balmer, I wonder if you have a minute for me to ask some questions?"

The librarian raised her eyebrow and nodded. "Sure, be happy to."

"When Mr. Harris and I were walking out to the area where the fights happen, we ran into a young lady coming out of the library." Mrs. Balmer nodded as she had seen the incident herself when Frankie left the library earlier.

"Mr. Harris said she's one of the smartest kids in the school, has the highest SAT scores he's ever seen, and she was leaving here with a thick book. Does she read textbooks for fun?" He smiled feebly at the librarian.

Mrs. Balmer smiled knowingly. The Sheriff wanted info on Frankie, but she wasn't sure why. Had he heard the town rumors about the Taylor family and the gossip about Buck's Bar? She wasn't sure of his intent, and she felt protective of Frankie.

"She's a very bright girl," she said hesitantly as she searched the Sheriff's face for clues. "She's probably read every book in this place and more, including everything at the town library."

Mrs. Balmer was proud of Frankie and her ability to absorb information almost with a photographic mind. But she wasn't sure how much she wanted to reveal about the girl she admired so much.

"Why are you interested in Frankie?" Mrs. Balmer asked in a guarded voice.

Sheriff Allen realized he needed to tread lightly, or the librarian wouldn't be his advocate for Frankie.

The Sheriff paused for a moment to consider how direct to be with Mrs. Balmer. She seemed to genuinely care for Frankie and maybe she already guessed his intentions. He couldn't tell but decided to risk it.

"Mrs. Balmer, I believe you can help me out. Frankly, I need to ask a favor of you." The librarian smiled and nodded.

"I'd like to speak with Frankie and have a friendly conversation with her, but every time I've seen her, she seems nervous and clams up."

Mrs. Balmer looked down at her desk and moved some papers around. She wasn't sure where this was going and what favor the Sheriff was going to ask of her.

"If you're willing, would you ask her if she'd meet me for coffee or maybe meet at the town library?" Sheriff Allen had picked up on Frankie's love of reading and sensed that libraries were safe spaces for her.

"It's not official business, I'd just like the chance to learn more about her." His brief smile told the librarian everything she needed to know.

Surprise was written all over Mrs. Balmer's face as she realized exactly what the Sheriff was asking. She let out a slow breath and looked at him intensely.

"Just to be clear, Allen, you are the Sheriff, and you can go to the trailer park and interview her anytime you want. You are the law, so you don't need me, do you, for an introduction to Frankie?"

She narrowed her eyes at the handsome young man and her lips suppressed a smile as she was determined to make the Sheriff reveal more of his intention.

The Sheriff stepped back and smiled. Mrs. Balmer was on to him and now they would play a cat-and-mouse game and he was about to lose.

"Precisely the problem, Mrs. Balmer. She won't talk with me if she views me as the 'lawman'." He air-quoted the words *lawman* to exaggerate his position.

"What do you want to talk to Frankie about that isn't related to your position as a 'lawman'?" Mrs. Balmer air-quoted the words lawman back at him.

"Ah, Mrs. Balmer, you've got me there." She had him and they both knew it. She was smiling at him now and was enjoying their little game.

Mrs. Balmer liked the young Sheriff and thought he must be lonely in this small town on the Eastern Shore of Maryland. He was relatively new to the job, an outsider who was working hard to make a name for himself as someone who cared for the townspeople.

It was evident he wanted to do his job well and kick off his career in law enforcement with a good start.

Mrs. Balmer was an intuitive type and she sensed the Sheriff had a depth to him that he rarely revealed. It was hard for most people to read what was going on behind the Sheriff's masked face. But she noticed a sensitive side to the young, handsome man and she hoped he was up to the job he had signed on for.

"As you suspect, I do have a personal interest in Frankie. I am intrigued by the situation she finds herself in and I want to help her out, but don't know how." Mrs. Balmer wasn't sure about Frankie's situation and was curious about what the Sheriff knew that she didn't know.

She wondered if the Sheriff had seen the title of the book Frankie took with her earlier in the day.

Mrs. Balmer smiled to herself about the irony of the situation - Frankie becoming aware of her physical maturity coinciding with the Sheriff's interest in her. She decided to be helpful.

"I'll help you, Sheriff," she said, anticipating his smile. "She's mature beyond her years, and very protective of her family. She's a brilliant girl with strong street smarts and she'll realize exactly what you're up to. You don't think there's an age gap here?"

Sheriff Allen looked up in surprise. He knew Frankie was in her late teens, but he hadn't thought about an age gap. Would she think he was too old?

Mrs. Balmer continued, "Well then, Frankie will decide on that question. What can I do to pave the way for your interest in her? She could use a friend, for sure."

The Sheriff rewarded her with a broad smile that brightened his blue eyes and made him stand up a bit taller.

"Thanks, Mrs. Balmer. If you would mention to Frankie that I was here and I'd like to stop by the trailer park on Saturday morning to chat with her, I'd be much obliged."

He surprised himself with his formality, and he felt like a kid again, asking permission for something beyond his grasp. He hated rejection and Mrs. Balmer saw a hint of fear in his eyes.

She was certain the Sheriff had a good heart and he seemed so earnest in his request. "I'll be happy to help you, Sheriff. Stop by on Friday afternoon and I'll have her answer for you."

She glanced down at her papers again and pulled her readers off her head. She waved them at him and added, "Be careful with this, Allen, the poor girl has already been through so much and doesn't trust anyone easily. You might push her away too soon if you come on too strong."

The school librarian's motherly instincts for Frankie were strong and she felt protective of the young girl and the Taylor family.

Frankie's family situation was made harder by their mother's death and Mrs. Balmer didn't want any other troubles for the family. She trusted the Sheriff to approach the situation with the best of intentions.

Mrs. Balmer's warning stayed in his head all week, alternating with the fear of rejection and the glimpse of hope that Frankie would accept his invitation.

CHAPTER EIGHT

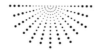

GOING ON A ROAD TRIP

*I*t was still dark when Sheriff Allen woke. No sleeping late on his day off, as he was too excited about what might happen today. *What might happen,* he reminded himself.

He grabbed a sweatshirt and jogging pants and prepped for his five-mile daily run, after which he would follow his weight-lifting program and stretching routine.

Sheriff Allen was in his mid-twenties, but in his short time in law enforcement, he'd seen too many out-of-shape officers and had determined that he would never drop his routines. He loved being in tip-top shape, and the ladies' glances at his toned body didn't escape him.

Sheriff Allen was in a good mood on Friday afternoon when Mrs. Balmer gave him the green light to drop in to see Frankie Saturday morning.

Friday night's sleep was interrupted by thoughts of Frankie being nice and friendly, alternating with the fear that he'd never see her and that her father, Buck, would run him off the property.

I'm just delivering papers, he reminded himself. *I'm just delivering papers, and maybe she'll come with me.*

After an agonizingly long morning, it was time for the Sheriff to head out and see if his plan would work.

He grabbed the envelope of documents he needed to deliver, jumped in his own black F-150 pickup truck, and headed to Buck's Bar and the trailer park where Frankie lived. His mind raced, and his heartbeat quickened when his destination came into sight.

Frankie heard his truck tires crunching into the parking lot and put her head in her hands. She was sitting on the side of the bed and wondered if she had lost her mind to agree with Mrs. Balmer to allow a visit from the Sheriff.

When Mrs. Balmer told her of his request, Frankie automatically said No and left the library.

It wasn't until she had time to hatch a plan that she returned to tell Mrs. Balmer that she had changed her mind and that "Yes, I'd be happy to have the Sheriff stop by the trailer park on Saturday morning."

But now it was Saturday morning and Frankie thought she might have made a mistake. She'd been getting dressed and undressed, changing from one outfit to another for a half hour.

Finally, she was exasperated at the fact that she even cared about how she looked and grabbed a pair of jeans and a white tee shirt.

Enough already, she thought. *I can't obsess about how crazy this is.*

Frankie wasn't going to allow Buck to interrupt her plan for the morning, so she walked out to the parking lot to welcome Sheriff Allen. She was surprised that he wasn't in his Sheriff's vehicle, and her eyes widened when she noticed him in a blue button-down short-sleeve shirt, black jeans, and a cowboy hat.

She raised her eyebrows with approval and called out to the Sheriff as he walked over her way.

"Good morning, Sheriff," she tossed her backpack over one shoulder as she approached. "Great morning, isn't it?"

"Sure is, Frankie Taylor," he smiled at her. "Thanks for giving your message to Mrs. Balmer. I appreciate it."

There was an awkward pause, and Frankie motioned toward Buck's Bar. "You wanted to talk, so maybe we could go somewhere for a cup of coffee?"

The Sheriff caught her by the arm as she started moving toward the bar.

"Hey, I was thinking about a different plan that might work." He looked at her for a moment, then reached into his truck and grabbed the documents in an official-looking envelope. "I have to run these documents up to Rising Sun, and I thought you might want to come with me, and then we could grab lunch on the way back. What do you think?" He looked at her hopefully.

Frankie stopped and looked at him with a questioning look on her face. "Well, I'm not sure. I thought we would have coffee in town, and I'm not sure what my father will say about that. He doesn't even know you're here."

"You can ask your father, but first tell me if *you* want to go, if *you* think it might be ok to run up to Rising Sun and then have lunch. What do *you* think of that?" He rushed through his rehearsed speech before she could use her father as an excuse not to go.

She took a long look at him and then smiled. The wheels were turning in her head, and she suddenly spotted an opportunity that appealed to her.

"Yes, I do want to go with you on your little road trip," she said softly, "I've never been to Rising Sun. How far is it?"

"It's only about an hour, and on the way back, we can stop at Chesapeake City and have lunch on the water." Frankie's eyes widened, and her face brightened with the idea of having such an extravagant lunch.

"That sounds great." She looked over at Buck's Bar and sighed. "I'll tell my dad what's happening and be right back."

Frankie disappeared inside the bar, and the Sheriff leaned against his truck and looked around the trailer park. The four trailers all needed some sort of repair, except for Buck's Bar, which appeared to be maintained better than the others.

The Sheriff noticed a slight curtain movement in one of the trailers and caught sight of a young boy looking out at him. He waved to the kid, who looked like he was around 13 or 14, and the boy swiftly moved away from the window.

Sheriff Allen smiled slightly and then turned as he heard the bar door open, and Frankie reappeared with her dad on her heels. The Sheriff straightened up and waited while Buck strode over toward him.

"Let me get this straight, Sheriff." Buck was pointing at his daughter. "You want Frankie to go with you to Rising Sun to take some papers there and then have lunch on the way back? Why would you want to do that?"

Buck was baffled by what was happening. Frankie hadn't told her father she was expecting the Sheriff this morning, and Buck was caught off guard.

"That's right, Mr. Taylor." Sheriff Allen was polite, but his tone was unyielding. "I have a quick trip to Rising Sun and would like some company on my day off. If it's ok with you, we'll head out now and deliver these documents before they close the municipal building at noon."

He wasn't going to take *No* for an answer. He was determined that a road trip and time with Frankie was an opportunity he would fight for.

Frankie chimed in, "It'll be fine, Daddy, it won't be a long trip, and I'll be back in time to finish all my chores. I think it'll be fun to get out of Kent County for a little road trip."

She smiled at her dad and reached up to kiss his cheek. Sheriff Allen moved to go around the truck and open the passenger seat door for her, and Frankie was right behind him. They were in sync now, both wanting to exit before Buck could make a scene.

Buck grabbed the Sheriff as he returned to the driver's seat of the pickup truck. "Sheriff, you're a good kid, and you've been good to us," he said in a low menacing tone, "but if you lay a hand on my daughter, I'll shoot your head off."

Then he smiled at the Sheriff and slapped his hand on the truck door. "Get out of here, you two kids, and be back by three for your chores, Frankie."

The Sheriff turned his pickup truck around, and Frankie looked back at the trailer park to see Debbie and Butch watching from the side porch of their trailer and Buck walking back into the bar. She let out a sigh of relief and then laughed out loud.

"Sheriff, you just manhandled the toughest guy in Kent County. Way to go." Frankie grinned at the Sheriff and rolled her window down to let the fresh air cool her face. She was excited, feeling like they had just made a fast getaway to a grand adventure.

A sense of freedom engulfed her and she glanced over at the smiling Sheriff.

"What did you say to your father to convince him?' The Sheriff had overheard a heated conversation in the trailer while he waited outside. Buck was known to be rough and tough when he needed to be.

"I told him you invited me and that I was going. It wasn't his decision, and I was going either way, whether he liked it or not." She smiled at him to ease his mind from the conversation she thought he might have overheard.

Frankie didn't tell the Sheriff what she had to say to secure

Daddy's approval. She hated to acknowledge to herself that she had to bring Mama into the picture to finally get her way.

That's what broke Daddy's resolve at the end of the argument. She wasn't sorry she said Mama would have been happy that the Sheriff asked her to go on a road trip. Frankie was just sad that it hit Daddy in the gut as hard as it did. He remembered when he and Mama went on their road trips, always escaping her father's fury.

Mama loved road trips.

"It's the best feeling of freedom you'll ever have," she'd told Frankie after describing a jaunt with Daddy from Philly to Cambridge, MD. "Nothing like the wind in your hair and the wide-open road in front of you. And no parents riding along with you."

She'd winked at Frankie and laughed her throaty laugh indicating a very happy memory.

The Sheriff settled in for the drive, and they chatted about the landscape and scenery along the way. He pointed out landmarks, rivers and lakes, notable farms, and historical markers that Frankie had never seen before.

When they crossed the Chesapeake Canal, Sheriff Allen pointed out a restaurant below the high bridge and told Frankie they would have lunch on the water's edge. She peered out the window down to the site and the excitement about lunch with the Sheriff increased.

She thought less about him as a sheriff and more about his transformation into a very handsome young man.

Frankie had never looked at him that way before, and she hadn't even thought about him as a guy. But, behind that Sheriff's uniform was one handsome dude.

They arrived in Rising Sun with plenty of time for the Sheriff to deliver his papers and conduct his official business. Frankie decided to stay in the truck and told him she'd wait for him. "How long will you be gone?" she asked.

"It shouldn't be more than 15 – 20 minutes." The Sheriff grabbed his papers and disappeared into the municipal office.

Frankie spotted a CVS Pharmacy just a block from the municipal office, and she jumped out of the truck and sprinted over to it.

She scanned the aisle headings and noticed the one she was looking for. Moving fast, Frankie spotted the pink and purple labels of tampon boxes and then caught sight of what she was looking for. She grabbed a pregnancy test and went to the checkout counter.

No other customers were in the store, and the young kid at the checkout counter was too embarrassed to say anything to her about her purchase. She buried it in her backpack and rushed back to the truck.

She settled in the passenger's seat, put the window down, grabbed a book from her backpack, and started reading. The Sheriff returned within a few minutes, and Frankie made small talk as they headed out of town.

"Are you hungry, Frankie, cause now we can go to lunch." Sheriff Allen was excited to take Frankie to a seafood restaurant he had heard about and was eager to try it out. He was a boy from Tennessee, so seafood was a treat for him. But on Maryland's Eastern Shore, the crabs and oysters were especially sumptuous.

"Do you like seafood?" He glanced over at Frankie as she nodded without hesitation.

"We don't eat out ever." She emphasized the word ever, as though it was the worst thing in her life.

"Daddy never lets us leave the place, except for school and if Tesh takes me to the library. I don't know much about seafood so you can help me choose the best thing to try today."

She smiled over at him, and his throat tightened up and his

mouth went dry. This was going so well; way better than he had hoped for. Frankie was light-hearted and fun to be with, and he couldn't believe how different she was from their prior encounters.

"You didn't think I would go with you on your road trip, did you?" She teased him and he laughed at himself for how often he was afraid she'd turn him down.

"You're right, Frankie. I was nervous about it and thought your dad would give me a hard time. I didn't expect you to be so adamant about going on this 'road trip.'" He air quoted the words 'road trip', as he had picked up that the term had some personal meaning to her.

"My Mama loved road trips." Frankie looked away from the Sheriff and gazed out across the water. "She would be happy for me to be on a road trip. Thanks for asking me to hang out with you today."

She looked back at him, and they settled into chats about what Frankie was reading and the Sheriff's daily work. Frankie was curious about everything, and she loved watching the Sheriff proudly speak about his work.

"The most important thing about my job is to protect people." The Sheriff was turning into the restaurant parking lot.

"By the way," he added, "would you call me Allen and not Sheriff? I'd like to be a regular guy on my day off." He looked at her to see if she thought his request was weird, but she just nodded and smiled as they left the truck and headed into the restaurant.

Sheriff Allen ordered a variety of seafood for them to feast on, and they devoured all of it with gusto. He handed Frankie a plate of shrimp and then grabbed her hand urgently as it appeared she would eat the whole shrimp, tail and all.

"No, no, not the tail," he was laughing out loud as he took the shrimp tail from her hand and put it on the plate.

Frankie laughed, too, as she realized what she'd done. "See, I told you we never eat out, let alone seafood like this. So delicious."

She leaned back in her chair and patted her stomach. "I'm stuffed. No more for me." She looked out over the water and relaxed with the sound of the water lapping the pier.

The restaurant was full of families and couples enjoying the beautiful weather, delicious seafood, the sounds of the water and the salty air.

Frankie imagined what life could be like if every day was like this. She compared it to her days at the trailer park and evenings working alongside her dad in Buck's Bar.

The difference between the two worlds made her think of Mama again. Was Mama's life like this when she was a kid?

Frankie wondered if she would ever know the real story of Mama and Daddy.

Still, if Mama's life was like this, she must have loved Daddy a lot to run off and marry him, knowing she could never go back to her family.

It was a new perspective for Frankie, and she felt a twinge of regret for what she'd said to Daddy before she left with the Sheriff.

"I'm going to finish this crab unless you want it." Sheriff Allen motioned toward the last crab on the brown paper-covered picnic table. "Then we can walk on the pier before we leave." Frankie nodded, watching him crack the crab and dig out the white crab meat.

He showed her the parts of the crab that were good and the poisonous parts, and she tasted a small bite he pulled out for her. "That's tasty, but I'm so full. While you finish, Allen, let me show you what I'm reading."

Frankie emphasized his name, rather than his title, as she reached for her backpack to show Sheriff Allen her book on computer science.

As she unzipped the backpack and tugged out the book, the CVS bag caught her eye. She felt a moment of panic as she shoved the bag deeper into her backpack.

"Never mind," she said, zipping the backpack closed. "We'll look at it later. Tell me more about the accident on Route 314 that happened close to the trailer park. You know, the one that happened a few months ago. We woke up when we heard the crash, and then the sirens and lights went on forever."

The accident was horrific and was what all the schoolkids talked about for weeks. One of the high school kids was killed, and his sister was in one of Frankie's classes.

The sister missed several weeks of school, and when she returned, no one knew what to say to her.

Frankie observed her sitting alone in the cafeteria one day and ate lunch with her. They were both silent the whole time, and when they got up to take their lunch trays back, the sister turned to Frankie and said Thanks.

Her eyes were sad and empty, and Frankie gave her arm a little squeeze. After that, Frankie sat with her at lunch until gradually the other girls were comfortable enough to eat with her, and Frankie got crowded out.

Allen described the accident scene, and Frankie saw the compassion he had for the families and the victims. He talked about his training and how he learned to manage his emotions at an accident scene.

Even with the training, the images stayed with him for a long time, and sometimes he dreamt about the accidents he'd seen.

Allen shrugged at the thought as he finished digging out the crab meat and devouring it. "Let's finish up here and walk the pier."

He motioned the waiter over, and soon they were out at the water's edge, looking at the yachts and sailboats in the marina.

Neither knew much about boating, but Allen had earned a

badge in tying knots in Boy Scouts, and he showed Frankie the various sailor's knots as they walked the pier.

He wanted to walk hand in hand but remembered Mrs. Balmer's comments from their conversation in the library and restrained himself.

He also wanted to do much more than just hold Frankie's hand, but being with her today, having light conversations, and watching her eat luscious seafood would have to do.

He checked the time and gestured toward the parking lot. "Time to go?"

Frankie slowed her pace and looked up at him with haunting green eyes. He took a deep breath and clenched his gut. His throat choked, and his shoulders slumped down.

"Yep, time to go. My dad will have my hide if I'm not back in time." They walked side by side to the parking lot, and for the rest of the drive home, both were quiet, with only occasional comments between them.

As they neared the trailer park, Frankie turned to Allen. "This has been the best road trip ever."

She laughed, "Actually, it's the only road trip I've ever taken. Now I know why Mama loved them so much. Thank you, Allen. You showed me a new world today." She fell silent and watched the passing landscape.

"Would you drop me off at the end of the drive, before the parking lot?" She looked at him shyly. "I don't want Daddy coming out to harass you when we show up."

Allen nodded, and when he pulled off the side of the road for Frankie to get out, he grabbed her hand. She turned her head, and he caught sight of a flash of fear in her eyes. His eyes widened as he noted her reaction.

"Sorry, Frankie, I just wanted to say thanks for going on the road trip with me. Do you want to go on another one with me?"

She nodded, then opened the door and got out.

She waited while he turned his truck around to head back to town. He stopped and put his window down. "You made my day, Frankie, and I'm going to start planning another road trip."

She flashed him a big smile and waved as he drove off.

Daddy was standing in the open door of the bar as she walked across the parking lot to the big trailer. "Hustle up, Frankie, you got work to do."

"Yes, sir, be right there." She rushed into the trailer and back to her bedroom. She unzipped her backpack and fished out the pregnancy kit.

After studying it, she put it in the back of her tee shirt drawer and covered it up. No one would find it there. Tomorrow she would figure out the rest of her plan. For now, Daddy was waiting, and he was probably mad at her.

She caught a look at herself as she passed the mirror in the bathroom and smiled. *My first road trip,* she thought to herself. *Who knew there was a hunk of a nice guy hiding in that Sheriff's uniform?*

CHAPTER NINE

A DEAL WITH THE DEVIL

Frankie and Debbie were sitting side by side watching the hugely popular sitcom *Happy Days* in the big trailer's living room. They were laughing along with the audience and Debbie howled with delight whenever the Fonz said "Aaayyy!"

The sisters loved the cool character in his black leather jacket, slicked-back black hair and thumbs-up gesture.

Debbie was enjoying herself after she'd had a string of days of morning sickness and missing school. Frankie was relieved to see her laughing again. Daddy insisted that Debbie went to school even when she was sick, but some days there was no end to the heaving in the bathroom. When that happened, Daddy would drop her off at school before eleven o'clock so she wouldn't show up as absent on the school records. He didn't want to worry about a social worker showing up on his front door looking for an absentee student.

Daddy had been on high alert since date nights started and he didn't want any rumors started.

Tonight, though, Debbie was relaxed and feeling better. Frankie decided to take the next step in her plan. She pushed her thigh against Debbie in a playful manner when the next set of commercials started.

"I'm glad you're feeling better. It's awful to see you so sick every morning. What do you think is wrong?"

Debbie shrugged her shoulders and took a sip of her soda. "I'm not sure, but I don't want to go to the doctor if that's what you're getting at."

"Nah, just had an idea about why you might be sick."

Debbie looked at her sister with a question in her eyes. "What do you think it could be? Do you think I'm going to die?" She shivered slightly and her eyes glistened.

Frankie felt a pang of sadness for her sister.

Ever since Mama died, Debbie's paranoia that she was going to die took over at the slightest sniffle or sneeze. She reached over to hug her sister and reassured her that she wasn't heading for her deathbed.

Frankie was certain that she was anything but sick; in fact, she was as healthy as a horse.

Frankie pulled out the big *Current Medical Diagnosis and Treatment* book from under the sofa where she'd hidden it earlier in the evening.

"Debbie, take a look at this chapter with me." She opened the medical book to a page she'd tabbed and pointed to a sub-head that read *Signs of Morning Sickness*.

She glanced at Debbie, who was wide-eyed and confused.

"You think I'm pregnant?" Debbie remembered Mama's morning sickness when she was pregnant with Butch, but this was different.

Debbie wasn't sure why she would be pregnant because she followed all the rules Daddy laid out for her about date night. She shook her head vehemently, denying what Frankie was reading to her.

Frankie stopped reading and turned to her. "Debbie, listen to me. I'm going to read each symptom and you tell me yes or no." Frankie began the list again and with each sign of morning sickness she stopped and looked at Debbie. "Yes, or No?"

Debbie reluctantly nodded yes to each symptom and Frankie closed the book and hid it back under the sofa.

"I think you're pregnant," she said softly. Debbie put her head in her hands and slowly rocked back and forth.

"No, no, no," she moaned. "Daddy will know I broke the rules. He'll be so mad. But it was only ever one time with Larry O."

"I don't want to be pregnant," she sighed.

Then she shifted to look at Frankie with a small smile as she realized Frankie was trying to help her. "Oh, now I get it. You want me to go to the doctor to see if I'm pregnant!"

Frankie grabbed Debbie's hand and pulled her close. "You don't have to go to the doctor, Debbie. I bought a pregnancy test kit for you, and we can find out now. Do you want to find out if you're going to have a baby?"

Debbie nodded and Frankie brought the test kit out of her bedroom and read the instructions. "Want to try it right now?" The sisters smiled nervously at each other and then dashed off to the bathroom.

As they waited for the results, Frankie considered the available options if Debbie was pregnant.

There was nowhere to send her for the duration of her pregnancy and abortion was not an option because there was no money and nowhere to go for those services.

Debbie would likely have to drop out of school and lay low at the trailer park. Which meant every day she would incur the wrath of Daddy.

Debbie kept popping up to check for the blue color on the test strip and Frankie kept pulling her back down to sit on the side of the bathtub.

"Stop, Debbie, I'm trying to think this through. You're annoying me."

Debbie's excitement was growing, and she jabbered on about being a mom and how thrilled Larry O would be that he was going to be a father.

She was sure he was the father, and that he would want to marry her and take her to a new house away from the trailer park. That's what he'd been promising her anyway and now they would have a family, too.

Frankie yelled at Debbie to shut up and when Debbie wouldn't quiet down, Frankie covered her ears until the kitchen timer she'd placed on the bathroom sink ticked the final seconds down to zero and the buzzer went off.

She quickly picked up the test strip and held it out to Debbie.

"Look at this. You're pregnant." She smiled at Debbie and hugged her. "You're going to have a baby and all that throwing up you've been doing is the same thing Mama had with Butch. You have morning sickness, not a disease that's going to kill you!"

Frankie was relieved and concerned at the same time. Debbie was hugging her, laughing, and started yelling, "I'm going to have..." when Frankie clamped her hand on Debbie's mouth and forced her to stop.

"Don't tell a soul about this yet." She grabbed the test strip from her sister.

"No one can be aware of this until your belly starts showing. Promise me you won't tell anyone until we figure this out."

"What's to figure out?" Debbie shot back at her. She straightened up, grabbed the test strip and headed out of the bathroom.

"I'm having a baby and there's nothing you can do about it.

You're probably jealous because you don't have a boyfriend who wants to marry you."

Debbie ran to her bedroom and locked the door. Frankie was furious and banged on the locked door and wiggled the doorknob to unlock the door. "Debbie, open the door and give that test strip back to me."

She heard Debbie moving her blankets and getting into bed. "Debbie don't go to bed yet," she said in a warning tone. "I want you to give me that test strip."

Debbie didn't reply and Frankie knew when her sister got stubborn there was nothing anyone could do to change her mind. It always took some persuasion for Debbie to rethink things and go with the plan.

Frankie grabbed the rest of the test strips from the bathroom and the *Current Medical Diagnosis and Treatment* book from under the sofa.

After browsing through the large book for an hour or so, she went to Debbie's bedroom and listened for the slow, low breathing that would indicate Debbie had fallen asleep.

She grabbed the emergency key she kept in her bedside table to free the lock on Debbie's bedroom door and cracked it open.

Debbie was sound asleep, curled up under her purple and pink flowered blanket, holding the test strip tightly in her hand. Frankie didn't have the heart to take it from her and closed the door softly.

God help us, Mama, she whispered to herself. *We are in for some trouble now.*

ebbie transformed into a new person as the weeks progressed in her pregnancy. She got up earlier, tidied up the big trailer, made breakfast for Daddy, and hummed to herself as she did the dishes.

She and Daddy weren't on speaking terms, after many fights between them about whether to tell Larry O that it was his child. Debbie knew Larry O was the only one who had broken the rules on date night and fought like a Mama Lion to be the one to tell him privately.

"This is our baby and I want to tell him when it's just the two of us." Frankie saw she was going to be stubborn about this but was not in favor of it at all.

"He'll make all kinda promises to you that he can't keep."

"No, he won't. He loves me."

Debbie's answer to every one of Frankie's arguments about the situation was that Larry O loved her and he would take care of everything. Larry O was Debbie's magic pill. She believed his love would conquer everything.

Frankie knew better. She was certain sleazy Larry O would never take care of Debbie and no child would ever be safe with him as a father. He was too unpredictable and careless to take on the responsibilities of a family.

Frankie knew his kind and could sense his intentions from the minute he walked in the door. She was always suspicious about Larry O and now he was going to be the declared father of her soon-to-be-born niece or nephew.

Debbie was four months into her pregnancy and no longer had morning sickness. Her curves grew more pronounced, her belly rounded, and her cheeks glowed. She moved gracefully and became fastidious about her body as it began to change.

"Frankie, would you bring home the big medical book from the library you had when we did the pregnancy test strip?" Debbie asked one day as they were doing laundry. "I'm scared about the baby and want to read about everything that might happen."

Frankie's emotions were in conflict whenever she thought about the baby growing inside Debbie's womb. Thinking of a niece or nephew would make her excited, but that was followed by thoughts of Larry O and the trouble he might make.

Her mind worked endlessly to figure out how to rid him from their lives.

The phone rang one day when she was stocking shelves at Buck's Bar. Daddy was out back at the burn pile and Frankie answered.

"Is this Buck's Bar?" A stern voice at the end of the line startled Frankie.

"Yes? Who's calling?"

"It's Mr. Erline from the Bank of Kent County. Who am I speaking to?" Frankie went on high alert as the stern voice spoke with urgency.

"This is his daughter."

"Can I speak to your father?"

Frankie checked out the window and saw Daddy at the far end of the field, tending the burn pile.

"He's out in the field. Can I have him call you back?" She grabbed a pen and paper to take a note.

"No, he doesn't have to give me a call. Just give him this message. Tell him his account is overdrawn again and he needs to have money here by noon tomorrow or we can't process his checks."

Frankie scribbled rapidly, trying to process his message. "Wait, sir, say that again?"

Mr. Erline repeated his message and added, "You go find him, ma'am, and tell him immediately so he can make this right."

"Yes, sir, right away," Frankie said and heard a click on the other end of the line. She hung up the phone and slid to the floor and studied her note. *Overdrawn needs money in the account,* Frankie thought she knew what it meant and an overdraft wasn't good. The man's voice made sure of that.

She found Daddy at the burn pile and handed him the note and tried to repeat exactly what Mr. Erline said. Her father stared at her for a minute and started shaking his head. She could tell he was getting angry about the message.

"He told you that? He gave you this message and told a young girl about her father's financial mess?" Buck started shouting obscenities and stalked back toward the trailer.

Frankie shouted after him. "How did this happen, Daddy? Is it trouble?"

Daddy just kept shouting and shook his fist in the air. Frankie stayed by the burn pile for a long time, poking a stick in the fire and wondering what Mr. Erline's message would mean for them.

Were they finished for good? Was this what Daddy always threatened would happen?

Frankie knew her father's anger wouldn't subside easily, and he was probably pouring himself a drink as soon as he got back to the bar. An idea flashed through her brain that was so terrifying and hopeful that she had to talk to her father immediately.

Fighting the fear in her gut, Frankie ran back to the bar. She threw the back door of the bar open and breathlessly said to Daddy, "I have a plan. Hear me out. It's time to call Larry O and have a talk. We have to tell him about Debbie and then he'll have to help us out with the money."

Daddy looked up from his glass of whiskey and snorted. "Call Larry O? Over my dead body, Frankie. Never will I stoop that low to call the weasel who did this to my daughter. If he broke the rules, as Debbie swears to, then the judge will make him pay for that baby. But first, I have a different plan that will solve this."

He glared at Frankie and then motioned for her to sit opposite him on a bar stool.

SATURDAY NIGHT AT THE TRAILER PARK

Frankie's whole body reacted, and her skin crawled as Daddy looked at her up and down. "Frankie, we all have to contribute to this family. You work hard here in the bar, but that's not cuttin' it anymore. You have to do more."

Frankie's voice squeaked out, "Like what?" She was terrified about what else she would have to do.

"We're losing a lot of money since Debbie is now devoted to having Larry O's baby." He turned away from her and swore under his breath at the father of his future grandchild. "Since date night stopped, we're out the money. You heard what the bank man said."

Frankie couldn't breathe when she realized what Daddy was trying to tell her. Her throat choked up and sweat broke out on her forehead.

She scrambled to her feet and hissed in a low voice, "Never, ever, ever, ever, will I do date night. Not in a million years. Never. I will run away or kill you first."

Buck came around the bar so fast she didn't have time to escape him. He slapped her hard and she stumbled back a step, grabbing the side of the bar to steady herself. He came at her again and slapped her harder, this time drawing blood from her nose.

She reached out to grab tissues from the top of the bar when a third slap sent her to her knees.

Daddy pushed her down on the floor on her back and pinned her arms to the oily linoleum. Her cheeks were on fire, and she squirmed to release his grip, as he yelled obscenities at her.

Frankie was like an animal caught in a trap, desperately trying to save its life.

When the whole scene was over and Daddy stomped off to the small trailer, Frankie curled up on the floor and drifted off in a mix of delirium and fever, frightened of the horror that was her certain fate.

Mama, I will never, ever, ever, ever give in, she whispered from her swollen lips. *Never, Mama, never.*

$\mathcal{T}$he bright sun brought Frankie to reality, and she groaned as she got up off the floor. She grabbed the phone book and thumbed through the thin pages. The phone rang three times before she heard his voice on the line. She hesitated for a moment.

"Hello, it's Sheriff Allen, who's calling?"

Frankie's voice broke as she said, "Sheriff, it's Frankie. I have a favor to ask."

"Frankie, you ok? What's going on? Of course, I can help. Do you need me to come out to the trailer park?"

"No, Allen, just a small favor." Frankie didn't give him any details about the fight she and Daddy had but asked the Sheriff if he could send a message to Larry O.

"Sure thing. I can find him." The Sheriff sensed there was way more to the story than what Frankie was going to tell him.

"Please tell him to call me as soon as possible. It's an emergency." She whispered into the phone and glanced out the window to make sure Daddy wasn't coming back to the trailer.

"I will, Frankie, I'll have him call you immediately. Just promise me you're ok." He held his breath as he waited for her answer and didn't release it until she said softly,

"I'm ok, Allen, it's not me I'm calling about. Thanks. Bye."

Allen heard the line go dead and moved into action. His Sheriff's sixth sense was on high alert, and he knew there was serious trouble at the trailer park. He'd find out about this sooner rather than later. But for now, he was relieved that Frankie was okay.

An hour later Frankie dragged herself over to the big trailer, showered off the blood and wiped the fog off the mirror in her bathroom to survey the damage. She felt fear and disgust as she saw her swollen eyes, her cut lip, and marks on her arms.

No school for at least a week, she thought. *May as well call child protective services right now, Daddy, since you hit me and Debbie's pregnant.*

She heard the phone ringing in the big trailer's living room and ran to answer it before Debbie and Butch woke up.

"Hello," she whispered, hoping the Sheriff had delivered on her request.

"It's Larry O." His tone was hard, and his voice was raspy. "The Sheriff told me to call you. Is Debbie ok?"

Frankie kept her eye on Daddy's trailer and heaved a sigh of relief. "Larry O, Debbie's fine, but I want to make a deal with you. Can you meet me at the back of the big trailer in a half-hour? Don't let anyone see you. We have to talk."

She waited on the phone as she heard him grab a cigarette and flick open his lighter. "Yeah, I'll be there. This better not be a setup."

"It's legit. A half hour. Back of the big trailer." Frankie hung up the phone, went back to her bedroom and crawled into bed. Finally, the tears flowed as she stared at her clock, watching every minute tick by.

---

*B*uck Taylor walked into the Bank of Kent County at 11:30 a.m. and asked for Mr. Erline. The bank teller went to look for him and said Mr. Erline would be right out.

"Have a seat and I'll brew some coffee for you, Mr. Taylor." The middle-aged bank teller gave him an annoyed look and her tight lips expressed her displeasure at being interrupted.

Buck sat and looked around at the high ceilings, shiny marble floors, leather chairs and finely crafted wooden teller stations with the big bank vault behind them.

This bank has lots of money, he thought to himself. *And they want mine, too.* His head hurt from drinking too much whiskey last night and his blood pressure was going up fast.

The door to Mr. Erline's office opened before the secretary came back with his coffee and he was motioned in by Mr. Erline himself. "Hello, Mr. Taylor, how are you today?"

Buck didn't expect Mr. Erline to be anything but curt and dismissive with him, but he nodded and muttered that he was fine, but not happy to be here.

Mr. Erline leaned back in his brass-studded, leather banker's chair and folded his arms. "You got the message I left with your daughter?" Buck nodded again.

"Sorry to have brought you in today, but 20 minutes before you walked in, I received another report that shows your account is in good standing after all. We made an unfortunate error, and your balance now covers the checks you have written. The girls in the back are processing them, and everything is accounted for."

He smiled politely, looking pained and not wanting any questions from Buck.

Buck looked at him with surprise. He wasn't sure if he was being gamed or if the bank had made an error.

"I can understand this seems confusing," the middle-aged banker was saying to Buck, "rarely happens, but the error is in your favor so that's a good thing for you. It's an unusual situation for us. Sorry you drove in for nothing, but I'm glad we got this worked out. Thank you for being a customer, Mr. Taylor." He stood up and extended his hand.

Buck looked at him with a blank expression on his face, turned quickly and left the fancy office in the fancy bank that had enough money but wanted his, too. He shook his head in disbelief.

Something very odd just happened, he thought to himself as he exited through the brass turnstile doors. An uneasy feeling settled over him as he headed back to the trailer park where he poured himself a drink at Buck's Bar.

CHAPTER TEN

FLAMES IN THE NIGHT SKY

The tension between Frankie and Daddy spilled over into everything that happened at the trailer park. Overnight, Butch went from being a young boy with a willing grin to an adolescent rebel with slicked-back hair and a continuous sullen look on his face.

Frankie stopped him one evening as he was leaving the trailer park, heading over to a waiting Ford Mustang revving its engine on MD Rt. 314. "Where you headed Butch and who's your friend?" She called from the open bar door.

Butch kept on walking and yelled back at her. "None of your business, Frankie. I won't be home tonight. Don't worry about me. I'll be just fine."

After he hopped into the passenger seat, the Mustang revved its engine and peeled out onto the highway, fishtailing as the rubber hit the road.

Frankie shook her head and closed the bar door. *There goes trouble,* she thought to herself. He had changed a lot since Mama died. He was growing up fast and Daddy wasn't noticing.

She wished she had the freedom to escape like Butch just did.

He never worked at the bar and Daddy never even mentioned it to him. Since Mama died, her spoiled younger brother seldom had to lift a hand to help, even though Daddy used to say Butch would 'run the joint someday.'

But now he was taking up with bad company. She was sure he'd be in trouble with the law before too long and she hoped she wouldn't have to ask Sheriff Allen for any favors.

Sheriff Allen had been knocking on her door off and on over the past few months and they'd gone on numerous road trips.

Allen loved taking her to new towns and exploring the back roads of Maryland's Eastern Shore. They went to seafood restaurants and festivals in St. Michael's and Cambridge. He could barely restrain himself when he was with her.

He had fallen for her, and it was too late for him to do anything but wait for her to feel the same.

Frankie felt very safe with him and relaxed when they were in his truck. They'd roll the windows down and Allen would turn up the radio as they'd sing along with Dolly Parton, Kenny Rogers, and Willie Nelson.

Frankie especially loved *On the Road Again* and imagined she and Sheriff Allen were just like Mama and Daddy on their getaway road trips that took Mama away from the mean family who didn't love her.

Frankie loved the feel of fresh air on her face and the freedom of escaping the drudgery of the trailer park for several short hours.

But Frankie didn't love the Sheriff the same way he loved her, or the way Daddy loved Mama. She saw how Allen looked at her with longing in his eyes and how his body tensed up when she brushed against him as he held the truck door open for her.

She was grateful for the flowers he brought her each time, but mostly she was thankful that he treated her like an equal. The kids at school thought she was odd and eventually didn't notice her anymore. After being ignored for so long at school and home, she was thirsty for attention and the Sheriff was certainly charming and a true gentleman.

But the love he felt wasn't there for Frankie. Occasionally he'd hold her hand when they walked the streets and once, he tried to kiss her, but she'd stiffened up and pushed him away.

He'd backed off after that, but his effort had ignited a fire in him for Frankie. It made him ache at night, and he couldn't just be friends with her. He wanted more.

Frankie was thinking about Sheriff Allen, and she was startled when the bar door opened and in strutted Larry O. She glanced out the bar window and was relieved that Daddy's truck was parked over by the small trailer, and he hadn't come over to the bar yet.

Her tone was guarded as she called out to him. "Hey Larry O, what are you doing here?"

He didn't say a word as he sat down on a bar stool and motioned for a beer.

Frankie popped a top and slid a bottle over to him. He lit a cigarette and took a long drag, then blew smoke in her direction. Frankie rolled her eyes at him and stayed silent. She'd play his game and not cave to his stare.

"I'm here to cash in on the huge favor I did for you and your loser dad." Frankie swallowed hard as Larry O continued staring at her. "I never told anyone about saving your dad's pride with the fancy-ass bank man and I'm not here for money. I just want to be with Debbie. I lived up to my part of the deal we made, and I've stayed away, but I just want one last time to be with her before I leave."

"Are you going to tell her you're leaving town?"

"No, I'm going to tell her I love her and I'm going to ask her to marry me."

Frankie gasped in disbelief. "That is unbelievably cruel. You can't do that. I know you don't love her. It will break her heart. Besides, she'll never leave the trailer park with you because Daddy won't allow it."

Larry O shifted his gaze and stared at the floor. "I've thought about it a lot, Frankie, and I think it's the best thing I can do for Debbie. She will be the happiest person in the world when I pop the question. Then you can handle everything when the baby's born and I'm not here. You figure out how to tell her I'm never coming back."

Frankie nodded, feeling panic rising inside her and her palms starting to sweat. She was shaky and anxious and grabbed the bar countertop to steady herself.

Larry O got up off the bar stool and headed toward the door. Halfway across the room, he turned to look at her.

"Have Debbie ready for a final date night this Saturday night and I'll meet her in the trailer after dark. I'm not coming in here first and your old man can't know. He'd kill me if he knew what I was doing. I'll park behind the date night trailer and go in the back door. Make sure you leave it unlocked."

He looked at Frankie with anger in his eyes. "No one else knows I'm the father of this kid, so I'm doing more than anyone else. That should count for something."

He reached for the door handle and stopped again. "One more thing. If it's a boy, name him Rocky. For the fighter in the movie, Rocky Balboa. The kid's going to need to be a fighter."

After Larry O left, Frankie felt so fatigued she had to sit down. She crossed her arms on the countertop and rested her head. She was faint and nauseous and barely made it across the room before she puked in the bathroom.

Her mind raced to find a solution so Debbie wouldn't have to go through the pain and cruelty Larry O was about to load onto her. Frankie saw no way out of this plan, which came from the deal she made with Larry O, the devil himself.

Once again, her part was evident in how Debbie was taken advantage of because she was easy prey. Frankie saw herself as part of the wolf pack now, guilty of the same abuse she had accused Daddy and Larry O of for so long.

She was no better than either of them, and the moral high ground she'd taken for so long crumbled under her as she curled around the bottom of the toilet in Buck's Bar at the trailer park.

Saturday night would be here too soon.

---

*F*rankie brushed Debbie's hair, and then braided tiny little cornrows along one side of her hairline and left the rest to flow freely. "You look pretty, Debbie. Larry O will be so happy that you got pretty for him."

Debbie smiled eagerly and smoothed her flowery dress over her belly as she nervously shifted her legs back and forth and wriggled under Frankie's hands on her hair.

"It's been so long since Larry O was here. I missed him and he hasn't even seen me with this baby belly."

Frankie's nerves were on edge, her left eye was twitching, and she paced back and forth, reluctant to leave Debbie alone. Finally, she kissed Debbie on the forehead and headed over to the bar for the evening shift.

If all went as planned, Debbie would go over to the date night trailer after dark, unlock the back door, and wait for Larry O's arrival.

Larry O would enter through the back door, and she'd give him 30 minutes before Frankie busted up their fake love nest party.

"Debbie, he'll tell you all about where he's been and what he's doing. Don't be nervous. It's not good for the baby." Everything these days was about what was good for the baby. Debbie was very possessive about anything related to the baby and wouldn't even let Frankie touch her belly when the baby kicked.

"He won't be able to stay long because he has to visit his mother, too, while he's back in town." Frankie hated how easily she lied to her sister, but she wanted Debbie to let Larry O go when his time was up.

If Daddy caught wind of what was going on there would be hell to pay for all of them. She couldn't imagine how furious Daddy would be if he saw Larry O with Debbie.

Frankie felt the pressure of Daddy's watchful eye as she worked the bar counter and Buck's Bar gradually filled up with the Saturday night regulars.

Her hands shook as she poured beers and mixed drinks. Her throat was dry, and she glanced over at the date night trailer frequently to check if the signal of Larry O's arrival was apparent.

Frankie had instructed Debbie to open the bedroom curtains in the trailer rather than turn on the lights so Daddy wouldn't notice she and Larry O were there.

But now Frankie realized that she couldn't view the bedroom window very well from the bar without making it overly apparent what she was doing.

As darkness descended and Daddy was deep into frying burgers, Frankie glanced over at him and mumbled that she had to go back to the trailer for a minute. "You know, that time of month again."

She sprinted over to the big trailer and sighed with relief when Debbie wasn't there. She looked out the window, over toward the date night trailer, saw the curtains were open and noticed the outline of two figures huddled together.

She checked the clock, sprinted back to the bar and made sure the clocks were synchronized. Every second was agonizing. The minutes dragged on as she delivered burgers and beer for 30 minutes. The noisy crowd took no notice of her, but her father did.

"You're acting crazy, Frankie. What's making you so nervous?" Buck looked at his daughter with suspicion.

"Nothing, Daddy, just not feeling well. My cramps are getting to me."

"Have a drink of this, it'll settle you down." Buck pushed a shot of whiskey toward her.

"No thanks, Daddy. I think I'll go lay down for a half hour and then I'll be back."

"Don't be sneaking out with that Sheriff, Frankie, or I'll have your hide when you're back."

Frankie nodded and gave him a little salute as she walked out of Buck's Bar. She went straight over to the big trailer, turned on the lights, and walked out the trailer's back door. Keeping an eye on Buck's Bar, she crept over to the date night trailer, knocked on the back door and ducked inside.

Debbie and Larry O were sitting on the edge of the bed and Debbie was crying. "It's ok, Baby. I'll be back. Hush, don't be sad. I'll be back."

Larry O wrapped his arm around Debbie and grabbed her left hand. He held it up to Frankie and laughed as he pointed to the ring.

"Debbie, tell her the good news. Tell her we're engaged. Tell her, Baby, we're getting married and gonna have a baby."

He laughed out loud and slapped his thigh like it was the best joke ever.

Frankie reached out for Debbie's hand and looked at the princess-cut diamond in a simple prong setting. "It's very pretty, Debbie. I'm so happy for you." She reached down to hug her sister and glared at Larry O over her sister's shoulder.

"I hate to break up the party, you two love birds," she said glancing over at Buck's Bar. "But I have to go back to the bar and Larry O, you have to leave. Debbie, I'll take you back to the big trailer. Let's go."

Debbie clung to Larry O and Frankie had to peel her off him as he struggled to push her away.

"Get out now, Larry O. And, have a safe trip, wherever it is you're going."

Larry O called out to Debbie as he stood up and slicked his hair back.

"I'll come back for you, Debbie. Don't forget me." He winked at Frankie and ducked out of the back door.

Frankie watched him run to his car parked down the street from the trailer. She grabbed Debbie's hand, and the two sisters ran to the big trailer and fell onto Debbie's bed, out of breath and chatting about the ring.

Debbie was thrilled and sad and was laughing and crying, all at the same time.

Frankie hugged her sister, telling her she'd be back to check on her soon.

"Debbie, I think you should take the ring off. If Daddy sees it, he'll be mad. You know he hates Larry O and doesn't want you to be with him anymore."

Debbie winced and sadly looked at Frankie. "It's the happiest day of my life and I can't tell anyone about it?"

"I'm so sorry, Debbie, but you can hold it in your hands while you go to sleep and when I come back, I'll put it in your little ring box and put it in your drawer. That way you'll know it's safe and Daddy won't find out about it."

Frankie waited until Debbie was in her pajamas and tucked her in, gently stroking her hair. "I'm happy for you, Debbie, and I can't wait to hear all about your evening. I have to go back to the bar and help Daddy, otherwise, he's going to come over here and be mad at both of us."

She kissed her sister and pulled the blanket over her shoulders.

"Good night, Frankie, love you." Debbie's hands were tightly cupping the diamond ring.

"Love you, too," said Frankie as she softly closed the bedroom door.

She locked the front door of the big trailer and made her way back to Buck's Bar where burgers and beer and Daddy were waiting for her.

That was easier than expected, she thought to herself, puzzled at the outcome. *It can't be that simple, can it?*

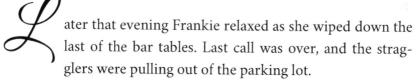

$\mathcal{L}$ater that evening Frankie relaxed as she wiped down the last of the bar tables. Last call was over, and the stragglers were pulling out of the parking lot.

Her father sat down on a bar stool and took a long swig of whiskey from his bar glass. He was exhausted and Frankie thought he was in a mean mood.

She hurriedly wiped the tables to finish up at the bar so she could go check on Debbie in the big trailer. She was exhausted, too, and wanted to crawl into bed and forget the world for a few hours.

Both Frankie and Buck stopped dead in their tracks when they heard tires crunching across the parking lot.

Frankie ran to the window and saw Larry O taking a hatchet to the locked front door of the date night trailer. He was screaming Debbie's name and saying he would save her.

Larry O hacked at the lock on the door until it opened, and he stumbled into the trailer before Frankie and Buck could catch up with him.

He was rummaging through the refrigerator when they stepped into the trailer, cautiously evaluating his condition. It was obvious Larry O had been drinking heavily.

Buck was out of breath and furious. "What the hell are you doing here, you lousy SOB?"

A string of expletives followed as he lunged across the dining area to grab Larry O, but Larry O was too fast for him, and Buck fell hard against the refrigerator door.

"You want me, then come and get me." Larry O was dancing around in the small dining area, his fists pumping in the air. "I'm going to beat the crap out of you and then I'm going to take Debbie with me."

Larry O threw some punches in the air and danced around, wanting Buck to take a swing at him.

Frankie was yelling at Buck and moved over to where her father was trying to catch his breath as she tried to hold him back. He pushed her aside, lumbered toward Larry O and took a swing at him.

Larry O stepped aside just in time and Buck staggered against the living room wall. He was laughing like a hyena who was about to finish off its prey.

He sucker-punched Buck in the face and Buck went down. He kicked Buck in the stomach several times as Frankie screamed at him to stop and tried to pull him away from Buck.

"Stand up, old man. You're going to pay for what you've done to your daughter. You're an evil man and you deserve everything

I'm gonna give you." He kicked Buck again as Buck tried to get up from the floor.

"I'm going to destroy you like you destroyed your daughter." Larry O was screaming at Buck and yelling at Frankie, too.

"You, Frankie, you're not innocent either, you skanky girl. You think everything is my fault, but you're guilty, too."

He turned to take a swing at Frankie, but she ducked, and Larry O tripped on the kitchen rug and slammed against the kitchen counter.

"This place is a hell hole and should be burned to the ground." Larry O took a lighter out of his pocket and grabbed a cigarette from his jacket pocket.

He lit the cigarette and held the lighter high. The flame increased as he waved it high above his head. "I'm going to burn this place to the ground."

He clicked the lighter shut and walked over to where Buck was groaning on the floor, trying to stand up, blood dripping from his lip.

Larry O kicked him again and Buck groaned as he slammed back down on the floor.

Larry O's curses were slurred, and Frankie was in shock at how suddenly everything was going wrong.

Larry O clicked his lighter again, and Frankie's world went into slow motion. Frankie saw Larry O hold the lighter up to the kitchen curtain which flamed so fast she was blinded by the flash of light. She shrieked with horror as Larry O moved through the trailer setting the curtains on fire.

She didn't understand Larry O's suddenly taking the moral high ground about Debbie and his violent outburst toward her father caught her by surprise. Her thoughts were hazy and scattered as she saw Larry O turning toward the back of the trailer.

The flames and smoke engulfed them in a matter of seconds,

and she tried to help Daddy up and out of the trailer. Frankie was coughing and fighting for air, her eyes were stinging, and she couldn't move her father. She yelled at him to get up, trying to drag him towards the door.

Frankie felt a strong hand grab her arm and pull her away from her father, dragging her out of the trailer door.

Smoke was billowing from the front door of the trailer as she was pulled out of the fiery inferno.

She heard Larry O scream at her that the trailer was going to blow. They ran across the parking lot as the date night trailer lit up the night sky with a loud explosion that tossed trailer walls, dining room chairs, and charred debris into the air.

Frankie wailed with pain and anger and struggled to run back to the trailer to rescue Daddy, but Larry O held her tight and wouldn't let her go.

They were covered in ash from the burning trailer and Frankie was in shock as she realized what had just happened. She was pounding her fists against Larry O's chest as she thought of her father burning up in the trailer, writhing in pain as he took his last breath.

"We have to go find Daddy," she screamed at Larry O, but he shook his head and pushed her against the outside wall of the trailer at the opposite end of the trailer park.

"You can't go in there. It's still burning and it's not safe. Let's go to the bar and call 911." He grabbed her hand and pulled her across the parking lot, dodging floating pieces of ash and still-burning remnants from the explosion.

Frankie grabbed the phone and called 911 as Larry O rummaged through the bottles at the back of the bar and took a swig from a whiskey bottle. She leaned against the bar counter and tears flowed down her face as she watched the horror that lit up the night sky.

"You're a murderer." She looked at Larry O with hatred in her eyes.

"You just killed my father. You were not supposed to come back here tonight. That was not part of our deal."

She was furious at Larry O and wished he had died instead of her father.

"You will rot in jail because of this, and I hope you burn in hell. You will never get away with this."

Frankie's face was hard, and she wiped the tears from her face and left the bar to view the catastrophic scene that used to be the date night trailer. She glanced back as she heard the bar door slam shut and Larry O ran past her, clutching several bottles of booze.

"You're a murderer," she screamed as he ran from the scene.

The date night trailer was charred beyond recognition and the trailer park was littered with ash, debris, and charred metal blown into the air from the explosion.

As she surveyed the damage, she thought of Debbie and rushed to the big trailer. Debbie was standing at the window, wide-eyed and frightened.

Frankie unlocked the door and rushed in to hug her sister and calm her down. She was hysterical as Frankie began telling her what happened, and she pushed Frankie away and ran outside to view the damage.

Just then, she saw Larry O getting into his car at the other side of the parking lot.

"Larry O, come back and get me," she screamed across the parking lot at him. "I'm over here, are you hurt?"

Debbie desperately wanted Larry O to come and rescue her. She couldn't navigate across the debris in the trailer park and was frantically waving from the porch of the big trailer.

Larry O stopped, threw her a kiss, slammed his door shut, revved his engine, and roared out of the parking lot.

Debbie clawed against Frankie's tight hold on her, and then in slow motion they lowered themselves down on the front porch and huddled there as the sound of sirens came closer.

Fire and smoke filled the night sky as the stench of burning metal filled the air.

***

Sheriff Allen was locking up his office when he heard the message crackling on the dispatch radio. "Full Alarm. Fire at the trailer park on Rt. 314. Possible fatality. Full Alarm. Repeat. Full Alarm at the trailer park on Rt. 314, north of town."

The shock of what might be happening went through the Sheriff's mind as adrenaline rushed through his body. His heart was racing, and he steeled himself for what he might find at the trailer park. He threw his paperwork on the passenger seat, as he gunned the engine and threw the vehicle into overdrive.

Sheriff Allen knew the horrors possible with a trailer fire.

Aluminum trailers are made of lighter building materials and can burn much faster than traditional housing. They are also smaller and more compact, allowing the flames to spread much faster.

With less ventilation, the smoke and fumes are almost always deadly to anyone inside.

The dispatch announcement had noted a fatality, and the Sheriff was focused on getting to the trailer park as soon as possible. He wasn't far out of town when he saw the glow in the distance.

His heart rate picked up as he realized the trailer probably exploded due to a propane tank under the trailer. He shuddered as he thought about what he was about to encounter.

The wail of sirens was coming fast behind him, and he sped up to arrive at the trailer park before any of the first responders. He was focused on only one thing. Was Frankie ok?

The scene was worse than he expected. The trailer closest to the road had exploded, throwing pieces of metal, wood, burning ash and debris all over the parking lot, covering the three adjacent trailers.

He stopped his SUV at the far side of the property, close to Buck's Bar which was fully lit with the front door hanging open.

He rushed to the bar, driven by his fear of what he would learn. Debbie was sitting on a bar stool with Tesh hovering over her, while Frankie was pacing back and forth.

When she saw Sheriff Allen, she ran to him and pressed against him while he hugged her tightly. She sobbed into his shoulder, choking out the news that Daddy was in the trailer when it blew up and he must be dead.

Sheriff Allen held her close, silently wishing there was a way to absorb her pain and erase the horror of the night. Sirens and flashing lights arrived at the trailer park, and he walked Frankie over to sit on a bar stool next to her sister.

He did a double take as he noticed Debbie was pregnant. He signaled to Tesh that he was going out to do his law enforcement duties and asked her to join him for a minute.

Frankie and Debbie sat side by side at the bar, arms wrapped around each other, stunned. Tears flowed as the Sheriff and Tesh stepped outside of Buck's Bar.

"Do you know what happened?" The Sheriff urgently asked Tesh as he surveyed the parking lot and the crowd that was gathering as the fire trucks, ambulance, and other emergency vehicles arrived.

Tesh told him the little bit she knew: The bar was closing when Larry O came to see Debbie. Frankie said he was drunk and hacked his way into the trailer and Buck heard the ruckus and they got into a fight. Larry O set the place on fire and ran off.

"That's all I got out of Frankie," Tesh said, piercing the Sherrif's gaze, wondering if he knew more.

"Looks like Debbie is pregnant?"

"Yes, sir. She sure is. Larry O found out somehow and claims it's his."

The Sheriff shook his head as the blaze from the burning fire lit up his face. "The rumor's true then." He gave Tesh a quick nod of thanks and hurried over to talk with the local police.

All the emergency responders were watching the firefighters trying to control and contain the fire so the rest of the trailer park would be safe. EMTs waited for clearance to check the trailer for the fatalities that were announced on the dispatch.

The Sheriff told the local police what he knew from Tesh's report. "We'll need to talk with the daughters," the Police Chief said after he learned that Buck Taylor was the only person in the trailer.

He surveyed the scene and glanced over at Sheriff Allen. "Your Frankie Girl ok to talk with us?"

The Sheriff's interest in Frankie was a topic of much small talk among the local townspeople. Allen thought their road trips had gone unnoticed, but now he realized people were talking about them and he felt embarrassed and ashamed.

His assumption that nobody had noticed was wrong, and he felt his face flush with the realization.

The Police Chief noticed and patted him on the shoulder. "I'm sure she'll be grateful for your help. Let's go and report what she has to say. This place is a total wreck and I imagine she is as well."

*D*ebbie, Butch and Frankie buried Daddy unceremoniously beside Mama at the little church by the lake. The minister said a prayer before they buried a small box of Daddy's ashes.

Frankie asked him to sing *Amazing Grace* and Debbie's sobs mixed with the haunting sound of Mama's favorite song.

Frankie and Butch stared at the ground and after Frankie paid the minister, they drove to a little coffee shop down the road where they had coffee and donuts.

"We're orphans now," Butch said.

Frankie nodded, her eyes welling up as she tried to hold back the flood of emotions. Slowly, a tear slid down her cheek as she felt the weight of their loss. It seemed as if a part of her had been consumed by the flames that had taken Daddy, leaving her empty and hollow, stripped of any emotions at all.

In the deep hole of her grief, she fought for strength to take the next step. "We'll all be okay," she said, her voice trembling but determined.

She reached out and grabbed each of their hands.

"We have each other, and I promise I'll take care of everything." Her words hung in the air like fragile threads of hope, and she saw nothing but overwhelming despair in their eyes.

There were no words for how shattered their world had become, but in that moment, Frankie remembered Mama's words from long ago. *You're a fighter, Frankie Girl, never forget to fight for love.*

The three siblings tried to piece together a life following the fire.

For several weeks the trailer park was the scene of an active investigation and Sheriff Allen stopped by almost every day to check on Frankie.

He was there the day Debbie's eyes widened and she let out a deep guttural groan that was the beginning of a long and hard 24-hour labor, ending with a c-section operation when the baby went into fetal distress.

A loud wail finally signaled the birth of Debbie's baby. Frankie and Debbie both cried from exhaustion and amazement at the tiny infant who was placed in his mother's arms when she returned from the recovery room.

Debbie stared at the baby, overwhelmed with all that had taken place.

"Frankie," she said as she fought back her exhaustion. "We need to give him a name. Can we name him Larry O?"

Frankie lifted the baby and cradled him in her arms. His dark curly hair and dark eyes reminded her of Larry O, and she remembered his request.

"Debbie, how about if we name him Rocky? You know, the guy in the movies who's a fighter and comes out a winner even when everyone is against him? How about that name?"

Debbie's eyes were half-closed as she struggled to stay awake. "Sure, Frankie, Rocky is a good name. Larry O would be a better name, but Daddy would have hated it. Rocky is a good name."

Frankie held Rocky in her arms as Debbie and Rocky both drifted off to sleep. His tiny fingers were wrapped around her finger, and she had to pry them open when the nurse came to take him to the nursery.

She fought back tears as she released him into the nurse's arms. He was already breaking down the walls around her heart and she felt a wave of pure love wash over her.

Mama, is this what it felt like for you? I've never felt this kind of love before.

CHAPTER ELEVEN

TRIALS AND TEMPTATIONS

*L*arry O's trial for arson and murder was announced soon after the investigation closed and within six months the small-town justice system placed his case on the docket. Frankie and her state-appointed prosecutor worked hard to assemble the evidence. But Larry O's defense attorneys were good, and some of the community thought the big city lawyers might prove him innocent.

Their defense hinged on the sisters' alleged deception of Larry O, leading him to believe he was the father of Debbie's child. According to Larry O's attorneys, this manipulation had pushed Larry O to a state of temporary insanity, making him incapable of being responsible for an accident like the one in question.

Their strategy was to establish that there was no ill intent on his part, portraying him as a victim of deceit rather than as a perpetrator.

It looked like Larry O could go scot-free from the arson charge of Buck Taylor's trailer and the murder charge itself, but Frankie had a plan that would stop the attorneys dead in their tracks. Or so she thought.

The question on everyone's mind in town was whether Debbie would be put on the stand. The prosecuting attorneys wouldn't commit, but the trial was coming up and the defense attorneys were asking for a decision.

Frankie had convinced Debbie to testify against Larry O and reveal what happened, but she wasn't sure it was the best decision. She lay awake at night playing out the scenes where Debbie was calm and clear, never wavering in her testimony.

But then her mind would lead her to the opposite conclusion–Debbie would take one look at Larry O and cave on her well-rehearsed answers.

Frankie's attorneys thought Debbie needed to testify because the prosecution's case rested on Debbie's testimony which invalidated Larry O's defense.

The pre-trial work was exhausting for Frankie and Debbie as they talked endlessly about what happened the night Daddy died.

Debbie often got confused about what she had seen and said things out of order or made contradictory statements.

Frankie was concerned about the stress on Debbie and thought Tesh might be able to help.

As the three women sat down to chat at Tesh's house, Debbie suddenly got sick and ran to the bathroom. The two women heard her from the living room.

Frankie went back to help her sister gather herself together and help her muster enough strength for another conversation about the trial and her part in it.

Debbie held her hand to her mouth and looked at Frankie with big, sad eyes. "I can't do this. Please don't let them put me on the stand."

Frankie wrapped her arms around her big sister and pulled Debbie's head onto her shoulder. She was caving in.

The anxiety was making both of them sick but in different ways. "Ok, Debbie, we'll talk to the D.A. and figure out a different path. This is no way to live. We'll find another way to find justice for Larry O."

Tesh noticed a change in Frankie's demeanor as the sisters walked back to Tesh's living room. "You ok, Debbie?" Tesh's voice was soft and carried her concern for Debbie.

"I can't let them put her on the stand," Frankie looked over Debbie's shoulder at Tesh. "I just can't do it. She's been sick all week and is getting worse. I can still take the stand myself if the D.A. thinks my testimony will work."

Frankie realized her big sister literally couldn't stomach the thought of being on the stand and facing Larry O.

Debbie didn't have it in her to betray the father of her child. Her perception of Larry O's love was naive, but very real to her.

"But Frankie, Larry O's attorneys will come after you like the snakes they are." Tesh's voice raised in volume, and she looked terrified. "Are you sure you and Debbie can't work this out?"

"We've tried everything, and it's too confusing for her." Frankie looked at her sister, whose eyes were downcast, and her lips quivered. Debbie nodded, wiped away tears from her eyes, and softly said, "I'm sorry, Frankie, I'm just not smart enough for this trial and lawyering stuff."

She moved to the sofa and sat down with a massive sigh before leaning over to rest her head on a pillow.

Frankie and Tesh watched her for a long time until she fell asleep. Tesh motioned Frankie to the kitchen table and grabbed tea from the fridge.

They spoke in low voices of the implications of Debbie not

testifying versus her taking the stand and stumbling with her words and making mistakes.

"My greatest fear in this trial," Frankie said, after they talked through many scenarios, "is that Debbie will turn on me if she's on the witness stand. She'll make me out to be the one who set everything up. I know she is still in love with Larry O. He asked her to marry him that night and she thinks he's still coming back for her somehow. Even though he came back later, he was drunk and out of his mind. She believes his crock of lies."

At that statement, Tesh's heart went cold. She sat back in her chair, and her voice was stern.

"Frankie, wake up! She's an innocent child in a woman's body. She's been taken advantage of by everyone around her."

Tesh had held in her feelings about the Taylor family for a long time, but her reserve was breaking, and anger was boiling up.

Her eyes flashed as she stared at Frankie. "What I've witnessed for years and haven't said anything about to anyone, except to my husband, has been horrifying. I have a few hard things to tell you, my dear, whether you want to hear them or not."

Frankie arched an eyebrow. "Debbie's been taken advantage of by everyone around her? That's harsh to say when you're looking right at me."

"Here's the thing, Frankie, you knew all along what was going on. Buck wasn't the only guilty one when he got the trailer ready for date night because you knew about it, too. I know you did. You're the smartest person around, and you can't tell me you didn't know what was going on."

Tesh was putting it all on the line as Frankie stared back at her in disbelief.

"You're accusing me of being complicit? I did not help Daddy pimp out my sister, and I did not know what he was doing in the beginning. I told you how I found out and that Daddy and I fought about it to the point where he hit me. One night, he beat me badly. *He* ruined my family, not me. There, are you satisfied?"

She looked at Tesh with sudden hatred in her eyes.

"You betrayed me. I thought *you* had my back. You're the only person I can talk to about this." Her eyes flashed in anger as Tesh looked away. Frankie took a few deep breaths until her anger slowly dissolved, and she was empty inside. "You *were* the only person I was able to talk to about this. I wish I had known earlier you felt this way. You *were* the only friend I had. I guess it's just Debbie and me now."

She stood up from the table and woke her sister on the sofa.

Tesh immediately regretted the outburst, and her heart broke. She loved Frankie in so many ways and didn't want Frankie to leave this way. She knew she had to break through to Frankie or this sudden rift would never be healed.

"Frankie, I'm so sorry I got angry. I didn't mean it like that. I've been frustrated, too, and only want this to work out for both of you." Tesh moved toward Frankie as Debbie woke from her deep sleep. "Please don't leave this way. I am so sorry."

Frankie busied herself with helping Debbie off the sofa before she replied to Tesh.

"I'm sorry you've carried those feelings and thoughts all along and didn't tell me before. Do you think I'm such a monster that I wouldn't do everything in my power to stop Daddy from date nights?

"I hated every moment of every Saturday night thinking about what might be going on across the parking lot. I puked my guts out for weeks before I hardened to it. I hated Daddy, and I started hating her, too." She gestured toward Debbie, who was putting the pillows back in place on the sofa.

"When my hate started creeping in toward her, an innocent victim, I knew I was in deep trouble." Frankie was holding herself together, remembering how difficult it was to justify what was happening at Buck's Bar.

"It's only when I started talking to Mama at night that I found peace and sleep. My Mama dreams gave me a way to think about it that allowed me to live with myself and Daddy. At least for a little while."

"Can we go home?" Debbie tugged at Frankie's sleeve. She was groggy with sleep and ready to return to the trailer park and continue her nap.

Frankie put her arm around Debbie and quieted her. She spoke in a low voice, "Tesh, when the anger erupted in me, I was no longer the Frankie you thought you knew. I was out of my mind that night with the horror of it all, and I'm not sorry I pressed charges. I'll never be sorry about that.

"We'll get justice for what Larry O did somehow, but not for the fact that Daddy died. Daddy deserved to die. The justice I want is for Larry O's cruelty to Debbie. How he deceived her by asking her to marry him, but never intending to make good on his promise to her. He only came back that night because he was so drunk."

Tesh held her breath to see what Frankie would do next. She wanted peace between them and knew she had created a barrier instead.

Frankie opened the door, gave Tesh a weary smile, and the sisters stepped out. Tesh let out her breath and wished they weren't leaving on such a sad note.

"Tell me you'll come back later, Frankie, so we can talk this out?" Frankie didn't reply to Tesh's question.

As they were leaving Tesh's house, Debbie paused and looked up at Frankie with a wary look, "Larry O didn't do anything bad to me, did he?" Tesh heard Debbie's question and her heart broke all over again.

*T*he only bright spot for Frankie as the trial preparation ground on was college. She was invigorated by the learning opportunities at the community college and especially loved her business and computer science classes.

Buck's Bar & Grill closed after Daddy died, but she finished high school with honors, despite the trauma and chaos created by the fire, investigation, and the ensuing trial.

On the day of her 18th birthday, with Professor Todd Burton's help, she became the guardian for both Debbie, Rocky, and Butch and their future together as a family was secured.

For the first time, Frankie felt accepted in school. Other students respected how quickly she grasped difficult subjects and she was well known for her growing skills at coding in the computer science class.

Long after the other students left, Professor Burton would find her completely immersed in a project, with her fingers dancing on the keyboard, pounding out line after line of code. Like a musician deep in the creation of a symphony.

"You make magic on the computer," he said to her one day when he saw a light on in the lab and found her there long after the other students had gone. "I have to close up the lab. Want something to eat?"

Frankie glanced at him and motioned toward the screen. "Give me five and then I'm out of here."

"Want to go for some pizza?"

Frankie ignored him until she was at a breaking point in her project. "Ok, that's done. Sure, pizza sounds great." She loved coding as much as the Professor did and some days, she would have stayed all night if he didn't come to close the lab down.

Over pizza and sodas, they chatted about his special project at the Community College. "MIT is loving what you're doing, Frankie. You're the star of the project and I'm blown away by everything you're turning in. You have a great future in computer science. MIT would love to have you after this project wraps up."

"Not so fast, Professor." Frankie took a bite of her pizza and grabbed the cheese as it strung out from between her teeth. "I need some help."

Professor Todd Burton's raised eyebrows showed his surprise. Frankie Taylor never asked anyone for help. She was a 'head down, I'll get it done,' kind of girl and nobody messed with her. If she was asking for help, it must be something big.

Todd knew they'd pushed the professor/student line a few times late at night in the computer lab, but he couldn't resist her when she showed him several of her projects.

She coded like a pro and was well beyond programming simple games like Pong, Pac-Man, or Frogger the other students were still struggling through. He thought she looked like a piano player at the keyboard, her fingers dancing lightly to a rhythm no one else heard.

"MIT sounds good, but I need to leave here sooner than that. I need to make money now because Buck's Bar isn't open, and I don't have credit for a bank loan. Besides, I hate banks."

She shuddered as she remembered the phone call she took for her father when his account was overdrawn. She'd had to do a shady deal with Larry O to fix that problem and he would say she still owed him a lot for it.

"There's just Debbie, Rocky, and me, now that Butch got sent up for the robbery he and his stupid friends did. They bungled it so badly, but as a juvenile he shouldn't have gone to jail. The thing is, he got stuck holding the gun, so he has to pay the time."

"What's your plan, Frankie? You always have a plan. You could easily find a job as a computer programmer if you want that."

Professor Burton's connections could quickly secure a high-paying job for her as a female programmer in a second. He was well-known in the field and Frankie's name was already floating around as news spread of her work in his well-funded program.

He hadn't expected a genius of her sort to show up at the small Community College on the Eastern Shore of Maryland, but he was thrilled, for many reasons, that she was there.

Frankie shook her head as she grabbed a second piece of pizza. "I need to be close to home until after the trial."

She smiled as she chewed. "You're right, though, I do have a plan. See what you think of this." She pulled a document out of her backpack and handed it over to him.

"It's an employment contract?" He studied it for a minute. "Ah, you went and talked to my friend George Duberman, didn't you? He hired you, just like I thought he would. He's no dummy."

Todd looked around the pizza shop before he scooted his chair over beside hers. No one else was there and he put his arm around her and took the pizza slice out of her hand.

"Tell me you're not going to take this job. How can you go to Philly and work and stay in class? Please don't tell me you're dropping out." He frowned at her and pushed the contract away.

Frankie was quiet as she picked up the pizza and tore a small piece of crust off the end.

"I don't see any other way to keep my family together unless I have a job where I can make money and climb the ladder fast. In this contract, I make a commission on everything I lease. I'll work hard until the trial is over and then maybe I can come back to class. They've delayed the trial again and I can't afford to not make money."

She hated the look of disappointment on his face and wanted to lighten up the conversation.

"I have a better idea, Frankie, and I think you'll like this one a lot." Todd shifted so he faced Frankie to see her reaction. He'd been mulling this idea over for a while but had shelved it due to the pressure Frankie was under with the Larry O case.

"I've noticed a lot of investors buying land in the area. I heard last week the Germans put in an offer to buy the farm adjacent to the trailer park. How about if I check in with my contacts and see if they'd be interested in buying the trailer park?

"I'm sure they'd love to add your adjacent five-acre piece on the corner to finish out their 2,000 acres. Then you'd be free to start over wherever you want, and your family would be taken care of, too."

Frankie looked at him with surprise. This was something she'd never considered, although her business classes were opening her mind to many new possibilities beyond what she'd imagined before.

"Sell the trailer park? Someone would buy it?" She paused for a minute to absorb what Todd was saying. He nodded as questions spilled out of her.

Todd assured her the property had high value, even though it was a small plot of land. The specific location would finish out the purchase already in the works and might happen relatively soon.

He covered all the details with her and mapped out how the deal would go together.

"Daddy would turn over in his grave if he heard this conversation." Frankie was processing everything so fast and beamed at Todd as she realized there was a future beyond the trailer park.

"Todd, you're a genius and I love, love that you've been hatching this real estate plan. I never would have thought of it."

Todd smiled. "You will think about nothing else but real estate if you ditch my class and go to work for George Duberman. As much as I hate the thought of it, real estate is a perfect choice for you right now. You'll love the pace and the pay-off for your hard work."

Frankie's eyes were bright, and she couldn't stop grinning at Todd. If everything he said came true, she would have a second chance at life.

Maybe she'd be able to take care of Rocky someday, too.

Todd threw some bills on the table and grabbed her hand. "Let's go for a drive and find a spot to watch the moon."

He and Frankie were on a natural high, excited at the possibility of selling the trailer park.

There'd be a lot of work to do before the deal was done, but for tonight she was his and he wanted to do more than talk about real estate.

After they pulled into a familiar wooded area, Todd spread out a blanket and they sat down, touching thigh to thigh. He wrapped his arm around her and pointed at the moon.

"It's a full moon, Frankie, even the celestial beings are celebrating with you."

She giggled and they collapsed onto the blanket, laughing with sheer delight at the thought of future possibilities.

Frankie stared at Todd. "This is amazing. You navigate the world so well and you have been so kind to me. There isn't anything I wouldn't do for you right now."

She leaned into him, but he held her at arm's length. "Just one thing, Frankie. Are you still going to ditch my class and take the job in Philly?"

She smiled at him and pulled him closer. "Of course, silly. I'm going to work my buns off for a year or two, get this trial behind us, and then I'll be back to code your programs. But right now, I think we should make some magic of our own."

She found his lips, her insides quivering as she heard a low groan escape his throat. They were no longer professor and student but equals, in a meadow under a full moon, with a bright future ahead for them both.

Frankie's mind calmed as her body took over, giving her much-needed relief from the endless pressures of fighting a legal battle with Larry O, taking care of her family, going to classes and visiting Butch.

She smiled as she stroked Todd's hair and melted into him, craving his hard body against hers. Her whole being moved into motion with him, and she cried out as love flowed through her. She was safe and happy for the first time since Mama died.

"Is this what love is like, Mama?" she thought to herself. *"If it is, I'll take a whole bucket full of it."*

*L*arry O's trial was delayed numerous times, but Frankie didn't waste time waiting for the final trial date. She left the Eastern Shore of MD and headed to a tiny apartment in Philadelphia.

Amid millions of people, she came to life for the first time in a long time. No one cared what she looked like, who she was, or what she was up to.

She realized she had been living in a fishbowl on the Eastern Shore, and the freedom to come and go as she pleased suited her life quite nicely.

Working hard was the prescription for her ailments and she thrived at work and caught the eye of George Duberman, Todd's friend who owned the company. He often found her in her office late at night and they'd chat for a couple of minutes before he headed out.

"You're the only person who works harder than me," he'd say to her with a chuckle.

She loved their short encounters and asked the older gentleman many questions about the industry. He noticed her interests and began leaving highlighted articles and books for her. She'd devour them and that fueled more conversations.

Soon, they were regular lunch buddies, and she was invited to meet his wife and daughter. He was proud of her and thought she was like he had been at the beginning of his career, hungry for knowledge he could turn into money.

There wasn't a minute to spare in Frankie's life as she climbed the ladder in Duberman's company. He made introductions to valued connections and she was a fast learner in knowing who to trust to share their industry expertise with her.

Her evenings were filled with networking dinners and "drinks for deals" as she laughingly called them when she reported to George Duberman. He was intensely interested in helping her with her budding career, but she never talked about her life outside of the real estate world. And he never asked.

She never mentioned the trailer park, her dead daddy and mama, her sister, her brother, or anything outside of her new life. It was like they'd never existed.

CHAPTER TWELVE

FULL MOON AT THE TRAILER PARK

Frankie pulled into the parking lot at Buck's Bar around ten on Friday evening after another long week of work in Philadelphia.

After she'd turned 21, she'd temporarily opened the bar on Saturday nights because the regular crowd had begged her to give them one night a week. She'd relented after a year or so of listening to them plead their case every time she came back from Philly.

Besides, the bar had a mortgage, and she needed the money. She finally understood the financial pressures that drove Daddy to drink and sell his soul to the devil.

She swore she'd never be like her father.

She noticed a light in Debbie's room in the trailer beside the bar, grabbed her bag and headed that way. She was happy to notice the door was locked and as she fished in her backpack for her keys, the door swung open.

"Frankie, I was worried you weren't coming tonight and Tesh

has already gone home," Debbie grabbed her sister and clung to her for a moment.

"Sorry, sis, I got a late start, and the traffic in the city was awful." Frankie looked past Debbie and noticed the place was tidy, everything was in its place. *Tesh knew I was coming,* Frankie thought to herself. *God bless that woman.*

After Daddy died and the chaos that ensued, Tesh offered to take care of Rocky. And Frankie was grateful for the selfless care she gave him.

They agreed that Rocky would not call Debbie his mother so that Tesh could fulfill that role for now. And if Frankie was ever able to, she would adopt him. Tesh did everything to not fall in love with the sweet infant from the moment she first held him. But her heart won out and she dreaded the day she wouldn't be his *"Teshie."*

Tesh's kindness to the Taylor sisters was beyond measure. At four years old, Rocky was rambunctious and full of life.

He loved playing with 'Auntie Deb' and always hugged her tightly before she left to go back home. He was a happy boy with a head full of black curls and deep brown eyes that melted Frankie's heart.

Frankie and Debbie talked for a while, chatting about Rocky and Debbie's activities during the week.

After Daddy's funeral, several of the church ladies had 'adopted' Debbie as their new project and they kept her busy with lunch dates, crafting, and local outings. She thrived from the attention and care she was getting, and Frankie was grateful that she wasn't sitting at home all day watching TV.

Before long, Debbie yawned loudly and headed back to her bedroom.

"I'm going to check the bar for a few minutes," Frankie said and headed over to Buck's Bar in the adjacent trailer.

The bar lights were bright and glaring to Frankie after her two-hour drive from the city and she turned the dimmer down to let her eyes reset. The inventory she'd ordered for the week was stacked up by the end of the bar and she sighed as she viewed the cartons of sodas, beer, and liquor.

That's a job for the morning, she thought.

She sat down on a bar stool and surveyed the place. Everything was the way Frankie left it the last time; the grill was cleaned, and the tables and chairs were in order.

She was pleased with the way the place looked and had a fleeting thought about what Daddy would think of Buck's Bar when she heard a car pull into the parking lot.

She walked to the front door, locked it and remembered she had also locked the trailer where Debbie was sleeping. Frankie glanced out the window and was surprised the Sheriff's SUV had just pulled in.

Sheriff Allen turned off the vehicle and got out slowly. He stretched, turned around to look at the three remaining trailers and then leaned against his SUV and waited for Frankie to make the first move.

Frankie watched him closely from inside the locked bar. Maybe I can wait him out and he'll leave, she thought briefly. But she also wanted to talk and thought it was harmless to have a short chat with the Sheriff and relax with a drink.

She unlocked the door and opened it halfway. "Hey, Mr. Sheriff, what are you doing here this time of night? You know the bar is closed." She stood by the open door, not inviting him in just yet.

"Yes, ma'am, I realize it's late and I hope I'm not bothering you." Sheriff Allen didn't move either. He was a patient man, and he knew her game.

Frankie looked him up and down and paused for a moment.

"You're not bothering me at all. I was going to invite you in for a drink, but I'm certain you don't drink on the job."

She gave him a small smile and pushed the door wide open. "Come on in, you are welcome in my bar."

Sheriff Allen smiled back at her. "Thanks, Frankie. I just finished my shift, and I was out this way and saw the lights. Thought you might be back in town to work the bar tomorrow night and wanted to say a quick hello."

The light from the bar created a halo around Frankie's hair and as she stood there waiting for him, Sheriff Allen thought she looked like an angel. *She is so beautiful,* he thought, *I can barely breathe.*

"You comin' in?" She stepped back into the bar and waited for him to make his move.

He paused to savor the moment and drink in her beauty. The light picked up the hues of her chestnut-colored hair and her smile brightened her green eyes as she waited for his answer.

His heart was tortured with what he wanted and what he knew he couldn't have.

He pushed off the SUV and headed toward the trailer trying to walk without noisily crunching the stones in the parking lot. Sheriff Allen was a head taller than Frankie with broad shoulders and a toned body and when he reached the trailer door he gave her a quick hug.

"Looks like someone's been working out," Frankie stepped back and eyed him up and down.

"Yeah, I have to pass my annual physical, so I've been putting in some time at the gym," Sheriff Allen grinned at the veiled compliment Frankie gave him.

Frankie stepped behind the bar and pulled out a bottle of Jack Daniels and mixed it with a Coke. "Have a seat at my bar, Mr. Sheriff. No drink for you though, right?"

She knew the Sheriff didn't drink but also that he wouldn't mind if she did. "It's been a hard week and I need to relax. It's good to see you, by the way. How was your week?"

As the Sheriff recounted his week Frankie surveyed the man in front of her. He had a kind face, with blue eyes and short blond hair. They had become road trip buddies, but Frankie never allowed the Sheriff to crawl into her heart.

Still, she would always be grateful for his assistance during the fire on the night Daddy died and how he helped during the investigation. He'd been there, too, when Debbie went into labor, and he took them to hospital when Rocky was born.

After that, she hadn't seen him very often. The two of them hadn't talked much about the horrific incident when her father died. Frankie wondered if it would come up tonight.

There was silence and Frankie suddenly realized she missed what the Sheriff told her about his week.

"I don't want to assume anything, Frankie," the sheriff continued, "but I haven't seen you for a very long time and I missed you. I know you are busy, but I wanted to catch up and make sure everything is good for you. Maybe go on a road trip sometime soon?" He tried to keep a neutral tone but realized his voice was a little shaky.

"Missed you, too, Sheriff," Frankie said lightly, hoping he wasn't going to get sappy on her. They both knew the undercurrent evident on road trips was deeper than friendship, but Frankie couldn't take the relationship as far as the Sheriff wanted it to go.

"I have two lives now, you know. One here with Debbie and Rocky, and one in Philly. Both are good and I wouldn't give one up for the other. Road trips are so lovely, though."

Frankie was sending mixed messages to the Sheriff but hoped he would understand her underlying meaning. But he was already feeling too much for her and the road trip reference gave him hope.

She took a deep drink of her whiskey and Coke and let the silence settle around them.

After a second long sip, she looked across the bar at him. He kept her gaze, paused, and took a deep breath. "Frankie, you're an amazing person. I don't know how you do what you do. I've seen you fight for everything you have and take care of your sister and brother with the fierceness of a Mother Lion. But who takes care of you, Frankie?"

His soft voice broke the silence, and a shiver went up her spine. He wanted so badly to help her, hold her close, and have her for his own. His restrained desire was evident in his eyes and his breathing gave away what was happening in his heart.

Frankie walked around the bar and sat on the bar stool next to him.

"You are so kind and big-hearted. I always thought the police were hard-hearted. You know, 'pigs'." She air-quoted the word to show that it wasn't her sentiment.

"Ouch, that hurt." The Sheriff swiveled his bar stool and leaned against the bar to take a look at Frankie. Her response had surprised him.

"Is that really what you think of me and my fellow lawmen? I'm deeply offended by that statement, Missie." He decided a lighter tone might be more appropriate to calm down the rising heat in his body.

Frankie laughed softly. "Nah, that's just what people called you guys in the war protests. I didn't mean anything by it."

It was better to keep things light now. She wasn't ready for any advances from him tonight. She just wanted a friend to talk with and no messy entanglements.

She felt safe with the Sheriff and was certain he would respect her need to keep him at arm's length.

The Sheriff saw the shift in her body and saw her facial muscles relax. He knew this was his night to be a friend, not a lover, and the realization disappointed him.

"Here's the thing, though, Frankie, I'm not the police, I'm the Sheriff. Big Difference."

"Tell me, Sheriff, because both are law enforcement, so I should be afraid of both of you, don't you think?" Frankie kept up the light banter between them.

Sheriff Allen knew most folks didn't know the difference and that his kind of law enforcement was often misunderstood.

"I won't bore you with the details, Frankie Girl, but here's the low down." The Sheriff listed how his duties were different from the police–he had jurisdiction over a county, not a specific city or town, his duties included the county jail, serving court papers, taking care of security at the courthouse and other duties that helped to protect the citizens of the county.

"As a Sheriff, I am the highest-ranking law enforcement officer in the county which some of the police officers don't like. Especially the older ones. They think I'm way too young to know anything. But we work together well, especially when we're teaming up for investigations into big crimes."

"Sorry, Allen, I didn't know those details. I'm sorry I made that stupid statement."

"Sure, Frankie, that's ok. I know you don't think of me that way. What can I do to help you forget about the week and just relax and let it go?" he said without any expectations, and the sincerity of his request was evident to her.

Frankie took a long, deep breath and let it out until her lungs were empty. Her shoulders slumped forward, and she laid her arm out on the bar and rested her head on it. "Thanks, Allen, for under-standing. You mean so much to me and I'm happy you are here to hang out with me. Let me tell you about my week."

An hour passed as Frankie recounted the meetings she had with city officials about a new project she was working on. It was a high-rise by the river, and she had named it Riverview Lofts.

That was just a working name, she explained, until they final-ized the paperwork and cleared the use of the term. She was excited about the project and Allen loved seeing the sparkle in her eyes.

Frankie loved her work and Allen enjoyed listening to her tell the details of her job. It always sounded glamorous and important and sexy. She viewed herself as 'the small-town girl with the big city life' and she always laughed when she used that phrase.

Her workload was intense, and she spent long hours in the office and on-site with building and remodeling projects.

Allen understood her lifestyle didn't allow for caring for Rocky and was amazed how she religiously came back to the trailer park every weekend to keep things intact.

The alcohol was relaxing Frankie, and she was glad he had stopped by. She didn't want to push him out the door, but she couldn't stop yawning.

"Frankie, you need some sleep," Allen noted after another big yawn. "I won't keep you up any longer. I'm so happy we got to talk. If you lock up now, I'll walk you to the other trailer."

He stood up and waited as she walked around the bar, poured another drink, and came back beside him. She set the glass on the bar, reached her arms up around his neck and then laid her head on his shoulder for just a second.

"Thanks, Allen, you are the best." Then she picked up her drink and headed for the door.

They walked quietly to the other trailer and the Sheriff paused at the door. He wanted to put his arms around her and feel those sweet lips against his own.

Frankie reached up again and gave him a quick hug. He wanted to hold on forever, but she released her arms and fished in her purse for her keys.

Allen stepped back and waited to exhale until Frankie was inside and he heard the door locking. He let out his breath slowly and headed to his car.

How long can I take this torture, he thought. Frankie's bedroom light went on and he banged his head against the steering wheel. *Pure torture.*

Frankie waited inside the trailer, listening for his car to leave the parking lot. As the tires crunched their way out, she slugged the alcohol, got in bed, and turned off the light.

Mama, is love possible with a man like Allen? She whispered. *He's not in love with the real me.*

*S*ix weeks later Frankie was feeling the pressure of Saturday night at Buck's Bar. It had been another long work week in Philly, and she was exhausted. It was full moon and she didn't want any trouble at the bar. She made a quick call to Sheriff Allen's office and left a voice mail asking if he'd send an undercover detective out later in the evening.

It wasn't long before all the stools at the bar were taken, most of the tables were filled and she was manning the place by herself.

As long as she kept the beer coming everyone seemed fine, but she couldn't seem to fry the hamburgers fast enough.

"Hurry it up, Frankie," a bearded guy wearing an Eagles hat

called from across the room. "I've been working all day and I'm hungry."

"Don't worry about him," yelled out another guy who was wearing a Ravens cap backward. "He ain't no good and neither is his team!"

There was loud laughter and snarky football team comments flying around the room and Frankie smiled as she flipped burgers and took more beer orders.

It would be a profitable night at Buck's Bar and maybe her decision to keep the bar open was a good one after all.

Most of these guys were regulars when her dad ran the bar and they had pushed her to reopen the bar after Daddy died and the chaos settled down. It was a lot of work for Frankie to come back to the Eastern Shore each weekend after a busy week in Philly, but she was committed to keeping the bar operational for the time being.

Coming home each weekend gave her a chance to evaluate Debbie's demeanor and to visit Rocky and Tesh. She fell in love with Rocky as soon as he was born and swore to herself and Debbie that she would take care of him forever.

He is the sweetest child, she thought to herself and smiled as she envisioned his dark curls and even darker, big round eyes.

Rocky lived with Tesh and thrived under her care and love. Debbie spent time with them when the church ladies didn't have her busy and Frankie visited on the weekend.

It was the best scenario Tesh and Frankie were able to create given the situation they were in.

Frankie's thoughts were interrupted by yells and a crash on the other side of the bar. She looked over just in time to see a beer bottle flying through the air and an angry guy pulling back to take a swing at someone across the table.

They were too far into the fist pummeling to even hear

Frankie's screams and one of them went down with the other one falling on top of him.

Frankie screamed for help and the two guys closest to the fight jumped up and went to break up the barroom brawl. Fists were flying as they all swarmed together, scrambling all over each other.

Frankie went behind the bar, grabbed her air horn and blew it loudly three times. That caught everyone's attention.

"Stop it. No fights, boys," she yelled harshly as she placed the air horn next to her father's pistol underneath the bar. "I'll kick all of you out of here if you can't settle down. There'll be no trouble in Buck's Bar tonight. You hear?"

She turned to check the burgers on the grill and started serving them into buns lined up in little red plastic baskets.

"No one gets beer until everyone sits down and shuts up." She looked across the room with a hard glare that dared anyone to cross her.

No one knew it, but she had Daddy's pistol behind the bar, and she would use it if she needed to. She searched the room for an undercover cop, hoping Sheriff Allen had heard her voice mail, but she knew all the faces in the bar.

The room quieted down as Frankie served the burgers and took more beer orders. Her nerves were taut, and her body was pumping adrenaline as she realized the precarious situation she was in.

It wouldn't take much for this group to take control, even if she had a gun. She was in high anxiety mode and wished the under-cover cop was in the room.

Conversations started again as the burgers were devoured and additional orders were placed. Frankie kept busy at the grill, breaking away to fill beer orders and pass out bags of Herr's potato chips.

The guys were hungry after a full week of work and Frankie knew they needed to shake off some tension.

She walked to the front door of the bar and counted 12 trucks in the parking lot. Most of the guys came together in twos and threes so she had a crowd to handle.

She surveyed the room from the door and thought everything seemed under control. Most of the guys had finished their first round of burgers and were leaning back in their chairs waiting for Frankie to serve up the next round.

She'd have four or five more rounds of burgers to cook before their appetites waned, their stomachs were full, and they started to relax as the effect of booze and burgers kicked in.

As Frankie walked back to the grill one of the guys reached out and slapped her on the butt.

She twirled around and slapped him in the face. "You do not touch me." She grabbed him by the shirt and brought her face to his. "Don't be a slimeball and never, ever touch me again."

A couple of the guys snickered and one of them yelled, "Frankie, calm down, we're just having fun with ya."

Frankie glared at him and went back to the grill. She knew from many years in the bar to be very careful how she talked with the guys.

Too much attention to a single guy would be noticed by the crowd and the guys always had each other's back. They would fight each other one minute and then defend each other the next.

Frankie didn't want to incite any more attention her way, so she focused on getting the next round of burgers grilled and out to the tables.

The conversation slowed as the next round of burgers was snarfed down. Frankie was in a cadence now of flipping burgers and setting beer on the bar.

The guys on bar stools would pass them back through the

crowd and Frankie kept flipping burgers and serving all the orders.

Frankie breathed a sigh of relief as she heard a vehicle pull into the parking lot. *Finally, the undercover cop is here,* she thought. *Now, I'll be ok.* She suddenly realized how tense she was, and she rolled her shoulders trying to loosen up and relax.

The front door opened, and she was shocked to see Sheriff Allen. The entire bar did a double take as the Sheriff stepped into the bar and scanned the room.

The shock turned into curiosity and suspicion at the Sheriff's presence and Frankie also wondered what was going on. In all the years she worked at Buck's, the Sheriff never came during bar hours.

Sheriff Allen walked over to the end of the bar and looked at Frankie. He didn't smile at her but gave her a nod. Then he looked back over the crowd and stopped to focus on one guy seated at a table in the center of the bar.

"Good evening, Harry, I thought you might be here." He nodded to Harry and motioned for him to come over to the end of the bar.

"What do you want with me?" Harry asked in a hesitant voice. He was a slight, younger fellow with long brown hair and a scar on his cheekbone. He fidgeted before he got up.

"I'm not in trouble, am I?" he asked the Sheriff.

The guys in the bar all laughed and a couple mumbled loudly, "Of course you are, Harry, you're a loser."

"No, sir, you're not in trouble." The Sheriff motioned to Harry in a friendly but firm manner. "Your family wanted me to find you. Can we step outside for a minute?"

The two men walked out the front door and down the steps into the gravel parking lot. No one in the bar said a word as

Frankie continued grilling burgers. Everyone was straining to catch the conversation outside, but they were too far away.

Whispers were heard around the room about what kind of trouble Harry was in this time.

It seemed like forever before Harry and the Sheriff came back and all eyes were on Harry as he went to his seat. No one said a word.

The Sheriff addressed Frankie and the rest of the bar. "Sorry to interrupt your Saturday evening, folks. I just needed to chat with Harry for a moment. I hope you'll respect his privacy, everyone. Ma'am." He tipped his hat to Frankie and turned toward the front door.

Frankie was quick to move toward the Sheriff before he reached the door. "Could I have a word, Sheriff?" She was worried about the rowdiness of the crowd and wondered if the Sheriff could watch out for the bar if he was in the area.

They stepped outside the door and the Sheriff said, "As crazy as it sounds, I wanted to stop by tonight because it's full moon and people get a little out of hand sometimes. My undercover guy is sick, so I was worried about you here at the bar.

"Then I got a call from Harry's family that his dad is dying, and they were asking for help to locate him. I thought he might be here, so I thought I'd come over, talk to him here, and check if you were okay."

Frankie glanced back at the bar, wondering how Harry was taking the news.

"I'll park down the street so I'm nearby if anything comes up. You have a gun, right? Use it if you need to."

He spoke urgently, then turned away and added, "Act immediately if anything happens. Flick the outside lights and I'll come over right away. These guys are amped up for some reason. Must be the moon."

A shiver went up her spine. She was already on high alert, her shoulder muscles were tight, and she was certain she would snap if anything else happened. She glanced over and saw the light in Debbie's bedroom.

"Hey Allen, would you go over and turn Debbie's light off? I don't want anyone to see her bedroom lights when they leave the bar. She's probably already asleep.

"Oh, and make sure the door is locked, please. Debbie doesn't always remember to do that."

He nodded and she returned to the bar to take care of burgers and beer. Everyone seemed to settle in, and the conversations were calmer and less electric than before. Frankie sighed and hoped the full moon wouldn't kick in the crazies tonight.

More rounds of burgers and beer were passed out and before too long a few of the old guys were nodding off.

A couple of young guys pulled out cards and before long the dollar bills were stacking up. Tables were pushed together to allow for more players, and everyone was either playing poker or watching money exchange hands.

Frankie was relieved that they were focusing on something to keep their attention off her. *What did Mama used to say,* she thought. *Don't go looking for trouble, it'll find you all on its own.*

Looking out the back window she mused about the myth of the full moon effects and then searched to see if Sheriff Allen's car was down the road.

Under the glow of the moonlight, she saw a slight reflection from his car and sighed with relief.

How kind it was for him to find an excuse to stop by and check on her. *He's too good for me,* she thought.

*S*heriff Allen sat in his car and rolled down the window. It was a cool night and the moonlight shimmered on the hood of his vehicle as he faced the east with Buck's Bar in clear sight.

He said a silent prayer for a quiet night and settled in for the duration.

But it wasn't long until his walkie-talkie crackled from the dispatch center. "Trouble in Rockhall, Sheriff. Boating accident. Possible fatalities."

The Sheriff groaned. "On my way," he replied into the mouthpiece. "Be there in about 20 minutes."

He whipped his SUV around and hit the gas. He went into crisis mode but then slowed down when he got to Tesh's house. He slammed his brakes and rushed to the door.

Tesh came to the door and he told her the situation. "Can you keep an eye on the trailer park tonight? There's an accident in RockHall and I've gotta go."

She understood his intent and the Sheriff rushed back to the SUV and gunned it into action. He was sure the accident in Rockhall would require his attention for several hours.

The accident in Rockhall was a tragedy. All-day drinking and boating rarely end well, and tonight was no exception. Speeding in a boat at night, even under a full moon, was a formula for disaster and the drunk boat driver had crashed into a buoy out from Rockhall in the Chesapeake Bay.

It was an ugly scene with people everywhere and flashing lights from the ambulances arriving at the same time the sheriff arrived.

Off to the side, four people on the ground were being tended by medics and one body was completely covered with a blanket. *It never ends well with booze,* thought the Sheriff.

He made his way through the crowd and checked in with the

medics and the volunteer fire police who were managing the crowd control. Another boater had seen the accident happen, fished out the bodies and pulled the boat to shore, otherwise, the Sheriff was certain they would have all drowned by now.

He was short-tempered and entirely unsympathetic to the victims of the boating accident. Each year a boating accident was predictable and entirely preventable.

He sighed and got busy with his job. The sooner the team cleaned up the accident, the sooner he'd be back to guard Buck's Bar.

That's where he wanted to be, and his chest tightened as he thought about the scene he had encountered earlier in the bar. Frankie seemed so vulnerable when he left, and he found it hard to focus on the scene in front of him.

Calls to the station, checking in with the hospital, taking a report from the witness, and other paperwork took him several hours. It was well past midnight when he saw Rockhall in his rear-view mirror. He flipped on the siren and lights for the next 20 minutes to speed his way back to the trailer park.

When he was a mile or two out, he cut off the lights and sirens and backed down his speed. He took a back road to circle past Tesh's house before he ventured to the bar. Tesh's house was lit up and she was on the front porch. As soon as his car came into sight, she rushed toward him.

Adrenaline shot through the Sheriff as he saw Tesh run toward his SUV. She was screaming, "Go to the trailer park, go to the trailer park. There's a terrible ruckus going on. I heard a gunshot. Go."

The Sheriff hit the gas pedal and laid rubber on the worn country road. His heart was pounding so hard he thought his head would blow up. He couldn't think. His police academy training kicked into high gear, and he gunned it to the trailer park, not knowing what he might encounter.

Images of Frankie bleeding to death in Buck's Bar flashed through his mind as he screeched to a halt at the edge of the parking lot. He noticed only one truck in the parking lot as he sprinted across the parking lot to the open door of the bar.

He was yelling for Frankie as he entered, expecting the worst. He stopped in shock at what he saw.

Tables and chairs were scattered everywhere, and Harry was slumped on the floor, beaten to a pulp. The Sheriff ran over and pulled on Harry's shoulder, trying to straighten him out onto the floor. He was still breathing but he'd been beaten up badly and there was blood coming out of his nose and glistening all over his face.

The Sheriff checked Harry's pulse and then crossed the gravel parking lot to the big trailer where he heard loud wailing noises. He saw the trailer door was wide open and in two quick steps he was up on the porch and into the trailer's living room.

Moans were coming from the back of the trailer, down the hallway, where he saw Frankie leaning over Debbie.

The room was a mess, with chairs tipped over and clothes strewn across the floor.

"Frankie," he called out with fear in his voice. "Is everything ok? Do you need an ambulance?"

Frankie looked up at him with an urgent plea for help. "Yes, please help me with Debbie. I shot her in the foot, and she needs to go to the hospital. I just called 911 and an ambulance is on the way."

The Sheriff rushed to her side and began examining Debbie who was moaning and crying hysterically. He tried to calm her down, but she was beyond reason and couldn't hear him. She was rocking back and forth, moaning, and groaning, and starting to hyperventilate.

Frankie was busy wrapping Debbie's foot, and the Sheriff followed her instructions to find wet towels to stop the bleeding.

"I was in the bar, and I heard Debbie screaming so I grabbed Daddy's pistol and came over to see what was going on."

Frankie's eyes turned dark as she recounted the scene. "Harry was all over her and she was screaming like a banshee in the woods. I was terrified and yelled at him to stop. He was on top of her and was ripping her clothes off and I attacked him to get him off her. Somehow the pistol went off and I shot Debbie in the foot."

Frankie was shaking all over as she realized how close Debbie had been to being sexually assaulted and how she wanted to kill Harry when she saw what was happening.

She tightened her arms around her sister and tried to soothe her as her stomach heaved. She was light-headed with the tension of it all. In the distance, she heard sirens coming their way.

"I don't know what happened to Harry." Frankie looked up at the Sheriff with horror on her face. "Did he escape?"

The Sheriff shook his head. "He's over in the bar, lying on the floor. When I got here, he was unconscious. Somebody beat him up badly and he's in worse shape than Debbie."

The whole scene was a mess and Frankie felt helpless to calm her sister down. And she wasn't feeling very steady herself.

"It all happened so fast," Frankie had to shout over Debbie's loud groans. "You should go check on Harry. He might need your help."

The Sheriff nodded and ran back to Buck's Bar where Harry was still lying motionless on the floor.

After checking his pulse, the Sheriff took inventory of the damage to Harry's body. He had a busted nose, cuts just below his left eye and his face was already swelling from the impact of some-one's fist.

The Sheriff lifted Harry's head and noticed a large bump on the back that was swelling and probably caused him to lose consciousness.

Harry moaned softly as the Sheriff lowered his head back down to the floor.

The bar was in disarray and the Sheriff surveyed the scene. He would eventually find the perpetrators who took the law into their own hands. They must have known what happened to Debbie and decided to snag Harry when he was running out of the trailer and delivered their own brand of justice.

He stood in the doorway as the ambulance pulled into the parking lot with its lights flashing and sirens blaring. He filled the EMTs in on the situation and guided them over to the bar where Harry was and then went back to Debbie and Frankie's trailer.

His plan was for the EMTs to tend to Harry in the ambulance and follow him to the hospital with the sisters in his car.

That was the fastest way to maneuver everyone to the hospital. But first, he needed pain meds for Debbie from the EMTs. It would be the only way to quiet her down for the 15-minute ride to the ER.

The EMTs moved swiftly and soon Harry was in the back of the ambulance and Debbie was lying down in the back of the Sher-iff's SUV. Frankie jumped in the passenger seat and the two vehi-cles pulled out of the parking lot at Buck's Bar with sirens screaming their way to the hospital in the center of the small town.

From down the road, Tesh saw lights flashing and heard sirens as they came and went. She waited until everything was quiet and then crept in to check on Rocky. He was sound asleep and didn't move when she kissed his forehead and tucked the covers in around him.

Earlier she had heard screams, shouts, and a gunshot but didn't know any details. She said a prayer as she paced the kitchen floor, flooded with anxiety and fear. *More bad things at Buck's Bar,* she thought to herself. *No good ever happens there. It's cursed.*

Her husband Edgar's hand touched her shoulder, and she turned to him as he wrapped his arms around her. He whispered softly, "Come to bed, my love. It'll all be handled in the morning." He led her back to their bed and held her close until morning came.

CHAPTER THIRTEEN

LAST CALL AT BUCK'S BAR

"I was sitting in the car, down the road close to Tesh's house, when I got the call about a bad boating accident in Rockhall." Sheriff Allen and Frankie were exhausted, sitting side by side on the floor of the crowded visitor waiting room at the hospital's emergency room.

Allen felt he needed to give Frankie an explanation of why he wasn't at the trailer park to protect her and Debbie before things went out of control.

"I was at the accident scene for several hours before I could get back to the trailer park because there was a fatality. I couldn't leave. I'm so sorry."

The room was full of people waiting to be seen by doctors or for news about their loved ones. Debbie and Harry were both in surgery, and Allen and Frankie were waiting for the doctors to come out with an update.

Frankie didn't move. She didn't acknowledge his comment, and Allen thought she might have dozed off. Her head was hanging down, and her chestnut-colored hair hid her pale face.

Allen felt a pang in his heart at the thought of Frankie and Debbie being so vulnerable at Buck's Bar and the trailer park. His blood pressure rose, and his frustration intensified about his failure to protect Frankie when she needed him the most.

Protecting people was his job; he had failed with the one person who meant the most to him.

"Frankie, are you awake?" He nudged her shoulder, and she turned to look up at him. Her gaze was full of anguish and pain. "I'm so sorry I let you down. I had no choice but to take care of the boating accident."

He wasn't sure if he should push his point at this moment, but then again, this would be the best time to ensure that Frankie would hear him out.

"I can't protect you, Frankie, and you can't keep up the crazy schedule you have. Working in Philly all week plus taking care of the bar and Debbie on the weekends is just nuts." Sheriff Allen spoke with a low voice.

"Can we go outside and get some air and talk?" Being in uniform with Frankie in the crowded waiting room was awkward and he wanted to have an unobserved conversation.

People were watching them closely, trying to figure out why the County Sheriff was here with the girl from Buck's Bar.

She got up quietly and followed him outside, and they leaned against the brick wall to the side of the ER entrance.

Frankie was rewinding the tape in her head of the night's events and playing them repeatedly, looking for clues as to when things went wrong and how they ended up at the hospital.

"What happened tonight was the worst thing I've experienced out of all the horrible things I've experienced. I could sense a rest-lessness in everyone at the bar tonight."

She detailed the scene again for the Sheriff and went through the escalation of behavior in the bar, explaining how Harry drank like a fish after the Sheriff told him about his father's condition.

"Harry's mood got darker and darker and the other guys were ignoring him."

"I think I missed how messed up he was. He took the news of his father dying so badly, which surprised me because he had not seen his dad for a long time. I thought he had written him off and hated his father."

The Sheriff nodded and kept silent as Frankie searched her mind for more details. "I thought I had settled everyone down, and the guys were beginning to leave. I guess I missed the fact that Harry kept drinking way more than he should have. I had no idea he would attack Debbie and I don't know how he got into the trailer."

Frankie's shoulders slumped as she heaved more and more responsibility on herself for how the evening played out.

"Frankie, please don't blame yourself. It wasn't your fault. You couldn't have known what Harry intended to do when he stumbled out of the bar."

The Sheriff turned and stood in front of her as she leaned against the wall. Her green eyes searched his, and a tear slid down her cheek.

A dam was breaking inside of her as the fear and rage from the evening subsided, and her heart filled with pain. She couldn't hold her emotions together anymore, and she moved toward the Sheriff as he reached out to put his arms around her.

"It's ok, Frankie, just let it out." The Sheriff looked around to see if they were being observed. He spotted his patrol car across the street and moved Frankie towards it. He helped her into the passenger side and lowered the back of the seat so she could rest.

When he got in the driver's side and looked over at Frankie, she had turned toward him and was curled up in the seat. She was heartbroken, with tears on her cheeks and Debbie's blood still on her shirt.

She whispered to the Sheriff, "Allen, do you think I'm a terrible person? I am the cause of so many bad things. I've hurt so many people. I didn't save my dad when I could have; now he's dead. I put Debbie in a bad position, and Harry must have broken into the trailer to assault her, and now I've caused even more pain for her."

She began to cry harder as the Sheriff froze. He searched his mind to ensure he had locked Debbie's trailer and suddenly became aware that he couldn't remember locking the door.

With a tight knot in his throat, he realized he may have left the door unlocked, which is how Harry would have gotten into the trailer without resistance. He didn't say a word to correct her but reached out to Frankie, and she leaned against him.

He held her tight as she cried until there weren't any tears left.

"You're not a terrible person, Frankie. You're just the opposite. You're the kindest person ever." He did his best to soothe her, but the possibility of not locking the door was going through his mind and would haunt him for a long time.

Frankie wiped her face and pulled away from the Sheriff to rest against the back of the seat.

"Will you go in and check on Debbie?" she asked. "I'm so tired, and my eyes are probably very puffy. They might not give me info, but I'm sure they'll give you an update."

After a pause, she said, "And check on Harry, too, if you can. I want to know if he's still alive."

Frankie slept lightly until the Sheriff returned through the brightly lit ER doors. The sirens of ambulances returning to the hospital kept her from a deep sleep, and she glanced up at Allen as soon as he opened the patrol car door.

"Everyone is in the recovery rooms right now," he said as he settled into the front seat and quietly closed the door.

"Debbie is sound asleep after the surgery on her foot. The doctor said she'll be ok. She'll have pain while it heals and might need some PT, but her foot will function properly. She'll be able to walk on it just fine."

Frankie reached out for the Sheriff's hand. "Thank you so much for being here with me. If you need to go and get some sleep, I can have Tesh pick me up in the morning. It's late, and there's nothing else to do but wait."

The Sheriff was exhausted, too, but he wouldn't leave Frankie's side.

"Harry isn't in the best of shape, though. Someone roughed him up badly, and he has a brain bleed from the punches and his fall. The doctor says he hit his head hard and has more than a concussion. He'll be in the hospital for tests until they see how badly his brain is damaged." The Sheriff hated to mention Harry's condition, but Frankie had a right to understand the whole picture.

He looked at her, searching her face as he asked her the question he'd been putting off.

"Will you press charges? How far do you want this case to go?"

Frankie stared at him as a million thoughts went through her mind.

She shuttered at the thought of Larry O's trial and how he had taken the plea deal she offered him. Daddy's horrible death flashed in front of her and the toll it had taken on Debbie and herself was heavy in her heart.

She couldn't bear to think of going through more trauma, but didn't Harry deserve to pay for what he'd done to Debbie?

"What about me shooting Debbie in the foot?" Frankie asked, thinking she might be in legal trouble for that mishap. She'd been an early suspect in Daddy's death but was quickly cleared by testimonies from the bar regulars.

With a new trial, she'd be back in the spotlight. She was sure the townspeople would remember her from the trailer park fire and might want to see her punished for this situation. She was certain people had a poor perception of her and would be suspicious of anything that happened in the trailer park.

After Daddy's death, the trailer park became the target of many rumors and speculation. The threats and comments had been vicious and menacing with sordid stories of pimping and prostitution running rampant. Lately, though, the townspeople had moved on to other rumors in the town.

Frankie noticed fewer threatening messages on Buck's Bar's answering machine when she returned every Friday night from Philadelphia.

The Sheriff's question about pressing charges against Harry made her shudder. In her mind, many scenarios came to light.

Charging Harry with sexual assault would bring up the possibility of a trial. Debbie's mental and physical health was extremely fragile. Frankie was working in Philly, Rocky was with Tesh, and she was visiting Butch in prison when she could. Another trial would be the breaking point for all of them.

She made a quick decision.

She looked at the Sheriff, withdrew her hand from his, and reached down for the handle to adjust the back of the passenger seat. Making a firm decision always gave Frankie energy and the determination to overcome a challenge.

"No, I'm not going to charge Harry with sexual assault."

Looking intensely at the Sheriff, her face hardened, and her eyes flashed. "Harry will have to live with his conscience, and God will be his judge. I need to protect Debbie and myself. I'm closing Buck's Bar. Tonight was 'last call' at the bar."

She pulled on the door handle and moved to get out of the car as the Sheriff's heart sank. He'd seen Frankie like this before and knew once she had made up her mind, there would be no discussion about her decision.

He knew it was the right thing to do, but being pushed out of her world and closed out of her life was the worst that could happen. He didn't want that. He desperately didn't want to be pushed away.

"Wait, Frankie, please wait. Let me take you home." His voice gave away his emotions, and she stopped and looked across the seat at him. "Or I can come into the hospital and wait with you."

She smiled at him softly. She knew his heart. "Thanks, Sheriff, but I have to do this alone. You've been so helpful, but you should go home and sleep. You have a job to handle tomorrow, but it won't include a case from the trailer park. Thank God for that. I can't put any of us through the trauma of another trial."

Frankie got out of the car and headed for the ER entrance. When she got to the door, she turned to wave goodbye and then disappeared through the sliding glass doors.

The Sheriff pulled away from the ER entrance with a knot in his throat and a sick feeling in his stomach. He knew the bar was the only thing bringing her back every weekend.

I've lost her now, and it's my fault. I failed to protect the only woman I've ever loved.

From inside the ER, Frankie turned and watched his car pull away. Her heart broke for him, but she knew she could never be the love he wanted her to be. Their love was not like Daddy and Mama's had been. She cried softly for both of them.

———

Following Harry's assault on Debbie, Frankie and Tesh took turns visiting the hospital, getting daily updates on the gunshot wound to her foot.

After five days, Debbie was released with PT instructions, and soon she was back in the trailer park, situated on the sofa in the big trailer.

Frankie and Tesh sat at the kitchen table while Rocky played with little metal trucks and cars at their feet, making vrooming noises and occasionally interrupting with shouts of, "Aunt Frankie, look at this."

"This episode has done her in." Frankie glanced toward Debbie, whose eyes were closed, nodding off under her favorite purple blanket.

Tesh nodded in agreement. Debbie was breathing deeply, still feeling the effects of pain medication and exhaustion from the incident itself.

"It's still a mystery to me how Harry got into the trailer and why he even thought of assaulting her."

The weight of Frankie's responsibility for the scene was heavy on her mind and the outcome troubled her deeply. She'd been turning the situation over in her mind for days.

Tesh searched for the right words to relieve her guilt. "Frankie, the details of what happened will never be fully known. I doubt that Harry even knows. By all accounts, he *was* out of his mind."

She took a deep breath before she continued. "It's best if you can let the situation go and give yourself some grace. You did the right thing by protecting Debbie and by not pressing charges. Nobody in this family can take another trial."

Frankie still had doubts about that decision, but Debbie's traumatized state was evidence enough to make her realize Tesh was right.

"Sometimes I blame myself for not getting Debbie help much earlier. But we were all lost after Mama died and Daddy's mind deteriorated from the alcohol and being broke. Then when Daddy died, I just wanted to keep Mama's little family together." Frankie stared out the kitchen window.

"It's been more than I can handle." Her voice quivered and Tesh reached out and grabbed her hand.

"You've done more than anyone could ever be expected to do," said Tesh, squeezing Frankie's hand reassuringly. "No one can ever fault you for what's happened here in the trailer park. You've been the only person with any sense at all."

Frankie shrugged her shoulders. "I'm not sure my brain even works anymore or that I've ever had much sense at all. After all, everything here is in shambles. I'm not able to take Debbie to Philly with me, Tesh."

She knew what she was about to ask was monumental, but she had no other options.

"I've been thinking about this for the past week. Will you take care of Debbie for me while I'm in Philly until I can figure this out? Maybe we could move the small trailer to your property for a couple of months, or until the summer, and by then I'll find a more permanent place for her."

Making this request to Tesh was the last thing Frankie wanted to do and she sobbed quietly at the thought. Her ability to protect Debbie was bankrupt. She had come to a dead-end and she had no other way to protect her older sister, keep Rocky safe, and allow her to keep her job in Philadelphia.

The desperation of the situation was gut-wrenching for Frankie, and she realized she was in the same shape her father had been in after Mama died.

He was broken-hearted and broken in spirit. But it was different for Frankie. She was empty and exhausted, but she wasn't broken and her spirit was still strong.

He made bad decisions, hurting them all, but she was not her father.

In the middle of her heartbreak, she was determined to break the curse the trailer park had on her family. It would no longer be home for them.

She was a fighter and would die trying before she gave in to her dirty past.

Tesh was relieved that Frankie was offering a solution. While it would be a hardship for her and her husband, she knew they could shoulder it for a short time.

Otherwise, despite Frankie's years of hard work to keep her family together, everything would be shattered.

CHAPTER FOURTEEN

THE SUNDAY MORNING SCHOOL BUS

*N*o charges were pressed against Harry, and Frankie closed the bar for good.

She considered getting a permit and burning it down, but when she called Professor Todd one evening, he talked her out of it.

"It would be a waste of time and effort," he reasoned. "Just have Tesh's husband board it up and paint a black X on it. If the Germans buy the property, they'll destroy it anyway."

Frankie was in Philly and Todd had gone back to MIT to collate his findings from the computer science project at the community college. They kept in touch, but both were extremely busy with their rising careers and occasional weekend getaways were all they managed to fit in.

And Frankie wasn't sure where she stood with the Professor.

Now and then he'd mention a female student or faculty member with a certain tone in his voice and she'd take note of it. She never asked any questions because they'd never talked about their status or mentioned commitments of any kind.

They kept their conversations light and easy and their time

together seemed too precious to do anything more than stay in bed and order room service.

Sometimes Frankie was confused after a weekend with Todd.

She couldn't ask him for anything more, they were both maxed out. But she wondered how he felt about her. Did he love her? Did she love him? She thought she did. Her feelings for him were much deeper than those she had at one time for the Sheriff. That thought always triggered guilt because she had hurt the Sheriff badly.

Todd had navigated many transitions for her without making a big deal out of the doors he opened for her. He had helped her become the guardian for her family members, gave her computer science and coding opportunities none of the other students got, had introduced her to George Duberman in Philly, and the biggest deal of all was the potential sale of the trailer park.

And, despite the huge influence he had in helping her create a new life, he never made her feel obligated to him. He was always thrilled that she grabbed every opportunity and worked hard for her achievements.

They were alike in many ways - intellectuals, high achievers, natural leaders, loved technology and were well-read in many areas. But there were also some key differences. Frankie didn't know much about Todd's background and had never met his family, but sensed he was the 'country club kid' compared to her 'trailer park' status.

Tesh asked about Todd from time to time and Frankie just shrugged her shoulders and said she didn't think they were boyfriend and girlfriend; they were good friends and colleagues, but they didn't have that kind of commitment.

When Tesh pressed her on the subject, Frankie just shook her head. "I don't know, Tesh, what's going to happen between us. For now, it's fun and he makes me happy. I love our time together and he makes me laugh."

Frankie stopped to check in on Rocky most weekends. He was the brightest light in her world and her love for him moved her to tears at times. He was growing so fast and constantly chattered about his little world. Frankie took him a Big Wheels truck or car every time she visited, and he was very proud of his collection.

When she pulled into Tesh's driveway one Saturday afternoon, six months after Debbie's assault, Rocky was watching for her from the dining room window.

He ran out and she swooped him up into a big bear hug, kissing him all over his sweet, smiling face. They walked into Tesh's house hand in hand, smiling and laughing.

"Aunt Frankie, will you play with me?" He tried to pull her down to the floor to play with trucks and cars. Frankie and Rocky created scenes of farms, fields, and roads. Frankie created sounds she'd never heard come from her mouth before.

She'd never played with trucks as a kid and after an hour she was played out. "Come here, Rocky, sit on my lap and give me a cuddle." Rocky recognized the signal; she was leaving soon.

"Don't go," he begged. "Stay with me and play. I have more toys for you." Frankie picked him up and hugged him and sent him off for more toys. She wanted to talk with Tesh about Debbie's condition.

"I'm concerned about Debbie." Frankie glanced over to Debbie, who was fast asleep in a recliner.

Tesh nodded in agreement. "She's very depressed and not interested in anything other than watching TV and napping. It's like she's shutting out the world as best she can. She doesn't even pay any attention to Rocky."

Frankie sensed the weariness in Tesh's voice and realized the burden she was bearing by caring for both Debbie and Rocky.

Just then they heard Rocky's bedroom door slam and Tesh grabbed him as he burst out of his bedroom and rocketed into the living room. "Tesh and Aunt Frankie need to talk, honey. You play with your toys for a while." The little toddler settled down and followed Tesh's instructions.

Tesh turned to Frankie. "Even though Debbie spends time in the trailer, she's as much of a handful as Rocky is and I can't take care of them both anymore. She's very needy and anxious."

Frankie was aware of the change in Debbie since she had been assaulted. She was numb and often looked at Frankie with a vacant stare. "I'm going to take her in for a psychiatric assessment and have the doctor recommend our next step. We need a plan, so she doesn't continue to regress."

Through her contacts in Philly, she had found a specialist who understood the nuances of Debbie's trauma. "She needs help and neither of us can give it to her. I'm worried now since it's been six months and she's getting worse, not better."

Debbie's condition was a sobering thought for both of them and Tesh reached out to hug Frankie. "You're doing the right thing, Frankie. She'd be better off in a place where she can be cared for by professionals who understand her special situation"

Frankie hadn't mentioned the possible sale of the trailer park property to Tesh and was reluctant to bring it up until the deal was final. It would change things for all of them, and she wasn't sure how Tesh would take it.

As she began to say her goodbyes, she held Rocky tight for a long time, knowing that the next few months held many challenges for all of them.

Finally, he wriggled free from her embrace and ran back to pick up some toys. "Aunt Frankie has to go to work. I'll come back soon. Do you want a truck or a car the next time I visit?"

His eyes lit up and he shouted out, "A truck. Rocky wants a truck." She grabbed him again and kissed his cheeks. Saying goodbye to Rocky was always the hardest part of the weekend.

*a*s Frankie rolled over in bed, her eyelids fluttered open against the harsh light shining through her bedroom window. Her head was pounding with an intense headache.

She glanced at the clock, noticing it was eight o'clock in the morning. It was a rare Saturday morning when she allowed herself the luxury of not setting the alarm and sleeping until she woke.

Frankie remembered what today was. It was jail visitation day, and she groaned.

Visiting her brother Butch was always a pain, and she would have rather gone back to sleep and forget about her brother Butch, Professor Todd Burton, Sheriff Allen, and the rest of the world.

After Butch's stupid robbery, she committed to her brother that she would visit him every other Saturday and she'd done her best to keep her promise. Today wasn't going to be a good time though and Frankie dreaded the scene she envisioned in her mind.

Today was the day she would break the news of the trailer park sale to him. He wouldn't like it, he'd probably make a scene, and she'd have to leave. *C'est la vie*, she thought and swung herself out of bed and headed into the bathroom for a shower.

Several hours later, she drove into the parking lot of the cold, dreary institution and double-checked if she had her ID and some cash.

Giving money to inmates was grounds for losing visitation rights, but Frankie always felt better if she had cash, just in case. She had no idea what the 'just in case' might mean at the prison, but she always took some with her. "Maybe I want to pay off the security guys," she chuckled. "Criminal intent runs deep in this family, for sure."

Frankie signed in and went through initial security where her purse was scanned, and her body patted down. She waited for the guard to open the first gate into the holding section between the two heavy steel gates that were called the holding pen.

Frankie usually waited until everyone else went through the two-gated system and then she would go through by herself.

She was aware that she viewed herself as superior to the other 'red-neck visitors' and enjoyed showing it with her Gucci purse and Jimmy Choo shoes. *No low-class visitation for my brother*, she thought and then almost laughed out loud at how ridiculous the idea was.

Several other people were waiting for the first gate to open, and so she hung back until she could go into the holding pen by herself. Just as she was about to step in, she was surprised when an older man signaled to the guard to hold the gate for him.

She was uncomfortable being in the holding pen with anyone else and looked nervously at the stranger who had invaded her space.

She glanced sideways at the older man who had arrived just in time to pass through the first gate with her. This was not the norm for her, and it made her nervous. She clutched her bag to her side and looked straight ahead.

The older man set his briefcase down and then reached up to smooth the thin hair on his balding head. He was a small man, wearing a dark suit which was complimented by a thin, pale blue tie. He smiled at her politely. *Just ignore him*, she thought as the heavy door banged shut behind them and locked with a loud clang.

There was silence for a moment, and she glanced again at the stranger. There was something familiar about him, and her mind searched for a clue as to who he was.

Something about his smile when she glanced at him that was vaguely familiar. She couldn't remember his name or place him in her memory and soon the lock on the second door of the holding pen unlocked and slid open, and she stepped into the jail's visitation room.

The bare room was filling with visitors, and a low buzz sounded through the room. Prisoners and visitors eyed each other up and down and began to settle into the routine of a visit.

"How are you?" and "You look great," and other preliminary chatter started the awkwardness of the visit.

Frankie saw Butch across the room and walked over to sit across the table where he was seated. Butch was in a minimum-security prison so they had no handcuffs or glass between them.

Her younger brother was a thin, wiry kid who nervously bounced his leg or tapped his fingers on the table. His brown eyes sought out Frankie's as she sat across the metal table from him. She took a beat and looked around the room before she acknowledged him.

The room seemed more heavily guarded today and she asked Butch about it.

"Nice to see you, too," was his curt reply. "Don't you want to know how I am first? Are you nervous about coming here to visit?"

"Not really," said Frankie. "I'm just a little off today, I guess. When I came in, there was a guy who looked familiar to me, and I couldn't figure out who he was."

Frankie looked around the room and couldn't locate the stranger she had been next to in the holding pen.

"He's not here in the visitor room, so he must have some kind of prisoner business to take care of. If he was a lawyer, he'd be here in the room, and he didn't look like the lawyer type."

She glanced around the room again and couldn't locate him with any of the prisoners.

"Not sure who you mean, big sis," sneered Butch. "I'm a little off today, too, by the way. I'm a little off this whole year, you know, being in jail and all."

Butch looked at her with a mean glare. He hadn't trusted Frankie since Daddy was killed, even though Larry O was the one who killed his dad. Frankie had been there when it happened, and Butch wondered why she hadn't been able to save their dad.

Even though everyone believed Larry O was guilty, Frankie let Larry O off with a plea deal. He was the one who should be in jail, not Butch.

But Frankie was still kind to him, no matter how messed up he was. Butch was grateful for that, but he wasn't sure why she kept visiting him.

It wasn't like they had this tremendous brother-sister relationship or anything. She was a 'rich bitch' now and why she bothered with him was beyond his understanding.

"Tell me how you're doing," she said softly, hoping he would settle in and relax.

Their visits always went this way. Hostility at first, and then Frankie sucking up to Butch until he couldn't resist his big sister and her smile.

Deep down, he loved his sister and looked up to her for taking care of him after their Mama died.

He was sure he was a 'good for nothing' kid, just like his dad always told him, but Frankie seemed to have more faith in him. She saw past the rough edges and the hardness around his heart.

Maybe there was something good in him after all. *Nah, probably not*, he thought. *I'm just a rotten person with no future.*

Frankie was telling him about her latest building project in Philly and how the construction was coming along. "You would love this building, Butch, because it has lots of glass and a great view of the city. You would love it at night," she said, bringing him back to their conversation.

"Remember how we used to lay out behind Mama and Daddy's

trailer in the summertime and look at the stars? You always said you would ditch the trailer park and go to the city."

"Yeah, I got out of the trailer park, all right," Butch said. "But not in the same way you did. I'd give anything to go back and live in the trailer park again. Are you saving one of the trailers for me?"

Frankie sucked in her breath and held it for a moment.

This was the opening she needed to tell Butch about the deal on the trailer park. If all continue to proceed well, the five-acre tract of land would be sold to a real estate developer who would pay her more money than Butch would think possible.

After he heard the news of the deal, she knew he'd want to claim it all as his, since Daddy said he was going to run the joint one day.

She was sure he would jump across the table and strangle her with rage if he caught wind of how much money was in the deal and that it wouldn't all be his. She looked around to locate the guards' positions in case Butch tried anything.

"Did you love it that much?" she asked softly. "I thought you hated it there, especially after Mama died." She looked at him carefully.

As a professor, Todd Burton had an intuitive read on people and taught her to spot micro-expressions on people's faces when they gave off signals that showed deception and fear. There was a fleeting shrug from Butch before he replied, and she realized what she was about to hear was a lie.

"Nah, Frankie, I never hated it there. It was always home to me," he glanced at her sideways and his hands tightened as he clenched and unclenched a fist.

"I always thought I'd be the bartender at Buck's Bar and make Dad proud. I'm planning on coming back home when I get released. I hope you'll keep a trailer for me. Will you, Frankie? Will you keep a trailer for your little brother?"

She changed her mind about breaking the news about the trailer park sale and wasn't about to answer Butch's question.

"Tell me some jail junk, Butch." Frankie sighed and resigned herself to defeat.

Today was not the day she would break the news to Butch because she couldn't deal with his anger and resentment just below the surface. She didn't want her already ruined weekend made worse with questions she wanted to avoid.

"Not until you promise me a trailer when I come back home." Butch continued to press. "You're all I have, Frankie, and I hate that for you, but you'll be there for me, I hope. I know you will because you always have been."

"You're right, Butch, you're absolutely right," she said. "Now tell me some jail junk."

Butch seemed satisfied with her brush-off and told her about the increased security because some "high and mighty" prison transfer was supposed to happen this week.

"Seems like the whole place is nervous with this guy being transferred through here." Butch was rubbing his hands together, and Frankie had guessed correctly that everyone was on high alert. The nerves from the security guys were contagious, and everyone could almost smell the adrenaline wafting off from them.

"Any idea who it is?" asked Frankie with a quick look around the room at the extra security detail.

"Nah, nobody does. Everyone has been tight-lipped," said Butch, looking around the room. "There's a lot of crap talk about who it might be, but no names yet. Word is that the guy is coming through, not staying, because of some glitch in the system. I'll be glad when it's done. Makes me too nervous when these transfers happen."

"Seems like everyone's uptight today," nodded Frankie. "I wouldn't want to be here when everyone is hyped on fear and adrenaline. Just stay cool, OK? Don't do anything stupid. You hear me, Butch?"

He smiled at her, "Of course, Frankie Girl, no worries. I'm good. You bring me anything today? Got some money for me?"

He grinned at her, wanting her to lighten up but knowing she was signaling her departure as she tucked her purse under her arm. He knew she wouldn't give him cash, but it was their little joke, and he always asked her.

"How much you got in that fancy bag of yours?" He pointed to her purse.

"Enough for me to make it through the week," she smiled back at him.

She didn't like to show off her money to him, but he didn't miss a clue about what she was wearing. She realized she had forgotten her 'fancy watch' and was glad she didn't have it on. She thought Butch was clever enough to steal it right off her arm in plain sight, and she rubbed her wrist subconsciously.

"Hey, kid, I gotta go," she said, standing to leave. Suddenly, a jolt hit her in her gut and a thought flashed through her brain. "Did you call me "Frankie Girl?" she asked.

She had a flashback to Sunday mornings and the big yellow bus pulling up to the trailer park to take her and her siblings to church.

"Oh my god, Butch," her voice was suddenly excited with the revelation of the stranger in the holding pen.

"I can't believe you just said that! Nobody calls me that anymore. Now I remember who the older man was in the holding pen. I think it was Mr. Bailer. I wonder who he visits in this jail. I can't imagine why he is here."

She scanned the room but couldn't spot the older man who stepped into the holding pen with her.

Frankie searched her mind to remember more about Mr. Bailer. He used to drive a yellow school bus bought by the country church Mr. Bailer attended. He picked the Taylor kids up every Sunday morning, transporting them to church for Sunday School classes. They were the last stop on his route, and several other kids were on the bus, although she couldn't remember them.

"Oh, that guy," nodded Butch. "Yeah, he comes in here a couple of times a month. He brings these little blue Bibles for the new prisoners. The guys love them because the paper is so thin, they can roll joints with them." Butch laughed out loud at the thought.

Frankie laughed, too, at how resourceful prisoners were, rolling joints from the pages of the Holy Book. "That's a crazy thought," she said with an eye roll.

"Do you ever talk with Mr. Bailer? Do you know anything about him? Does he still drive the bus?"

Frankie peppered Butch with questions about the bus driver who had called her Frankie Girl whenever she climbed the bus steps to go to church. She loved the brief exchange they had each Sunday morning.

She suddenly realized it was the only time in the week that someone actually saw her, looked her in the eyes, and saw her. A lump gathered in her throat at the memory.

"I remember the yellow bus, too," Butch was saying. "That was the best, getting out of the trailer park on Sunday morning and going to the little church with the other poor kids. Remember how we used to make fun of the 'normal kids.' I guess we actually wanted to be like them."

His voice trailed off as he remembered the noisy bus and the quiet church where people seemed to like him. He never understood why Mr. Bailer would pick up all those kids, but Daddy loved getting them out of the house after a late night working at Buck's Bar. And all the kids loved the candy Mr. Bailer passed out on the way back home.

Frankie smiled at Butch and saw a sadness in him. *He never had a chance,* she thought. *Daddy spoiled him rotten and let him off the hook with everything, which eventually landed him in jail.*

"Things were too easy for you, Butch. You always had everyone spoiling you."

Frankie wanted him to understand why he was here. He was guilty of a crime, for sure, but he was never taught how to work for a living. Daddy didn't expect much of him, and Mama up and died on him when he was 12. What kid would survive that? She shook her head and glanced at the clock on the wall.

"OK, bud, I'm headed out. If you see Mr. Bailer, talk to him and tell him Frankie Girl said *Hi.*" She stood up to leave and looked around the room. Maybe she'd run into him again on her way out. She hoped so. It would be nice to chat with him again.

Then she caught herself and realized that Mr. Bailer might not want to talk with her. He had been so kind to her family, and for what outcome? The younger brother in jail, the older sister pimped out, a mother who died of cancer and a father blown up when a trailer exploded. He'd realize they were kids not worth saving. That his efforts had failed. That the Taylor kids were a waste of his time and the church's money.

"Two weeks, Butch. I'll be back." Frankie watched Butch shuffle to the exit and wait for a guard to escort him out. Even though it tore her heart out, she always waited for Butch to leave before turning away. The small wave and sad smile from him always got to her, but she never left first.

"Bye, Frankie," he said softly with appreciation in his expression. "I like that you keep coming to visit. I don't know why you come, but I appreciate it." He turned to go.

"Butch, I hope the prisoner transport thing goes well," she added. "Remember to chill out and stay low."

"Got it, Sis," he said with a grin. "Ain't nothing getting to me." He turned to go, and the guard escorted him out. After the gate clanged shut and the lock clicked, Frankie waited for Butch's little wave before she turned to leave.

As she left the parking lot, she was disappointed that she hadn't seen Mr.Bailer on the way out. The Sunday morning school bus rides brought back happy memories.

But Butch's anxiety had rubbed off on her, too, and she shivered at the thought of a prison filled with high-octane nerves, just waiting to explode.

CHAPTER FIFTEEN

AMAZING GRACE

"Frankie?" George Duberman shifted his gaze from the 20th-floor view of the Philadelphia skyline to where Frankie sat casually at the side of his desk. "I have an opportunity for you, and you'll really like this one. I think it's perfect for you."

Frankie leaned forward. Whenever her boss mentioned her name and the word opportunity in the same sentence it was a good thing for her. She loved calling him Dubie, although no one else dared to use that kind of intimacy with him except his cronies at the old, stodgy Cricket Club.

Dubie took Frankie to the club when she first started working for him in Philly. Professor Todd Burton had introduced them, and they met for lunch at the club, which Frankie thought was stuffy and pretentious.

Now, with a lot more experience, she'd come to understand it better as the preferred spot for deal-making, but back then it just seemed boring and full of old, white men.

When she thought about it now, the five years she'd worked for Philly's best real estate developer had flown by. George Duberman had taken an early personal interest in her and helped her climb the corporate ladder.

He spotted her bright mind and fast learning abilities and opened doors for her. She'd capitalized on the opportunities he presented.

The two had an easygoing relationship, although he was frequently gruff and stern with his other employees.

Frankie would humor him when he was grumpy, cajole him when he was stubborn, and often thought of herself as his younger female self or his spoiled long-lost daughter.

She often helped him with personal requests most team members would have refused to do, but Frankie was happy to help and Dubie sincerely appreciated it.

"Dubie, what's the opportunity?" She was curious and as usual, cut to the chase of their conversation. "Spill it. I'm ready for lunch. You can share my sandwich or take me to Parc."

She knew where they'd end up; Parc was a favorite restaurant for both of them and right around the corner from their office.

Once they were seated and placed their order of salads and salmon, Dubie got down to business. He drew out the buildings on a napkin and went through the numbers. Frankie immediately saw the uniqueness of this opportunity and was excited because of what it could do for her and George Duberman's company.

The opportunity was a short block of row homes, called brownstones, close to Rittenhouse Square and needing renovations. Dubie was proposing that part of the deal would be to make a brownstone available to her for an excellent price and to include her in the contract as an equity partner.

Frankie tried to stay calm and hide her excitement, but she couldn't hide the big grin on her face. Inside she was doing a happy dance and felt a swell of love and admiration for her boss.

Dubie looked up from his salad and smiled at her. "You haven't lost your appeal for the excitement of real estate, especially the money part. But this is even more than that, isn't it?"

"We've always said it's the money I love in real estate, and it's the aesthetics you love," Frankie noted, although she knew Dubie loved both aspects. "What I love is this deal has both in spades.

The thought of someday living in a brownstone was hard for her to believe. It had been her dream since she moved to Philadelphia and fell in love with its historical architecture.

Leaving the Eastern Shore had been painful, but she was making a home in Philly and the long hours and hard work were worth it, especially since she had developed a close relationship with Dubie.

He could be difficult, but she understood his combination of righteous anger and stubbornness when his high standards weren't met. She saw the same traits in herself.

Mama flashed through her mind as they finished lunch and chatted about brownstones and Philly's architectural beauty.

If only Mama could see me now, Frankie thought as they paused before the check came. *I hope she'd be proud of me. Mama understood the power of money and walked away from it, but that's not what I'm going to do.*

Frankie hadn't thought about Mama in a long time. Too many other concerns were crowding her mind, and she was always on the move. Between working long hours, visiting Butch and Debbie, and going back to the Eastern Shore to check in on Tesh and Rocky, she had little time for herself.

In addition to daytime hours, her job required evening galas and business deal dinners. She loved the pace, and it had earned her accolades in the Philadelphia Business Journal's *30 Under 30* with a spot on the front cover.

Dubie was very proud of her for that home run, and she was sure his influence made the media coverage happen.

After a long day, though, Frankie was often empty and exhausted. She couldn't put a finger on the feeling, but she'd look out over the city and feel like she was a dot in a big universe.

Why am I here? She often thought to herself. *I'm a nobody, working hard to fake everyone else out. So far, so good.* She'd shrug her shoulders, let out a loud sigh, and later she'd pull the covers over her head, thinking of innocent little Rocky, the Sheriff or Todd Burton.

The Sheriff was a steady, honorable man who loved her, but she had crushed his heart, and that chapter was closed.

Todd Burton was like a steamy romance novel with adventure and risk, and she couldn't get him out of her mind for long. She wasn't quite settled with Todd, but he was never far from her thoughts.

No need to rush, she'd remind herself. *There are too many other things to take care of.* Soon sleep would come, and the alarm would ring way too early.

---

*D*ebbie was packed and ready to leave when Frankie showed up for her regular weekly visit to the Forest Hills Care Facility. "Where are you going?" Frankie asked her sister. She wasn't prepared for this unusual development. She looked around for the assistant and noticed there wasn't anyone close by in the large craft room.

"I'm ready to go home. Look, my stuff is all packed." Debbie motioned toward the small purple roller bag Frankie bought for her when she left the Eastern Shore to live at Forest Hills. The transition had been hard for everyone, but Debbie suffered the most.

The facility's healthcare professionals were kind when they

explained to Frankie the depth of trauma Debbie suffered at the trailer park.

The impact of Harry's sexual assault was severe and the shot from Frankie's gun left Debbie confused and frightened. Debbie had been inconsolable and needed to be restrained and drugged in the hospital.

After the incident, Debbie was never the same. She slipped into a dark place and Frankie sought professional help to make Debbie's life manageable. Their professional recommendation was to move her to full-time care in the Forest Hills Care Facility.

Debbie fought the move to Forest Hills at the beginning and had difficulty settling in. The aides would find her wandering the halls at night, being disruptive at mealtimes, and packing her suitcase repeatedly.

Frankie remained steadfast in refusing their recommendations for heavy meds to control her mood swings. Eventually, Debbie settled down and seemed content and well-adjusted.

Frankie was disturbed that Debbie was waiting with her packed suitcase today since things had been going better the past few months. She gently wrapped her arms around her sister and hugged her for a long time. Debbie finally shrugged her off, picked up her suitcase, and started for the door.

"Whoa, Debbie, slow down. Where are you going?" Frankie blocked her sister's path out of the room. "Tell me what's going on."

Debbie stopped as Frankie blocked her path and put her head on Frankie's shoulder. There were tears in her eyes, and her chest heaved as she began to sob.

Frankie held her close and stroked her hair until Debbie's sobs began to subside. Deep in her soul, Frankie knew Debbie's pain and had deep compassion for her inability to communicate her feelings.

Debbie's mood today was troubling, and Frankie continued to hug her until she was quiet, and her sobs had stopped.

"Look at me, Debbie," Frankie said softly as she pulled Debbie's chin up and wiped the tears off her cheeks. "Are you having a bad day? Tell me how you are feeling."

She moved Debbie over to the sofa, and they sat in the sterile, colorless room. *Next time I visit, I should bring flowers.* Frankie thought, scanning the room, and making a mental note for her next visit.

Debbie sat on the sofa, slumping down until she was lying with her head on Frankie's lap. She stroked Debbie's hair, fussed with her collar, and started humming a song that came to her mind from many years before.

Amazing grace, how sweet the sound...she hummed the rest of the song, and Debbie began to relax. "Do you remember this song, Debbie?" Frankie paused to remember the small church she and Debbie went to on Sunday morning on Mr. Bailer's church bus.

Debbie smiled and started humming along with Frankie. She remembered the Sunday church services, too, and how kind Mr. Bailer and the other church people were. The kids were lovely, too, but that seemed so long ago.

She yawned and reached for Frankie's hand. "I remember that song, Frankie. Do you remember we sang it at Mama's funeral?

Frankie's eyes welled up at the mention of Mama. *If only Mama hadn't died, if only she hadn't left us so early. So much would be different today.*

Frankie was overwhelmed with homesickness for Mama, and tears flowed down her face.

She sat on the sofa, with Debbie's head in her lap, humming *Amazing Grace* time after time until Debbie was sound asleep. She didn't move for over an hour as tears continued to fall from her cheeks onto her shirt and disappear into Debbie's hair.

She wondered what Mr. Bailer and the church people would say to Debbie at this moment.

What would they say to a young woman who had been made fun of all her life, who had hoped for love from Larry O? A young woman whose escape plan spiraled out of control when she became pregnant.

What would their words be when Daddy's death and the lead up to Larry O's plea bargain just before the trial sucked the life out of Debbie, leaving her a shell of her former self.

And the final blow was Harry's assault on Debbie. What would Mr. Bailer say about that incident?

Frankie looked down at her sister and tucked a strand of hair behind her ear. Debbie's dark black hair trailed down the side of her lap, and Frankie stroked it tenderly as she considered the despair she had just witnessed in her sister.

I may need to reconsider meds, she thought. *Debbie needs relief and peace of mind.*

No one had entered the craft room the entire time Frankie and Debbie were in the room. The fluorescent lights shone brightly on the polished linoleum floor, and the industrial-grade furniture was uncomfortable for Frankie.

Her foot was asleep, and her back was aching. She hated to wake her sister, but she had to get back to work. There was more paperwork to complete at the office before heading home for a shower and dinner.

She nudged her sister and gently woke her. Debbie sat up and stretched, yawned, and looked at Frankie. "Oh, you're still here." She straightened her skirt, stood up, and reached out to hug Frankie. "Can you come to my room with me?"

Frankie nodded and picked up her sister's suitcase. They went down the hall to Debbie's room, unpacked her clothes, and Frankie turned on her favorite TV channel.

205

Frankie gave her a quick, final hug and turned to leave. She stopped at the door and looked back at Debbie, who was already absorbed in a late afternoon TV show. Her sadness slowly eased, and Frankie was grateful that Debbie was cared for.

On her way to the front door, she stopped by the nurse's station and asked about possible medication for her sister. She didn't want her drugged, but she did want some relief for Debbie.

It seemed that Debbie relived trauma and grief daily and needed a solution and the relief that a low dose might give her. The attending nurse assured her she was doing the right thing for Debbie and that the doctor would call her in the morning.

As she drove home through the city, she found herself humming the beloved hymn she and Debbie remembered. *Amazing grace, how sweet the sound...*

CHAPTER SIXTEEN

A FARMER'S BREAKFAST

Several weeks later, Frankie thought she had glimpsed Mr. Bailer when she was signing in for a jail visit. He was on the other side of the holding pen, and she saw him through the bulletproof glass-plated doors.

"Do you know that man?" She asked the security guard. He nodded.

"How long does he usually stay? I hear he distributes Bibles?" The guard nodded again and said, "He only stays for an hour, then he leaves."

Frankie was thrilled and planned a short visit with Butch. She checked her watch and noted the time.

Her visit with Butch was brief. She was distracted. He was moody and sulked when she tried to have a conversation. She wasn't in the mood to placate him so they agreed to a short visit so she wouldn't miss Mr. Bailer.

Butch was interested in the former Sunday Morning Church school bus driver, too, although he had made no attempts to speak with him when he saw Mr. Bailer visiting.

Frankie's spirits lifted when she saw Mr. Bailer exit the jail and head toward the parking lot. She called out to him and introduced herself. "I'm sorry to interrupt you, but I remember you from the country church by the lake. You used to drive us to church on the school bus. I'm Frankie Taylor. Do you remember me?"

Mr. Bailer looked her straight in the eyes and immediately said, "I sure do, Frankie Girl. How have you been all these years?"

She sighed. "Mr. Bailer, how much time do you have?"

"For you, Frankie Girl, I have time. Do you want to go to the diner for a cup of coffee?"

A short time later, Frankie and Mr. Bailer were seated in a booth at the local diner ordering coffee. She felt a bit awkward and apologized for ambushing him in the jail's parking lot.

"No worries, Frankie. I'm happy to see you. I remember you well from way back then."

"Are you hungry?" she asked politely as she pulled out menus from between the salt and pepper shakers and handed one to Mr. Bailer.

He shook his head. "Just coffee for me. Usually by now, I've had eggs, bacon, and toast." He smiled softly. "I've been a farmer most of my life and I'm used to a solid breakfast, lunch, and supper."

Frankie looked at her menu as she observed Mr. Bailer with an occasional side glance.

He was a gentle man and had always been kind to the Taylor kids when they climbed on the yellow school bus every Sunday morning. They were always rewarded with a Peppermint Patty candy on the ride back home.[KDG56]

Now, years later, although his hair was thinning and the wrinkles around his eyes had deepened, his smile was still soft and reflected the kindness in his eyes.

His blue button-down shirt and gray pants, combined with his black-rimmed glasses, gave him the look of an everyday man. An honest man who did an honest day's work.

"Why did you drive the bus every Sunday morning and pick us up?" she asked.

Mr. Bailer looked at her and took a moment before he answered.

"Frankie, I haven't done big things in my life. I've been a farmer. I got up early, worked hard all day, raised ten kids and that was enough for me most of the time," he said quietly, as though he was summarizing his life for the first time.

"A farmer's life isn't easy. We struggled financially and sometimes we were in debt. But through it all, I knew life had more meaning than money. I had a stirring in my heart to bring kids like you to church each Sunday because there's a path to love and salvation that I wanted to share."

Frankie stiffened at the mention of salvation. She wanted none of that talk. No church talk for her.

"What do you think of all of that now, Mr. Bailer?" She asked in a sarcasm-tinged tone. "What do you think of those efforts? My brother is in jail. Debbie's been institutionalized and my dad and Mama are dead. It doesn't seem like much of your path to love is available to me."

She looked away and felt her chest tighten as she fought hard against Mama's memories flooding her mind. She suddenly felt overwhelmingly sad as she realized how much she missed her Mama and oddly enough, even her dad.

"It's hard, Frankie, isn't it, to see any good in your situation, although you've become very successful. Look at you. You have a great career; you're making money, and you were just on the cover of a business magazine. Look here. My daughter, Sheryl Ann, sent it to me."

He pulled out the Philadelphia Business Journal and showed her the picture and the article. "I was going to show it to your brother, Butch, on my visit today, but I didn't see him."

Frankie, of course, had already seen the cover article with the stunning shot of her and her latest high-rise building. She was touched that Mr. Bailer cared enough to bring it to show Butch and that one of Mr. Bailer's daughters remembered who she was.

She took a deep breath and dug into her eggs and bacon and tried to get rid of the lump in her throat.

She was moved by Mr. Bailer and his calm presence, and it scared her. She didn't want to cry in front of him, but she was so sad and felt so empty that she could barely eat.

"Mr. Bailer," she said. "I may be successful, but I am so empty I wonder if I will be able to love another human being ever again in my life. All my money isn't making me happy. Even providing for my sister and my nephew hasn't filled my heart up. I'm happy I can be the glue in the family, but I'm exhausted by what it takes to make everything work. Maybe you have the best world possible on the farm."

She smiled sadly as a tear slid down her cheek and she brushed it away.

"How can you have love, anyway," she continued, "if everything in the past makes the future meaningless? Not a day goes by without me remembering my Mama and the rest of my family and the ugly things that happened at the trailer park."

Frankie's mind was filled with images from the past and she was fighting the feelings coming from the images touching her heart.

It was the middle of the morning in the small diner a mile down the road from the jail. The quiet was broken only by the sounds of the cook at the grill and the burbling noise of fresh coffee brewing.

Frankie swallowed hard. "You have a deep belief in God, Mr. Bailer, but the stuff that happened when I was a kid makes me think God doesn't exist, and if he does, he surely didn't care about us."

Mr. Bailer looked up from stirring his coffee and gazed at her. "No one can say 100% that God exists, Frankie. Sometimes I've wondered about that myself. I've had times of depression and doubt, too. Just like you. But I can't let go of what I've been led to believe over the years."

He took a sip of coffee and continued. "Every time doubts came up in my mind and I thought I couldn't go on any longer, someone appeared to show me a path to love. Maybe I'm that person for you, Frankie."

Frankie felt a sob starting deep down inside her and she was fighting it hard.

She did not want to lose her composure in front of Mr. Bailer, but she was so empty maybe he could help.

"What is this path to love?" she whispered as a tear slid down her cheek again. "What does it mean - a path to love? I don't want religion. I don't want to be churched." She stared hard at Mr. Bailer, fighting her feelings of emptiness.

"Religion isn't the path to love, Frankie. I've tried that, too." Mr. Bailer took a long sip of coffee. "I can only tell you that opening your heart up to a power greater than us is the beginning of the path. When you have walls around your heart, you are locked in your own prison."

Frankie's thoughts went to her brother, Butch, who was in prison and deserved his sentence. And she thought of Larry O and her father, who both deserved to be in jail, but one was free and the other one dead. And what about Harry? Should he be locked up? What about her – was she a guilty accomplice, too?

"What happens on this path to love?" she asked. "Why should I even consider it?"

Her thoughts went to the Sheriff, who loved her like Daddy loved Mama, but she had crushed his heart. She thought about Professor Todd, who had opened her heart to love but she wasn't sure where she stood with him.

Then she thought of Tesh, and her heart melted. Dear, sweet Tesh had loved her more than anyone except for Mama.

Tesh had taken care of her and Debbie since they were kids. They'd spent hours together at Tesh's house, giving Mama a break from working in the bar with Buck. And now, Tesh was taking care of Debbie's child like he was her own, without ever complaining.

As she thought about Debbie, her older sister who had endured so much trauma, Frankie knew she was close to losing her composure.

She was about to break down and sob as she felt the hurt that was buried so deep inside of her. It was agonizing to consider continuing her high-flying stressed-out life with no love in it.

And even though Rocky loved her with a sweet innocence, Frankie had a hard time accepting that love and kept her love for him tight within her. Besides, someday he might find out the truth about her and hate her for who she really was.

No one knew her deepest, darkest secret and it would be better if no one ever found out about it.

Her focus came back to the room as Mr. Bailer said, "Frankie, Frankie? I'm sure I don't have much of the story of what's happened in your life. After you stopped getting on the bus on Sunday morning, I overheard Debbie and Butch talking about some things that were happening at the trailer park. If what I heard was true, it was bad and should never have happened. I'm sorry for what's in your past. I'm sad for your pain and suffering. Especially for what happened in your family and especially for you."

Frankie was startled. "Why me? Why me, specifically?" she asked.

"You're successful in real estate, right?" he asked. She nodded yes.

"Well, when you were a kid, you were fierce. You had a warrior spirit and for a girl, it got noticed. I watched the other kids stay away from you because they were afraid of you. And, if they ever said anything about Debbie or Butch you were always by their side to protect them. You learned very early on to protect them, and you learned to watch out for yourself and everyone in your family."

Frankie leaned in and said in a low voice, "Yes, Mr. Bailer. Exactly. That's why I'm in the position I'm in and why no path to love for me exists for me."

"Do you remember what we used to say to each other every Sunday morning when you got on the bus?" he asked.

Frankie thought for a moment. She remembered the big yellow bus rumbling to a stop on the side road of the trailer park. She loved seeing that bus and thinking it was a ticket to freedom for a few hours while her dad slept in.

"Sure do," she said with a smile. "I'd say, 'Good Morning, Mr. Bailer' and you'd say, 'Good Morning, Miss Frankie Girl.' Then I'd say, 'That's right, I'm a girl and don't you forget it.' And you'd laugh and say, 'Grab a seat, this bus is moving on.' Then we'd high-five and I'd grab the seat behind you. I loved knowing you would always be nice to me and that we had a little routine. It was such a small thing, but it had a lot of meaning."

"You were a sweet girl, even though you were tough," said Mr.

Bailer with a smile. "And now I can see you're still tough, but deep down I still see a sweet girl hiding out in you."

Frankie held her palm up, as if to silence him. "No, Mr. Bailer, you're wrong about that. Nothing sweet can be found inside of me. I'm rotten to the core and nothing good is inside of me, except for maybe what I'm doing for Rocky and Debbie. But there's nothing, nothing, nothing, nothing good about me...."

Suddenly, Frankie was so overwhelmed with the emptiness in her life. Every challenge she had fought against in her life hit her with a jolt.

She had taken the protector role so early and for so long it seemed second nature to her. But being with Mr. Bailer touched something deep inside of her and the tears started flowing and she couldn't stop them.

She put her head on the table and wept for what seemed like a long, long time.

After her tears subsided, she looked up at him and shook her head. "I'm not sure why I'm so emotional. Sorry about that. It's just that you remind me of when my Mama was still alive. She's the only one who ever talked about love. She could see the good in everyone and when she didn't see anything positive, she'd make it up."

"Frankie, a path to love for you is available to you," he said and tapped on his heart. "When you're ready to learn more about it, will you contact me? Can we have breakfast again and talk some more? I don't want you to keep your heart in prison. I want you to have love. You deserve to have love."

Frankie lifted her head, her eyes filled with tears again and her heart was broken open.

Here was the kindest man she had ever known and he was offering her a way out of the prison her heart was in.

He wasn't like anyone else she knew, and her rule was never to trust anyone. But Mr. Bailer? She wanted to trust him.

She used a napkin to wipe her eyes and face and fished a lipstick and mirror out of her bag.

"Mr. Bailer," she said with a sigh, "I'm going to take you up on that offer. I'm going to meet you again for breakfast and learn more about the path to love. After all," she said, "I've got nothing to lose."

Mr. Bailer's gaze held hers. "Frankie, I go to the prison every other Saturday morning. If I see you at the prison in two weeks, we'll go to breakfast after you visit Butch. If you're not at the prison, your decision will be clear."

He picked up his coat and left $20 on the table. "This should cover it. I'd stay here all day and chat if I could, but one of our cows is having a calf any hour now and I need to get back to the farm. But I don't want to walk out of here unless you'll be ok until we meet again."

He stood up and looked down at her with a concerned look on his face.

Frankie was certain he knew some of the secrets in her heart, but would he still want her to find a path to love when he knew who she really was and what she had done?

She dropped her gaze and again she was filled with shame and regret for what had happened at the trailer park.

She wondered silently if she could ever escape the hell in her mind, keeping her from love and keeping her heart in prison, as Mr. Bailer called it.

She looked back up at Mr. Bailer who was waiting for an answer. She nodded and said, "Yes, Mr. Bailer, I'll be at the prison in two weeks. We'll have breakfast and you can tell me more."

She held out her hand and he took it in both of his. His farmer's hands were rough and warm, and his eyes were kind. "I'll be there," she said. "I'll be there."

After Mr. Bailer left the diner, Frankie sat silently for a long time with tears trickling down her cheeks. She was startled when the waitress tapped her on the shoulder and said, "Everything ok, Miss? Can I get you anything else?"

Frankie glanced up at her and wiped her cheeks. "No, ma'am, I'm fine. I'll be on my way now, but I hope to be back soon."

CHAPTER SEVENTEEN

PRACTICING REDEMPTION

*T*wo weeks later, Frankie was up early, excited to visit Butch, but more excited to have breakfast with Mr. Bailer. He was waiting for her at the jail's front door, and they agreed to meet at the neighborhood diner, a mile south of the prison.

Mr. Bailer waved Frankie over to a booth at the diner and poured her a steaming cup of coffee. He slid the small dish of creamers over as she poured in two spoons of sugar.

Frankie hungrily looked at the menu and pointed at the breakfast special of two eggs, bacon, and toast. "That's the one for me. I'm as hungry as a horse." She grinned at Mr. Bailer, hoping he picked up on her reference to farming.

Mr. Bailer smiled and pushed his menu away. "Nah, Frankie, I'm not hungry this morning. I have something going on in my stomach. Gonna pass for today, but you enjoy yourself. You look like you need some meat on your bones." He reached over and pinched her wrist, then took a sip of his hot tea.

As the waitress took Frankie's order, he studied the young

woman. She was a complicated tangle of emotions and intellect and he sensed she had a desire for more in life than what the big city gave her.

He watched as she gazed around the diner and then settled in for their chat. "I had a rough visit with Butch this morning."

Mr. Bailer raised his eyebrows as he waited for her to continue.

"A while back, we had a horrible night at the bar and Debbie was almost assaulted by one of the guys who was drunk. I reached her in her bedroom just in time to pull the guy off her, but I had Daddy's gun and somehow it went off and a bullet ended up in Debbie's foot."

She looked at him with wide eyes, wondering what his judgment of her would be. "I had to tell Butch about it this morning and he was enraged. It took the guards to calm him down."

Mr. Bailer's look of concern kept her talking. "Debbie's foot is okay now, but she is messed up and in a bad way right now. We recently moved her to the Forest Hills Care Facility and she's receiving good care. It's hard to visit her in an institution, but that is the only option we have now.

"The drunk who assaulted her, his name's Harry, he got beat up badly by some of the guys at the bar and is messed up in the head. Butch knows who he is and swears he'll kill him when he gets out of prison."

Seeing that Mr. Bailer wanted the whole story, she continued. "That night was the worst night ever and I decided to close Buck's Bar for good. I should never have opened it after Daddy died, but the guys begged me to do Saturday nights, so I did. That was a mistake."

"Here you are, hon." The waitress slid the breakfast special on the table and Frankie dug in.

Between mouthfuls of runny eggs, greasy bacon, and buttered toast she told Mr. Bailer of the horrors of the evening, starting with the Sheriff showing up to tell Harry about his dying father and the chaotic energy in the bar that night.

"In the past, I'd hold my own with those dumb drunks, but I got scared that night." Frankie paused to grab some coffee and continued with the bacon and eggs.

"The Sheriff told me he would be down the street, which didn't happen because of a boating accident in Rockhall."

The words tumbled out as Frankie's mind played back the scenes from the evening.

"Somehow I missed Harry being so drunk, but I guess the news about his father passing away just was too much for him." She chastised herself for not paying close enough attention to the bar scene. She thought she might have prevented Harry from attacking Debbie if she'd been on high alert.

"It's all my fault, Mr. Bailer. Again." Frankie slowed down her frenzied chewing and took a huge gulp of coffee.

"I was so done with the bar and that night I determined to find a better way. That night was last call for Buck's Bar. Mama would hate what happened in the place she loved."

Mr. Bailer looked at her with compassion in his eyes. "Frankie, you are very hard on yourself. That evening was not your fault. You couldn't have known what was going to happen."

"That's just the thing, Mr. Bailer. I should have known. I should have been able to stop Harry before he left the bar. I should have protected Debbie. I am her guardian. I am responsible."

"That's a lot for a young woman to handle."

Frankie motioned to the coffee and Mr. Bailer poured her another cup of coffee.

"In addition to that, I ruined things with the Sheriff because I told him to leave me at the hospital. He wanted to stay with me that night and I sent him away. He's a great guy but our relationship complicated my life."

"How does your heart feel about this complication?" Mr. Bailer sipped his hot tea and held her gaze.

"My heart? What does my heart feel? Does that matter?" Frankie was confused.

No one ever asked her how she felt about things. *Feelings don't matter when everyone else is more important.*

Mr. Bailer tilted his head, tapped his chest, and smiled at her. "Your heart, Frankie, you have one, that spot that goes a little pitter-patter when you're taken out by a handsome guy."

Frankie smiled sheepishly. "Right, that little pitter-patter thing. Can't do that anymore. It's last call on that, too."

Mr. Bailer's smile disappeared. "No, Frankie, you can't give up on love because of what happened. Life is more than survival or taking care of people and beating yourself up. You've had a rough life, but you can't give up."

Frankie thought Mr. Bailer was getting a little teary-eyed.

She leaned against the back of the booth and relaxed. Her stomach was full, her hunger pangs were gone, and she was enjoying Mr. Bailer's company.

He listened to every word she said and took everything in. No one had focused so keenly on her words before.

"What's happened with Harry? Are you going to press charges?"

Frankie shook her head. "No, I decided not to press charges because it would have been overwhelming for Debbie. And we couldn't afford the time, money, or trauma to go through another trial."

Flashbacks of Larry O's trial, aborted at the last minute by his plea bargain went through her mind, and she shuddered at the horror of another trial.

Mr. Bailer noticed her reaction. "If you don't press charges against Harry, will he just go free? No justice for Debbie?"

Frankie paused, knitted her eyebrows, and looked at Mr. Bailer quizzically. "Are you suggesting that we should have pressed charges against Harry? I didn't expect that from you."

She was confused by Mr. Bailer's suggestion.

"Surely you're not saying I should have pressed charges and gone through another trial?" Frankie added. "Debbie was out of her mind, and she would never have survived another trial. She is in bad shape, as it is."

"How will you seek justice for Debbie? Will you let Harry off for his crime?" Mr. Bailer paused. "Or will you forgive him?"

"If you mean, will I go and kill him myself for justice? Never. But will I forgive him? Never."

"I want to tell you a story, Frankie, and maybe you'll understand how forgiveness might bring a different result for you and Debbie, and even Harry, too."

Frankie didn't believe it was possible, but she would hear him out. He was kind to her, and she was curious about this new perspective on forgiveness.

"When I was growing up, around age 11 or 12, the neighbor adjacent to our farm hated my father. They had a falling out about a property line between our farms. The neighbor accused my father of moving the property line to add more to his farm.

"My father swore up and down that he didn't do it and he had documents to prove where the property line was. But the neighbor was convinced my dad had done him wrong and persuaded all of the nearby farmers to take his side on the issue."

Mr. Bailer poured more hot water into his cup and swirled his tea bag around for more flavor.

"That must have been hard for you and your dad," Frankie murmured as she cupped her hands around her coffee cup.

"It was, for sure. I thought my dad should fight for his case. I hated that he let the neighbor rile up all of the other farmers against him. It seemed unfair to me, and I wondered if my dad was a coward. If he was a weak man."

Mr. Bailer's hand trembled as he pulled the tea bag out of his cup and placed it on the saucer. Frankie noticed his troubled face as he remembered the scene from so many years ago.

"As the neighbor's anger about the issue grew stronger, my dad tried to placate him by offering to move the line to where he thought it should be located. Even though my father had the documents to show where the property line was, he was willing to bend to the neighbor's anger on the issue.

"The neighbor was trying to sell his property because he was going broke, so the property line was a major deal to him. It meant more money if the property line was moved. To this day, I can't comprehend the lies he told to convince the other farmers that my dad was wrong, but that's how it played out.

"One day, a pickup truck drove up the lane with two farmers in the cab and three in the back of the truck. My dad wasn't home. Just me and my mom.

"They drove in, yelling and screaming, a few of them had rifles and my mother was very upset. She yelled at me to come in from the yard and we stood on the porch as those farmers, our neighbors, drove up and cursed at her and yelled slurs against my dad.

"She stood her ground and took all of it in as they whooped and hollered and yelled bad things about my dad. She stared them down and didn't say a word. She just grabbed me and pulled me close to her on the front porch."

Frankie was leaning into Mr. Bailer's story and imagining him as a young boy; feeling the emotions he had as his mother stayed silent in front of the boisterous crowd.

"Then she did something so courageous, people talked about it for a long time." Frankie's curiosity elevated and she took a deep breath waiting for the ending to be revealed.

"My mother walked over to the truck, opened the driver's door and motioned for the driver, our hateful neighbor, to step out of the truck. All the farmers quieted down at this point, wondering what she was going to do. She pushed him over to me and told him to tell me, straight to my face, what my daddy had done that was so bad that a truck full of angry men would drive over with shotguns and rifles."

Mr. Bailer shook his head remembering the day. "The neighbor couldn't do it. He couldn't look me in the eye and tell me why he hated my dad. It was like the kindness of my mother pricked a hole in the balloon of his anger and he just fizzled out.

"Then my mother looked at the other guys and asked them, one by one, if any of them wanted to tell me, straight up, why they hated my dad. Not one of them would even look at her. They were too ashamed.

"Here's the important part, Frankie, that changed my life. My mother looked at the formerly angry neighbor and held out her hand to him." She said, 'We don't want to hold any grudges against you or any of our neighbors. We believe in forgiveness, and we forgive you all today."

"Just like that?" Frankie asked with a puzzled look on her face.

"Well, that wasn't all of it, Frankie, because then she talked to them about making peace in the farm community and not holding a grudge. She promised them my dad would make right whatever the angry farmer thought was wrong.

"She asked them if they all would work together to fix this problem. She reminded them that their wives and children were watching them and learning from them how to be good neighbors and good fathers.

"She took them to church with her little sermon on forgiveness and redemption. She stood up for my father and wouldn't back down." Frankie was totally enthralled by Mr. Bailer's story.

"Eventually she coaxed the men in the truck to come and have a piece of pie on the front porch. Turns out they knew my dad wasn't home and they were bringing a dead skunk to throw on the front porch to send him a message. They hadn't considered my mother might stand up to them and not hide in the house."

Mr. Bailer's eyes were tearing up again. "I was so proud of her that day. I learned about courage, forgiveness and redemption and took it to heart."

A quietness settled between them as they had their own thoughts about Mr. Bailer's story.

Frankie wanted to hear the rest of the story and Mr. Bailer's mind was full of images of the angry men who backed down when a courageous farmer's wife spoke truth to them.

"These were not callous men, Frankie, they were farmers who loved their community but just got mixed up in a petty argument that was getting out of hand. I think my mother saw their hearts and knew they were like little kids playing king of the hill in a sandbox and the angry farmer just had a temper tantrum that got out of control.

"He was under a lot of stress and took it out on my father." Mr. Bailer looked across the table at Frankie and dabbed a napkin at his eyes. "I didn't mean to get all sappy on you, kid, but the memories of my mother are getting to me these days."

Frankie smiled at him, wondering about the ending of the story. "So, what's the final ending? How does forgiveness fit in?"

"The angry farmer came back later after my father was home and apologized. They sat on the front porch until it got dark, talking through their issues. It turns out the angry farmer was broke, and his wife was going to take the kids and leave. He was like a scared rat in a trap. He had nowhere to go, no one to turn to. He was too proud to ask for help, so he stirred up anger instead."

"What did your father do? Did he forgive him like your mother said he would?"

"Yes, Frankie, he did. The angry farmer broke down and cried and my father sat with him until he pulled himself together. My father helped him make a plan to keep his family together and eventually helped him secure a loan and bring his farm up to standards."

Mr. Bailer sat up a little taller when he talked about his dad. "My father was a very good farmer. He taught farming habits and practices to the neighbor and helped him learn how to make money from his farm.

"That's the redemption part of the story, Frankie. After my mother offered forgiveness and my father showed grace, the man was able to redeem himself and restore his life to a better place."

Frankie mulled over this new concept of forgiveness and redemption. No one in her world had ever chosen those options over a fistfight and a lifetime grudge.

"Does this work, Mr. Bailer? Is it even possible that this would work for a person like me? Could I forgive Harry and help him to redemption and maybe find some redemption myself?"

A lightning bolt idea struck Frankie as she thought of forgiving Harry and how difficult that would be to explain to anyone.

Everyone she knew would agree she and Debbie had every right to stick it to Harry and send him to prison.

Mr. Bailer saw the wheels turning in her mind. "You want to practice this with Harry?" He smiled at her, knowing that Frankie was already two steps ahead of him in her plan.

"I do," Frankie said, with a deep feeling of gratitude and love for Mr. Bailer. "I want to learn how to do this thing called forgiveness and redemption because nothing else has worked so far. I'm looking for your path to love, Mr. Bailer. I need a new way to live.

I can't keep going from one crisis to the next. I don't want to be the person I've been."

Mr. Bailer motioned the waitress over and he paid the check. "Let's go to the park for some fresh air. My bones are getting stiff."

Frankie and Mr. Bailer spent an hour in the park with Frankie practicing her kindness and redemption speech with Harry. As they walked round and round the perimeter of the park, Mr. Bailer shared with her the process his parents taught the angry neighbor.

Finally, Frankie asked to sit on the park bench and take notes. "This is a lot for me to absorb at one time. I need to have specific steps of what to do or I will never be able to make it through this with Harry. If I'm not prepared, I will overreact and spout off something stupid and make him even more angry at me."

"Don't overthink it, Frankie. Just use your heart to guide you. Prepare yourself first and make sure that you genuinely forgive him."

"How do I take steps to forgive him so easily? He is in the wrong. He did something terrible to my sister." Frankie wasn't going to let go of this wrongdoing without some consequence.

"Here's the thing, Frankie, you have to set aside your anger to look at it from his side. Not to excuse what he did, but he got smacked in the face that night with a lifetime of emotions when he heard his father was dying. He wanted to run away from all the feelings he didn't want to have, so he got drunk. You can only truly forgive that bad behavior if you have empathy for what he was going through. Even if you think he was dead wrong."

Frankie shrugged, not sure that she had any empathy toward Harry.

"Forgiveness is a powerful thing," Mr. Bailer said, "but it's not always easy. Sometimes it takes a bit of effort and a few specific steps to understand the power of it."

He reached in his pocket and pulled out a pack of Juicyfruit gum and offered a piece to Frankie, then continued.

"First, you have to acknowledge the hurt. You can't forgive someone if you don't even recognize the pain they've caused you. So, take some time to sit with your feelings, and think about what happened and how it made you feel."

Frankie shifted on the park bench and looked across to where families played on the swings and little kids played tag with each other.

Some people's lives look so perfect, she thought to herself. *And, mine is far from it.*

"Next," Mr. Bailer said after, "you have to decide to forgive. It's not enough to just say you want to forgive someone. You have to make a conscious choice to let go of the anger and hurt, and to move forward in a positive direction."

Frankie was scribbling down notes to use when she tracked down Harry and gave her forgiveness speech. Just thinking about it made her stomach turn, but Mr. Bailer's words convinced her to give it a try.

He paused for a moment, then went on. "After that, it's important to communicate your forgiveness. Depending on the situation, this might involve talking to the person directly or simply acknowledging your forgiveness to yourself. But it's important to make it clear you've let go of the hurt and anger, and you're ready to move forward. In your case, that would mean letting Harry know why you didn't press a case against him."

"Finally," Mr. Bailer said, turning on the park bench to look directly at her, "you have to take care of yourself. Forgiving someone can be hard, and very emotional. Make a special effort to take care of yourself: sleep and rest are vital, eat well, and schedule some downtime. You have a busy schedule, and you need to take care of yourself when you're forgiving someone."

He reached over and touched her shoulder. "You're too thin, Frankie, and you look like you haven't had a lot of sleep lately. A good night's sleep before you approach Harry is important. Do you know where he lives?"

Frankie nodded and told Mr. Bailer she had info on Harry with the help of the Sheriff. A flash of road trip images and the tall, blue-eyed man made her nostalgic. She hadn't seen him since Harry messed up their world and missed the Sheriff, even though she was the one who pushed him away.

"The Sheriff is a good man," Frankie said softly. "He was a godsend to me and helped me in many different ways."

Frankie looked at her notes and then gave a summary to Mr. Bailer to make sure she got it right.

"Step one, feeling the hurt myself isn't hard for me because I feel the pain of that night every time I visit Debbie in the Forest Hills Care Facility. Step two, deciding to forgive - well, you've convinced me of that with your mom and dad's story. Step three, it's important to me to have a forgiveness talk with Harry. That will make it real for me. If I just say it to myself, it won't be concrete enough. Step four, take care of myself."

Mr. Bailer nodded. "You have it right. Sounds easy, right? When you talk to Harry you will discover deep feelings of forgiveness you don't even know are possible to feel. It will be a cleansing moment for you when you release your anger towards him. You will feel lighter and less weighed down by how hard your life has been. In forgiving him, you will forgive yourself."

He motioned to the children in the park. "You may even find joy in simple things like a playground."

He smiled at her and then pointed to her notepad. "These steps are a giant move forward for you, but it's not the end of the process."

She looked at him quizzically. "What's missing?"

"Do you remember the role my father played in the angry neighbor incident?" Frankie shrugged her shoulders, not quite remembering the details.

"My mother showed forgiveness to the angry neighbor, and then my father showed him what redemption was. And that made a lasting difference. Redemption had the impact that ultimately changed him and helped him restore his life."

Redemption was completely new to Frankie, and she wrote the word in bold letters on her notepad.

"Redemption is about moving beyond the mistakes of the past and working towards a better future. It's about taking responsibility for your actions and making a conscious effort to grow and change."

He went on to explain that redemption often involves making amends for past mistakes and working to improve relationships with others. "It's not always easy," he said. "But the rewards are tremendous. When you work towards redemption, you're not just improving your own life. You're making the world a better place."

Frankie scribbled notes, feeling a sense of hope and purpose.

"Remember," Mr. Bailer said, his voice warm and reassuring. "Forgiveness and redemption go hand in hand. When you forgive others, you allow your spirit to release bad feelings and your soul to experience growth and positive change. When you work towards redemption, you make things right that were wrong in the past and you create the possibility of a better tomorrow."

As they finished their conversation on the way out of the park, Frankie felt a sense of determination and hope. She knew forgiving Harry wouldn't be easy, but she was ready to try this new idea and take the steps towards redemption and a better future for both of them.

She hugged Mr. Bailer, and they said their goodbyes. She

thought he felt a little thin and noticed he looked pale and tired. "Mr. Bailer, are you doing ok? You need sleep, too, don't you?"

He smiled at her and said, "Yes, Frankie, I do. I'm a little worn out myself, but I'll be ok. I can't wait for our next coffee meeting to hear how your journey of forgiveness and redemption is going."

He waved to her when he got to the edge of the park, and she watched him as he reached his car and drove away.

The kids in the park laughed as they played. Frankie sat back down on the park bench and thought of Rocky. Next time she went to the Eastern Shore, she'd take him to a park. She realized she hadn't seen him for a while, and she missed his hugs and laughter.

Plus, all this talk of love reminded her of Professor Todd Burton.

CHAPTER EIGHTEEN

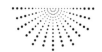

PARIS - THE CITY OF CHOICE

$\mathcal{P}$rofessor Todd Burton ordered a 'bourbon, neat' at the bar as he waited for Frankie to join him in Philly's latest five-star restaurant.

She'd called him several days ago, asking about when he was coming to town. "This weekend, of course," had been his immediate answer.

He missed Frankie and her green eyes and her special brand of quick wit.

Even after five years of their loosely defined relationship, Frankie was still an enigma to Todd. When he met her at the Eastern Shore Community College, she was young and naive.

Watching her enter the restaurant tonight from across the room, he saw a sophisticated, savvy young woman who turned heads as she walked his way.

He stood to greet her with a hug and a kiss on the cheek. She lingered in his hug and smiled warmly at him.

"So happy you came to town. It's been a while and I've missed you." Frankie was always direct and to the point with him and he appreciated it.

"I've missed you, too. Thanks for the invite."

He released her from his arms reluctantly and she ordered a glass of Chardonnay and sat on the bar stool facing him.

"You look marvelous." He loved her sophisticated style and how the choice of a jade jacket with a black sheath dress showcased her eyes.

He caught their reflection in the mirror behind the bar and gestured toward it. "Look at us. The professor and the student have both grown up. We're getting old, Frankie Girl."

Frankie laughed and they relaxed into their conversation, sharing recent developments in their lives. They were sitting knee to knee and Frankie's hand wandered over to Todd's leg and rested there for a moment.

She knew what this did to him and enjoyed how he widened his eyes at the gesture. He moved closer to her and put his hand on hers.

"You know what you're doing to me, don't you?" He growled softly as he saw the teasing look in her eyes.

Frankie smiled and took a sip of Chardonnay without breaking her gaze. She uncrossed her legs and turned toward him, forcing his legs apart on the bar stool as she fit her knees between his. They were face to face and she was slightly flushed as her lips parted in a half smile.

"As I was saying," she kept the conversation going as she heated up the body language. "We have an open house for the Riverfront project in about a month and we're at 60% occupancy. I'm pushing the team to ramp it even higher, but we're getting some push-back on pricing."

Todd reached over and tucked her hair behind her ear on one

side. "You really want to talk business right now?" He wasn't hearing a word she said, only what her body was telling him.

"Of course, I have some exciting news to share with you."

"I can't focus when you do that," Todd said as she crossed her legs directly between his. They both loved the urgent torment they forced on each other, no matter how long it had been since they last saw each other.

Frankie loved that about Todd – his easy-going, low attachment manner cleared the way for them to be lovers without obligation. The arrangement was tantalizing, exciting, and usually spontaneous, but lately, not quite enough to keep her satisfied.

She realized she was looking for more from Todd but had no idea how to ask for it so she kept the flirting game going.

"Just focus on my lips; up here." She reached over and pulled his chin up from where he'd been staring at her legs. "The conversation is up here, for now." She swung around to face the bar and Todd followed her lead.

"As I about to say, Todd, before you got all heated up and lost your focus," continued Frankie with a wry smile. "The good news is we are getting close to closing the sale of the trailer park and I have you to thank for that!"

She leaned over and kissed him on the cheek and then trailed her finger from his chin to his chest and tapped him lightly.

"You are the one who saved the trailer park from complete ruin. So, I owe you one and I'll buy you a fancy dinner tonight." Frankie ran through the details of the final sale and the financial gain that she, her sister, and her brother anticipated if the deal went as planned.

As legal guardian for both siblings, she needed to be cautious about how to safeguard the money when she invested on their behalf.

Todd motioned to the bartender for another round of drinks,

but Frankie pushed her wine glass aside and signaled to the bartender that she was finished for now. She continued explaining her plan for the trailer park sale, and the closing date schedule, and then gave Todd a quick update on Debbie.

"It broke my heart the other night to see her so confused and in so much despair."

Todd had never met Debbie, but he knew the story of their childhood and how the last years had been so hard on her sister. It was evident how much Frankie cared for her sister, and he put his arm around her to comfort her.

"I finally gave in on the meds for Debbie and I hope that gives her some relief without being too sedated. I don't want her to be a Zombie." That was Frankie's fear all along and she had fought the medication for long enough. The doctors would do the right thing for her sister, she hoped.

They fell into silence as Todd sipped his bourbon and Frankie freshened up her lipstick, pulled a tissue out of her purse and dabbed her lips. Then Todd remembered his good news and he turned to Frankie with a broad smile on his face and his eyes brightened.

"I have good news, too, Frankie, and I have you to thank for this news." He reached over and touched her chin and trailed his finger down her throat. She shivered at his touch and laughed lightly and caught his hand and kissed it.

"What's your good news? I can't wait to hear and what do you have to thank me for?"

Todd was ecstatic about the phone call he'd received minutes after his last conversation with Frankie. This was big news for him and an elevation in his career.

"The computer science program I ran at the Community College got so much attention, in part because you were the first female in the project." Todd was so proud of Frankie back then;

she was his star student and was far ahead of the rest of the class.

Frankie nodded and urged him to continue. "The fact that you also quickly mastered programming and coding got everyone's attention and helped put the project on the map."

Todd was beaming at her now, remembering how exciting his time as Frankie's professor had been.

Their long hours together coding simple, then more complex projects created an intimacy between them that was as electric as anything Todd had been a part of.

And, after the project was over, it paved the way for an even more intimate relationship between them.

"So, here's the big news. I was just asked to be the keynote speaker at TECH 2.0 in six months, out in L.A. and I'll be presenting the case study of what we did way back then." Todd was smiling with pure delight at his news and Frankie high-fived him and gave him a big hug.

"That is so cool," she said as she signaled to the bartender that she'd take the check. "Tell me more about the project and how it all turned out."

"Frankie, you ditched us after a year and a half to go to the big city for your real estate career, so you never saw the final success we had. But you did the right thing because you were rocking it. Coding came so easy to you. You were a natural at it."

Todd raised his bourbon glass in a toast to Frankie and she laughed as she raised her empty wine glass. "To us and the great program you helped me build for computer programmers everywhere. And, especially for the girls who want to learn how to code. Not enough of them yet, though."

Todd continued with his success story and Frankie was thrilled for him because this presentation would secure his professor position at MIT and give him even greater opportunities. Professor

Todd had spent so much time with her and had educated her about business and real estate and she was forever grateful to him for that.

She reached over and linked her arm to his. "Todd, I am so happy for you. You truly deserve all the accolades from the audience when you come off that stage. I'll be there in spirit to cheer you on." She smiled brightly and lifted her glass again to toast him. She was swept up in his excitement and loved seeing him so happy.

"Hey, Frankie, why don't you come with me and hear the presentation firsthand? You'll hear the feedback and accolades yourself. You deserve to be on stage, too. Please say you'll come with me." Todd turned to her and took her hands as his excitement overwhelmed them both. He looked at her with anticipation.

Frankie was delighted to be asked to accompany him. They'd never taken a trip during their time together and this would be a big first. And she'd never been to California or L.A. and it was an exciting thought.

"I'd love to go with you, but I'm not sure it's a good idea for me to be at the conference." She frowned slightly as she realized how the audience might view the two of them being together and the inference it might have on Todd's career in academia. Todd's face sobered as he realized she was referring to some of the rumors that swirled around the professor and his student at the small community college.

Frankie didn't want to kill his mood. "How about if we go on a different trip to celebrate after you're back? By then, the trailer park will be sold, and my responsibilities will be lessened, and we can get away for a week."

Frankie realized this was the first time she had asked Todd for any commitment to spend time together in the future. Their time together was usually spontaneous and never a planned trip. She waited to see Todd's reaction; afraid he wouldn't want to commit.

"Great idea," he said, brightening up. "It won't be the same as if you were in the crowd, but I will give you the complete rundown of what happened. What you're saying is true, and I agree that it might be a bit awkward given our relationship."

Frankie's heart swelled at his response, and she realized they had taken a baby step toward giving their relationship more meaning.

She moved closer to Todd, put her arm around him and stroked his thick, dark hair. She wasn't sure if this was Mr. Bailer's idea of a path to love, but for right now it sure felt good.

After drinks at the bar, they were seated in a plush corner booth, secluded behind leafy ferns and leisurely talking their way through dinner. They sat side by side as Frankie gave Todd updates on Rocky, Butch, and the scene on the Eastern Shore.

She hadn't stayed in touch with the Community College crowd like Todd had, but knew the people he talked about and some of the other students who were accompanying him to TECH 2.0.

The computer science project was completed over a year ago and it skyrocketed Todd's career. He was always lavish in his praise of Frankie's quick mastery of programming and coding and sent her every article and paper that he wrote on the pilot program. She was so proud of his work and her part in it and how generous he was in sharing credit for the project's success.

"Frankie Girl," he said as he pushed his empty dinner plate to the other side of the table. "Where do you want to go on our celebration trip? Somewhere exotic?"

Frankie's heart soared at his question. *He is committing to a trip,* she thought to herself. *Baby steps to commitment!*

"Think big, Frankie, what's your dream destination?" Todd smiled and pulled a pen out of his jacket and grabbed a paper napkin from under his wine glass. "Give me your top five dream places to go for a celebration week."

Frankie was caught off guard, but several came to mind immediately. "Ok, number one is the Caribbean Islands, like Aruba or the Dominican Republic. Number two would have to be Hawaii and number three would be Paris."

Then she laughed and reached over to grab the napkin where Todd was writing down her selections and she crossed off one and two and circled Paris. "Yep, that's it. Paris. The city of lights. That's where we'll go!"

Frankie had no idea why she chose Paris but now it seemed like the perfect choice.

She had images of strolling the Parisian streets arm in arm and having coffee at an outdoor cafe. Maybe walks through the galleries and museums each day, and lavish dinners and the theater each night.

"So, we're going to ditch the island theme?" Todd took back the napkin and stuck it in his pocket. "You start planning the trip, lovely lady, while I start planning on some dessert."

Frankie's smile was followed by a deep, throaty laugh from Todd as he moved closer to her and pulled her into his arms. He twirled her hair in his fingers and traced a line down her throat as she felt her body melt into his.

Being with him felt different this time and she knew she was opening to love. She hoped Todd wouldn't be careless with her heart and she was glad they had six months to plan this trip together.

She gave in to his caresses and sensed his breathing quicken as he moved his hand down her back and tightened around her waist. He kissed her cheek and then turned her chin to meet his lips, just as the waiter rounded the corner with the check.

A polite cough got their attention, and they straightened up and laughed as if they'd been caught like kids doing something naughty.

Frankie grabbed her purse to pay the bill. "Tonight's on me, Professor, we're starting the six-month celebration of your big presentation."

Todd nodded his thanks as he moved his hand under the table to find the edge of her dress and started inching it up her thigh. Frankie twisted under his touch and fished out bills from her purse to pay for dinner.

The waiter turned to leave, and Frankie called after him, "Thanks and keep the change."

She turned back to Todd, smacked his hand on her thigh, and with a huge grin said, "Dessert at my place?"

CHAPTER NINETEEN

CONFUSION IN ROCKHALL

*F*rankie drove up and down Main Street in Rockhall several times, crossing through the Franklin and Marshall Streets intersections, looking for a row home on the east side of town.

The address for 109 Franklin Street was scrawled on a scrap of paper handed to her at the neighborhood bar several blocks down.

She'd slipped the bartender a ten-dollar bill in exchange for a tip about where she could find Harry.

It was time to have a chat with the guy who traumatized Debbie six months ago and landed her in the Forest Hills Care Facility.

She finally located the building and slowed down to look at the house. *Not too bad*, she thought, *maybe he's living with a relative.* She thought she'd play detective for a while and scope it out before she made any moves toward Harry.

Besides, she needed time to think before she talked with him. She was nervous herself and didn't want to scare him off.

Frankie and Harry didn't know each other that well. He wasn't a regular at Buck's Bar, just a skinny kid who showed up occasionally. Back then he was a fidgety 21-year-old who wasn't experienced in the art of holding his booze.

The Sheriff had dropped into the bar that dreadful night and told Harry that his dad was dying. Now was the time to visit if he ever wanted to see his dad alive again. Harry and his family were estranged and had no contact with him for years. All they knew was that he was living in a dump somewhere on the Eastern Shore, and if they wanted him to know about his dad, they should contact the local Sheriff.

Frankie figured something snapped in Harry that night. The mixture of his raw emotions and booze must have sent him over the edge.

But why he stumbled over to Debbie's bedroom in the big trailer was still a mystery to Frankie. Her mind ran through a hundred scenarios of what might have raced through Harry's boozy brain that night, but nothing made sense.

Her mind was also fuzzy about how Harry entered the locked trailer that night. She'd checked the door the next day, and it didn't look like there was a forced entry.

Since she'd decided not to press charges against Harry, there had been no crime scene investigation that might have revealed his entry into the big trailer. Had the Sheriff forgotten to lock the door to Debbie's trailer? That seemed impossible since he was so anal about those kinds of details.

Frankie's mind wandered as she surveyed the row home where Harry was supposedly living. It was a plain two-story house with black shingles and a brown door.

The small elevated front porch had a lattice to hide the gap from the ground up to the porch bottom and was adorned with faded plastic roses. Floral curtains were visible through the windows, and as Frankie gazed at the house, she thought she saw movement behind the curtains.

After several moments of checking out the rest of the house and a tiny patch of flowers by the front step, she decided to come back another time.

She started her car, checked her side mirror, and started pulling out when she noticed the front door of 109 Franklin Street opening and an elderly woman exiting with a rug in her arms.

It's Harry's grandmother, she thought. *That makes sense. He's living with her because no one else would take him in.*

Frankie pulled into the street and drove by the house. Harry's grandmother shook the rug slowly, not once looking in Frankie's direction.

Frankie was sure she'd been spotted by the older woman and wanted to investigate further, so she drove around the block and parked her car in the spot she'd vacated. The elderly woman was gone so she watched the house for ten minutes, then decided to carry out her mission.

She headed up to the front door and knocked loudly.

The door opened as far as the interior security chain would allow. "What do you want?" The elderly woman was gruff, and Frankie saw she was expecting a bad encounter.

"I'm a friend of Harry's, and I was told he lives with you. Is he home?" Frankie decided getting to the point would save them both time.

"What do you want with him?"

"I have some news for him about my sister, and I thought it would be important to him." Frankie was trying to keep her tone friendly and non-threatening.

"What kind of news?"

"My sister was hurt a while back, and I thought Harry would want to know that she's ok."

Frankie stepped back to show she wouldn't be forceful with the elderly woman. "Are you his grandmother?" she asked.

"What's it to you?"

"If it's all the same to you, ma'am, I'd like to talk with Harry for just a bit. I'm sure he would want to hear my news."

Frankie thought she'd give this one last try and then walk away. She couldn't tell for sure but felt Harry might be on the other side of the door, listening to the conversation.

"Just tell me the news, and I'll pass it on to him."

"Thank you, ma'am, but I can't do that. It has to come from me personally. I'll come back another time." She smiled slightly, gave the woman a nod, and turned to go back to her car.

Frankie was reaching for the car door handle when she saw Harry coming out of the house. He stood on the porch looking at her, not saying a word.

"Hey Harry, do you have a minute?" She didn't move away from the car but waited for his reply.

"What's the news about your sister?" He didn't move a muscle, just stood there with a blank look on his face.

"I don't want to shout at you from down here on the street. Do you want to come down, or should I come up to the porch?"

Frankie wanted a closer look at Harry to see his condition and if he was possibly high or doing drugs. She wasn't going to talk with him if he was wasted.

Harry moved down the porch steps and over to the front of Frankie's car. "Nice wheels," he said as he leaned against the hood. "What's up with your sister?"

"I want to tell you some things about her, Harry. Would you get in the car, and we can talk?" She motioned to the passenger seat of her Honda Accord and got in the driver's seat.

He stared at Frankie for a minute, then pulled the car door open and joined her.

"Did Debbie die?"

"No, she's not dead. Debbie's foot healed from when I tried to shoot you and accidentally shot her instead."

Frankie had a flashback of the pistol going off in her hand and felt the horror of seeing Debbie's foot blasted and blood gushing everywhere. She shuddered slightly and rubbed her forehead to calm herself.

"Debbie was traumatized that night and had a mental break-down." Frankie turned toward Harry. "She's in a facility outside of Philly and being taken care of, but she'll never be the same."

Harry raised his eyebrows and stared at her. "And that's the good news you want to tell me. You're a hard ass, Frankie. I can't believe you tracked me down to tell me that crap."

Frankie grabbed his arm to keep him in the car. "No, that's not it. There's something else."

Frankie had rehearsed this part of the conversation for months with the help of Mr. Bailer. Harry already knew she was not pressing charges, but she wanted him to understand why.

"Harry, what you did was horrific and cruel. There's no doubt about that, and I'm sure you've relived that night many times."

"No, I haven't. I was drunk." He shrugged and folded his arms tightly. Where this conversation was going was a mystery to him. He respected Frankie as a tough, scrappy girl from Buck's Bar, though, who could hold her own. He decided to hear her out.

"Right, you were drunk. Which is no excuse for what you did. You were out of your mind with the news of your father, is that why you did it?"

"I have no idea. I told you I was drunk." He wasn't going to make this easy for Frankie.

"Here's what I think." Frankie kept her tone neutral and looked up at his grandmother's house. "You're here with your grandmother because you have nowhere else to go. You don't have a job, no money, and no future. Do I have that right?"

Harry nodded and looked over at Frankie with a flicker of interest in his eyes.

"I'd like to help you change that."

Harry's eyes shifted back and forth from Frankie to his grandmother's house and back to Frankie. He had a look of suspicion on his face. "Why would you do that after what I did to Debbie? Are you messed up or trying to trick me?"

"Not trying to trick you, and I'm not messed up. I've learned a few things about life, Harry, and I no longer want to mess things up for people. I want to help people. I want to make up for all the crap I've done and how I've hurt people. And you're the best one for me to start with."

Frankie looked at Harry and saw the disbelief in his eyes.

She continued, "I just want to clean up stuff in my life and want the same for you. Mr. Bailer is a man I met when I visited Butch in jail, and he's helping me look at life differently. He talks about a path to love, which I'm learning about, and he suggested I start by forgiving you."

She took a deep breath and released her fear of Harry's reaction. She didn't need an answer today, and this small step was a good beginning for both of them.

"You can think about it. I'm sure you think I'm trying to pull something over on you, but I'm not. Call me if I can help." She handed him a small piece of paper with her phone number.

She reached into her backpack. "Mr. Bailer wanted me to give this to you, too. He gives them out at the prison." She handed Harry a small pamphlet, and he jammed both papers into his hoodie pocket.

"Little Butchie is in jail?"

She nodded. "Yeah, he got stupid drunk one night and was

involved in an armed robbery. Ten years with early parole for good behavior."

"Too bad for him."

Harry was confused as he silently got out of the car.

This was the last thing he expected to happen when his grandmother told him someone was scoping out the house.

He stood on the sidewalk as Frankie pulled away and then he headed to the bar. He needed a drink to help him figure out this unexpected incident.

CHAPTER TWENTY

DEAR FRANKIE

*P*hilly workdays were filled with meetings, paperwork, and more meetings. She loved the fast pace and the heavy workload Dubie placed on her. Happy hour and a light dinner with friends capped off the night, usually followed by a chat with Todd Burton or Tesh.

On a quiet evening, it was a paperback and a glass of wine. The days flowed into weeks, then months and Frankie's life settled into a normal routine. Something she never had before.

But normal didn't stick around too long and she knew it was gone when she checked her mailbox one morning and found a letter from Tesh.

Dear Frankie,

I fall into bed at night exhausted, knowing the next day I'll do it all over again. I love Rocky as my child, and I wouldn't give back the time I've had with him since he was born.

After Rocky's birth, you and I both came to the same conclusion that Debbie couldn't parent a child properly. You were back here on the weekends, but your work took you to Philly during the week, so you couldn't care for him either. Butch got himself locked up so that was one less person you had to take care of, but you did the right thing and went to visit him regularly.

When you asked us to care for Rocky, we said yes immediately. We never doubted our decision and every night we thanked God for having this sweet little soul in our home.

You are a hard worker with a heart of gold, and I love you in so many ways. Like a daughter, because I'd do anything for you. Like a sister, because you're like next of kin to me. And like a best friend, because we've weathered so many storms and beaten back many hard times together.

I saw you lose your Mama and stay strong for the rest of the family. You took her place at the bar and worked evening shifts when you should have been a carefree teenager doing homework and being a cheerleader.

Debbie would have been neglected by any other sister, but you took the best care of her possible. And you're still taking care of her.

I can't say I understand what happened between you and your father and Larry O that night when the trailer exploded, and the fire's escalation took your father's life. The situation knocked you down hard and I wish I had been more supportive.

You stood back up to take care of Larry O's justice and suffered public shame and humiliation to do the right thing by not letting Debbie take the stand and letting him take a plea deal.

Rocky loves you so much and lights up when you walk in the door. Auntie Frankie is his favorite. He loves it when your car pulls up to the house and goes crazy wild when he knows you're visiting.

Alfred and I knew this day would come. We've known since we agreed to take Rocky into our home and hearts and love him like our own son. We were never able to have children, so Rocky filled that void and we are forever grateful to you and Debbie for sharing him with us.

But now, we've been fortunate to have little Ricky join our family. I can't wait for you to meet him. He and Rocky are best buds and hopefully will be lifelong friends. Like brothers, that's our prayer.

God bless little Ricky's heart; he's been through so much in his young life that we're amazed at how he's thriving. He called me Mama yesterday for the first time and it broke my heart and made me smile all at the same time.

However, we have concerns as Rocky nears first grade. We fear he'll need more than we can give him. Not in terms of food, shelter, or love, but we think he needs to be with a family that looks like him and is his blood relation.

Due to the circumstances, we do not have legal guardianship and will have difficulty doing the school registration and paperwork that comes with public education.

It's a touchy subject to talk about race regarding Rocky and us, because we love him like family, but we have to be real about it for his sake. The few times I've taken him to the grocery store or taken him and Ricky for ice cream, people stare at us with looks that are more than just curious.

It's a small town here on the Eastern Shore, and the townspeople have long memories involving the trailer park.

I'm sure you understand he'll be under scrutiny at school due to the notoriety of Larry O's trial and its surprise conclusion. You were so brave to keep Debbie off the stand and push for Larry O's plea bargain. No one understood it except you and me. Debbie would never have survived the cross-examination. It would have been cruel beyond words to subject her to public humiliation.

This is a hard letter to write, Frankie, because we have a long history together and I never dreamed I would be writing this letter.

The timing might seem odd to you since you and the Professor are headed off to Paris, but I wanted to give you time to think about this matter. Rocky's school registration will be required several months after you're back and we need to make plans.

Please don't take this the wrong way and think I'm abandoning

*Rocky. Quite the opposite, I have his best interest in both of our minds as
we talk about options, although I think there's only one real option.*

*That option is for Rocky to be with you in Philadelphia, as his legal
mother. It's the answer that keeps coming back to us when Alfred and I
pray about it. It won't be easy, but you would be the one person in the
world who loves him like no other.*

*Think about it, Frankie, and call me if you want before you leave for
Paris. Otherwise, I'll wait to hear back when you and the Professor
return.*

Traveling mercies and have fun. He seems like a nice man.

Love,

Tesh

Frankie stared at the letter and reread it several times as she
sipped coffee before getting dressed for her Saturday morning
visit to Butch in jail.

She folded the letter, put it back in the envelope and slipped it
into her purse. A million questions raced through her mind, and
she was overwhelmed by the idea of taking care of a five-year-
old boy.

How could she add one more thing to her schedule, she wondered.

And, with Paris just around the corner, she had hoped to have a
carefree time with no worries at all. Now, Tesh's requests and
Rocky's future weighed heavily on her mind.

It was Saturday morning and after Frankie stopped by
the jail to visit her brother Butch, she headed over to
the diner where she and Mr. Bailer frequently met. His car wasn't
parked in his usual spot when she pulled into the parking lot so
she fished out a lipstick from her purse and applied it to her lips,
double-checking in the mirror to make sure everything looked

fine. *Not too fine,* she thought to herself. *No need to be fancy for Mr. Bailer, after all.*

She decided to go into the diner and start with a cup of coffee and was surprised that Mr. Bailer was at their regular booth in the corner.

"Mr. Bailer, where's your car? I didn't see you in your usual spot" Frankie slid into the booth and saw he was drinking his preferred cup of tea. "How are you?"

"Good to be with you, Frankie Girl." Mr. Bailer put sugar into his tea. "I got here early and my spot was taken, so I'd thought I'd have some tea before you arrived. How's your brother?"

"He's doing well and he's looking forward to a hearing coming up in a month or two. He's hoping for early release for good behavior."

She leaned in toward him and spoke in a hushed voice. "I'm sure you can't do this, but if you could, would you say a good word at the jail on his behalf?"

She took a sip from the coffee cup the waitress brought over when she entered the diner. "I've learned so much about forgiveness and redemption from you in our breakfast meetings and I'd love for Butch to have a second chance."

Mr. Bailer smiled at her. "He deserves a second chance, for sure. You will help him with that." Frankie nodded, thinking of the challenges her younger brother had throughout his life.

She suddenly brightened, remembering to tell Mr. Bailer about her upcoming trip to Paris. She pulled out her itinerary from her purse and traced the trip highlights on the map she brought to show him. She was animated and excited to share the details of the many excursions she and the Professor had planned.

"So excited for you, Frankie, and I'll miss you when you're gone. I'll be out of commission for a few weeks myself but nothing as exciting as what you're doing." He busied himself with his tea bag as Frankie noticed a slight quiver in his lips.

"Everything ok?" Concern edged into her voice.

"My systems seem to be gumming up," he said, attempting to keep the conversation light. "I've had a few tests done and I'm scheduled for an operation in two weeks."

Frankie sucked in her breath and reached over to touch his hand. "Mr. Bailer, I hope you'll be ok. I'm so sorry you're not feeling well. Can I come visit you when I'm back from Paris?"

He nodded and pushed his plate away from him across the table. "My mother used to make the best pancakes, but I don't seem to be able to stomach much food anymore. I've been thinking of her a lot lately. My brothers and sisters always said I was a lot like her."

Frankie smiled and patted his hand before she released it. "You are the kindest person I have ever met. You changed my life and others' as well. How else would I have been able to forgive Harry and his assault on my sister? That was major."

"How is Harry, and your sister, too? Update me on everyone. Including the little one. What's his name again?"

Frankie's face turned serious at the thought of Rocky. She told Mr. Bailer about the letter she'd just received from Tesh and how confused and conflicted she was by the request to raise Debbie's child, Rocky.

"I understand Tesh's situation," Frankie said as she poured herself another cup of coffee. "I want to do the right thing, but it is so overwhelming to think about my job, my responsibilities with Debbie and Butch, my trip to Paris and my blooming love life." She smiled wryly at the thought of the professor.

"I have to thank you for this trip to Paris, you know." She tapped his hand for emphasis. "You planted the seed to start this path to love and you gave me the courage to ask for more from the professor. It's been almost six months since you and I practiced my little speech, and I had the guts to ask him to go on a trip with me. I was so excited about this trip, but now I have to think about Rocky and how to respond to Tesh. I hope I don't ruin it for the Professor."

Mr. Bailer looked at Frankie with love in his eyes. "You have the answer about Rocky deep in your heart, Frankie. The path to love is not just for lovers. It's for love of all kinds. Every kind of love opens up your heart and increases your capacity to feel deep empathy for others. Do you sense that since you've been working on forgiveness and redemption?"

Frankie nodded and a rush of gratitude for the man across the diner table ran through her. She knew the answer to Tesh's request.

There was never any doubt she would have Rocky at some point. It just was earlier than expected and her life was still in transition.

The sale of the trailer park wasn't completed yet. Debbie was adjusting to her new meds and beginning to stabilize but still had occasional episodes of utter despair and sadness.

Frankie's job was exciting and demanding, but so busy she was wrapped up in work 24/7.

"How can I fit the care of a super active little boy into my life?" She gave Mr. Bailer a questioning look. "Is the path to love a superhighway where you drive at top speed all your life?"

Mr. Bailer chuckled. "The path to love is more like a winding road up the mountain. It's not an easy path, but the road will continue to call you because there's joy and peace at each milestone. The views are beautiful, and when you stop to look at the view, your heart will be filled like never before."

"That's a big promise."

"It is, Frankie, and it's a big reward."

"What's your reward, Mr. Bailer? Where do you find your joy?" Frankie was testing him out on his big promise of the path to love.

"That's a good question and not an easy one to answer." Mr. Bailer looked down as he grabbed a napkin to wipe his mouth.

"These days my reward and my joy come from simple things. From talking with the inmates at Butch's jail. Being with my children and watching my grandchildren play with the farm animals. And, yesterday, helping a calf being born. I get a lot of joy from our meetings, too."

He suddenly teared up and wiped his eyes.

"What's wrong with me these days, Frankie Girl, I'm emotional so much of the time. I didn't mean to get sappy on you."

Frankie was moved to tears herself as she began to realize there was more to Mr. Bailer's tears than just this moment. The gravity of his health situation hit her hard.

"This operation is serious, isn't it?" she asked with a catch in her voice, not wanting to hear the answer.

"Yes, it is. The doctor says I have pancreatic cancer, but they're hopeful this operation will help them clean it out of my system. That's my prayer, that the operation is successful, and I can continue to bring joy and hope to other people. Just think, Frankie, when I think about what you've done with Harry, Butch, Debbie and others makes my heart burst. That's plenty of joy for me."

Tears were sliding down Frankie's cheeks and the lump in her throat choked off her words. She was afraid to ask more questions about his health.

The thought of losing the friend who had changed her life broke her heart. His talk of a path to love changed her life forever. She wiped her cheeks and gripped his hand.

"Don't cry too much for me," he continued as he cupped his hand over hers. "I'll be out of the hospital before you're back from Paris and you can bring me some chocolates or whatever the best sweets are from France. You might remember that I have a sweet tooth". He reached into his pocket and pulled out two Peppermint Patties and pushed them over to her.

She smiled through her tears and promised with a nod of her head. Her heart was heavy, and she paused to take a sip of coffee. "I'll come visit you as soon as we're back. I will think of you every day and send good wishes to you from Paris. I wish I could do more."

"Thanks, Frankie Girl, but it's up to the doctors now."

"Mr. Bailer, I'm going to call Tesh as soon as I'm home. You've helped me decide what to do. I'll tell her I will bring Rocky to live with me. I will adopt him as my son. He will be on my path to love." More tears slid down her cheeks and she moved across the booth to sit beside Mr. Bailer. She put her arms around him and laid her cheek on his shoulder.

"Does it always hurt on the path to love?"

"Many times, it does," he said with a sigh. "There are many hard times on the path to love, for sure. Sometimes it doesn't feel like it's worth it. A lot of times I questioned what I thought was true about forgiveness and redemption. I guess I couldn't give up after I started seeing how it changed people's lives."

"Like your neighbor, the farmer who hated your dad at first?"

"Yes, exactly like that. Someday you'll tell someone about the path to love and you'll tell them about Harry, and how you forgave him and helped him change his life. Forgiveness and Redemption. It's life's best medicine."

"That's true about forgiveness and redemption, Mr. Bailer, but before I tell them about Harry, I'll tell them about you. I'll tell them about Mr. Bailer and how he changed my life. Then I'll tell them Harry's story."

On the way back to her apartment on Rittenhouse Square, she was on a rollercoaster of emotions from the day.

Her trip to Paris with the professor gave her excitement and anticipation.

Tesh's letter had filled her with anxiety, but her decision to raise Rocky as her own gave her joy and peace.

Mr. Bailer's upcoming operation filled her with concern and a feeling of helplessness. There was turmoil and joy at the same time.

This feels like a rocky road, not a path to love, she thought to herself. *Am I strong enough to walk this path, Mama? Will you walk with me?*

*S*ix months of planning, replanning, a few fights here and there and Frankie and the professor were packed and ready to fly to Paris.

Pre-flight jitters were making Frankie jumpy, and the professor suggested they go out for a drink before they settled in for the evening.

Their mid-morning flight allowed for a reasonable start to the morning and Frankie was happy for a chance to relax before she checked her suitcases one last time. Her passport and their itinerary were stashed in a special purse she'd purchased just for the trip.

Frankie and Todd walked hand in hand across Rittenhouse Square and found a seat at the bar of their favorite restaurant. They chatted about the trip and the details of each day's activities.

Frankie was excited to tour the ancient architecture and historic landmarks and the Professor had connected with several of his MIT alums who were living in Paris. They were going to have a meetup and introduce Todd to the tech scene in France.

Frankie relaxed with the first glass of wine and then suggested they drink champagne.

"What are we celebrating?" Todd motioned the bartender over and placed an order.

"We have two things to celebrate tonight."

Frankie pointed to the mirror behind the bar. "Do you remember when we were here six months ago, and you told me to look in the mirror and that we weren't the student and the professor anymore? Then, later, you told me about the TECH 2.0 conference and asked me to go with you?"

Todd nodded and smiled at Frankie; that night was etched in his brain.

Six months ago, on that night, he'd agreed to go to Paris with her. It was an unusual commitment for him to make. He liked to keep things light and easy in his female relationships, and Frankie hadn't asked for anything from him before that night. So, when she asked him to go to Paris with him, he didn't hesitate at all.

Since that night there had been a shift in the energy between them.

His commitment to her had deepened and their time together reinforced what he already knew about Frankie's bright mind.

What he noticed more now, though, was her kindness and compassion and how she took care of everyone around her. She was letting her guard down, and the walls around her heart were softening.

A wave of emotion washed over him, a feeling of wanting to protect her and take care of her.

It was a new feeling for the MIT playboy, as his colleagues called him. But they had never met Frankie and had no clue how meaningful a deeper relationship could be. He was clearly falling for her, and he couldn't stop now.

He put his arm around her and pulled her closer while they waited for the champagne.

"The conference was great, and everyone was impressed by your advanced projects. As they should be. But we've already celebrated that, Frankie Girl. What else are we celebrating?"

Her green eyes were bright and dazzled him with their intensity. She leaned in against him and softly traced her finger from his ear down his chin to his chest. "Do you know that it's only 18 inches from your head to your heart?"

She tapped him on his chest several times as Todd nodded, wondering where Frankie was going with this question and wishing she wouldn't have stopped at his chest.

"There's one part of my life I haven't told you about, Todd, and I think it's time to do that before we leave for Paris. I'm not sure I'll do a good job of explaining this, but if I do it right, we'll have a lot to celebrate."

The champagne arrived and Todd was relieved that he could pause a minute and calm himself. He was surprised and a little unsettled at Frankie's comment but waited for the bartender to fill their glasses before raising his glass.

"Cheers, I think, but not quite yet?"

She smiled and took his hand. "No need for concern, Todd, what I have to say is all good. It's just different for me to talk to anyone about it. But, now that we've made more of a commitment to each other, I feel I need to tell you about this."

Frankie took a deep breath. She could tell from Todd's face he was uncertain about what she was going to say and was bracing himself for not-so-good news. To put his mind at ease, she reached over and put her hand on his arm.

"I've been visiting my brother Butch since he was sent to jail a few years ago. I think you were back at MIT the summer that all went down. He was part of a robbery and says he was handed the gun just as the police came in. Not sure what the real story is but he got sentenced as a minor because of the gun."

Todd nodded as he had heard bits and pieces of Butch's story. He'd never met the kid, but he knew the Taylor children's childhood was filled with hard times, and he could understand that Frankie's brother might have gotten caught up in a robbery and taken the hit for the gun.

"One day when I was visiting Butch, I saw an older man visiting the prison who I remembered from when we were kids. His name is Mr. Bailer and he used to pick us up on Sunday mornings at the trailer park and take us to church in a big yellow school bus."

Frankie went on to describe the little church by the lake and the church kids, and then she stopped.

Her eyes welled up and she took a sip from her champagne glass.

"What's wrong, Frankie? Tell me the rest of what you want me to understand. What's moving you so deeply?"

"The day I saw Mr. Bailer at the prison, I remembered how kind and gentle he was and I wanted to talk with him but I was afraid I wouldn't catch him on the way out. Butch said he came to the prison some Saturdays to give the prisoners Bibles so on my next visit I asked the security guard about him. She told me he was already visiting prisoners and passing out Bibles in the jail but that he only ever stayed for an hour. I waited until he was leaving and introduced myself."

Frankie wiped her eyes and remembered how she ambushed Mr. Bailer in the parking lot.

"We started having breakfast after our jail visits and chat about things over coffee. There's never been anyone else like him in my life, and he has slowly, over time, and despite my resistance, showed me a new way to think about everything."

"Everything? Like what, everything?" Todd was intrigued but needed to hear some specifics.

"Mr. Bailer talks about a path to love. I thought he was going to push church and the Bible on me, but he knew a better way to approach me to hear him out. He asked me lots of questions about my life, what I wanted, what made me happy, what made me sad. Questions like that. And then he listened. No one has ever cared more about what I said than Mr. Bailer."

Todd noticed Frankie's tone of voice changed when she talked of Mr. Bailer. Her voice relaxed with respect, admiration, and love. Her face softened as she continued.

"I fought the path to love for a long time until Mr. Bailer explained forgiveness and redemption and told me about several incidents in his life that convinced me it was worth a try."

Frankie's confidence grew as she continued telling Todd about Mr. Bailer. She was relieved that her fear of Todd being dismissive was unfounded and his genuine interest showed in his eyes.

"The first forgiveness was the one I gave to myself. I've had a very dark secret for a long time, never told anyone. But Mr. Bailer's stories of love and forgiveness created a longing in me, and I was exhausted from everything that happened in my life that was so wrong."

"Frankie, you weren't responsible for all those horrible situations. What happened to your father and your sister was not your fault. You're clear about that, right?"

Todd was concerned that Mr. Bailer was putting guilt on Frankie that she didn't deserve.

"You're right, Todd, that's not what I needed to forgive myself for. Mr. Bailer said that forgiveness starts inside us first, and then can go out to others. The day I broke down and told him my darkest secret was the day things started to change. He didn't judge me at all. He didn't flinch when I mumbled my way through it.

"He looked at me with the kindest eyes and when I finished crying, he handed me his cloth hanky. When I pulled myself together, I was so relieved and light, like a heavy wet blanket had been taken off me and I could finally breathe again."

Frankie sighed, remembering the day she thought Mr. Bailer might reject and condemn her. But just the opposite happened. He helped her see her darkest secret came from a place of survival, from an instinctive, natural response any human being would have.

"After forgiveness, he taught me about redemption, which is the next step on the path to love. It's taking action to make things right. That's when I decided to find Harry to forgive him and help him find redemption. That experience had so much impact on me and totally freaked him out!"

Frankie laughed, remembering the look of bewilderment on Harry's face the day she found him at his grandmother's house in Rockhall.

Todd was listening intently, swirling the champagne in the fluted glass, taking everything in. He'd never heard Frankie refer to a deep dark secret and it was evident she wasn't ready to share that part of the story.

"Here's what I want to celebrate, Todd, and why I told you about Mr. Bailer. I also told him about you." She suddenly felt very shy and glanced over at him to gauge his reaction.

"You told him about me? How so?"

"I told him I wanted more from you but wasn't sure how to ask or even if I had the right to want more with you."

"What did Mr. Bailer say?"

"He said there were many ways to love someone, and that romance was one way. If I was serious about wanting more from you, I should decide what I want and ask for it. He and I practiced for an hour one morning after breakfast. We left the diner and walked to a park, and I practiced what I was going to say to you."

Frankie's face turned bright red.

263

"So embarrassing and silly when I think about it now."

"Now it's all making sense." Todd laughed out loud. "I invited you to the conference in L.A., but you said no. Then you asked me to go to Paris with you instead. You took advantage of an opening I gave you to ask me for more of a commitment. What an opportunity I gave you!"

Frankie nodded vigorously, they both laughed and then clinked their champagne glasses.

"Cheers to Mr. Bailer's path to love," Todd murmured as he kissed Frankie's cheek. "There's more to this story, I'm sure, and I'm happy we have time in Paris so you can tell me everything."

"Yes, Todd, I have so much to tell you. Like how happy I am we're going to Paris."

He pulled her to him, their bodies both responding to the discovery of each other's hearts.

"Remember the distance from your head to your heart?"

She nodded and her eyes sparkled at his comment as she melted into his arms. Todd hadn't rejected her revelation of the path to love, he seemed to understand and embrace it.

"Let's pay the bartender's bill and go back to your apartment and start exploring the space between your head and your heart. Let's explore the path to love."

He chuckled as she swatted him on the arm.

"It's not really like that, Todd, but I like your interpretation for tonight."

She waited for Todd to pay the bill and thought to herself, *"Thanks Mr. Bailer, please, please, please don't be sick. Please have a successful operation."*

She shivered slightly and wrapped her coat tightly around her. She'd tell Todd the rest of the story when they got to Paris. For now, she was happy to be on the path to love with the professor.

*T*hey walked through the park to the other side of Rittenhouse Square to Frankie's apartment building. As they walked through the glass revolving doors, a movement at the far side of the lobby caught her attention and she gasped when she looked over and saw Larry O.

Her hand flew to her mouth to muffle a scream and she grabbed Todd's arm tightly.

Larry O stared at her for a minute. "I figured you'd be back eventually, Frankie. I've been wanting to talk with you." He looked at the professor and said with exaggerated politeness, "Sir, I don't mean to interrupt your evening, but can you give us a minute?"

Frankie held on to Todd's arm. "No, Larry O, he's not leaving. You can say what you need to say in front of him. What are you doing here? You promised you'd leave me alone. That was part of the plea bargain."

Larry O nodded and sat down on a chair in the lobby area. "This is a mighty fine place you live in, Frankie. You've done well."

He motioned to the security guard at the far end of the lobby who was watching closely, "Your security dude didn't want me to wait, but I said we're related and so he said I could wait for a half hour. Lucky for me you got here now because my time is just about up."

"We're not related, and your time is up." Frankie moved to the back of the chair across from where Larry O was seated.

"I'll give you ten minutes to say your piece and then the security guard is going to escort you out if you don't leave of your own free will. I'm listening. The clock's ticking."

Frankie tapped on her watch and noted the time before she sat down across from Larry O. Todd moved behind her and stayed standing, watching a scene unfold that he knew nothing about.

More of Frankie's past is coming to haunt her, he thought. *We need to get to Paris and get her out of this town.*

Larry O calmly surveyed the couple and noted how protective Frankie's date was.

He'd never met the professor in person, but back on the Eastern Shore, the professor was known around town for his computer science course. The man looked like someone he could easily take in a fight, but then Larry O remembered seeing the professor enter a karate studio one day. He wasn't sure what that would mean in a physical brawl. Tonight was not the night to find out.

He shifted his focus to Frankie.

"I'm not here to bother you, Frankie, I'm not here to do you any harm. I'm going to keep the deal we made several years ago." He settled back in the lobby chair. "I just want to know where my baby is."

Frankie's world went into slow motion as she considered what Larry O was asking.

Did he mean his son, Rocky? Or was he referring to her sister Debbie? What manipulation was Larry O trying to pull over on her this time?

She gripped the sides of the chair to steady her nerves and collect her thoughts.

"Larry O, tell me what you're up to. What is it exactly you're here for? What do you need?"

"Like I said, where is my baby?" He moved forward in his chair and Frankie's knuckles went white.

"Your baby, as you call my sister Debbie, is in a facility, being taken care of by professionals because she can no longer properly care for herself."

Frankie stared at Larry O, searching his face to see if she had noted the right 'baby' he was asking about.

"When did that happen?" Larry O returned her stare.

"When we made our plea bargain deal and the judge let you off, things were ok for a while. But later, Debbie was almost sexually assaulted, and she had a breakdown that eventually put her in a facility."

Larry O turned away from Frankie's continued stare and her harsh voice.

"What happened to the baby?"

"Adopted." Frankie hoped he didn't hear the quiver in her voice. She glanced at Todd for reassurance.

"A boy?"

"Yes. We named him Rocky, just like you asked."

Larry O groaned and dropped his head. Frankie didn't expect his reaction and her palms were sweaty as her heart began to race. "He's in good hands, Larry O. It's for the best."

"Do you have a picture of him?"

"No, I don't, but he has his mother's big brown eyes and your dark black hair."

She stood up and stepped back beside Todd. "I think it's time to go, Larry O, unless there's something else you need from me."

"Thanks, Frankie, I won't bother you again. I'll keep my end of the deal. You kept me out of jail with the plea bargain, and that means a lot to me."

He got up from the chair and held his hand out to Frankie. "Best not to mention my name to Debbie. I do miss her."

Frankie shook Larry O's hand and took a deep breath.

"Larry O, I wish you all the best. I appreciate you honoring your part of the deal. We did the right thing for everyone when we came to an agreement. Go live your life in peace.

"Everything is cleared up and I trust you are sincere when you say you will keep your word. Your son will grow up in a loving home and Debbie is well taken care of. The past is over. We all have new lives now."

Larry O glanced at Todd and nodded politely. "Hope I didn't ruin your evening, sir. My time's up. Bye, Frankie. I always admired your spunk. You're a smart girl."

Frankie, Todd, and the Security Guard watched as Larry exited the revolving door. Frankie heard the soft click of the lock securing the door in place and heaved a sigh of relief.

She gave a thumbs up to the Security Guard, walked over to the elevator and punched the UP button.

She leaned into Todd as they waited silently. He wrapped his arms around her and held her tightly as tears slid down her cheeks.

As the elevator whisked them up to the 22nd floor he tilted her chin up and wiped away the tears. "Tomorrow we'll be in Paris, my dear Frankie. We'll be far away from all of this, and you can finally take a deep breath and relax."

Frankie's thoughts were on Larry O, and she wished she could have helped him.

Long before everything went crazy at the trailer park, he had covered her father's debt at the bank. Even though she had made several deals with the devil, Larry O's money had kept the bar afloat at a crucial time.

"Thanks for being here, Todd. You helped me stay calm. I feel bad for Larry O, but I didn't expect him to take the news about Rocky like he did."

She wasn't ready to give Todd the latest news about Rocky yet, but she didn't want to mislead him either. Her decision to adopt Rocky affected them both and Todd deserved to get a clear picture of everything about the situation.

She would tell him as soon as they settled in at their suite in Paris.

She lightened up when her focus turned to their trip tomorrow. "Let's have a glass of wine and then finish packing," she said as she swung open her apartment door. The view of the city at night was spectacular and she never grew tired of the lights that gleamed in her 180-degree view.

"Sure thing." Todd went to the wine cabinet and pulled out a bottle of Merlot. "My bag is packed except for what I need tonight, so take your time and relax. That was an intense conversation."

They settled into comfortable positions side by side on the sofa. "Todd, you are a very patient man and I love that part of you. I could feel your presence behind me downstairs and I knew you had my back in case Larry O would have tried to pull something."

"He was cocky at the beginning, but by the end he looked more like a wounded animal."

Frankie nodded and her tension began to dissolve with her first sip of wine. "Rocky's situation is on the list for discussion in Paris. Along with more of Mr. Bailer's path to love." She smiled at him. He took her wine glass and set both of their glasses on the coffee table.

"Let me massage your neck, Frankie, and help you loosen up and relax. Let's enjoy the rest of the evening and you can finish packing in the morning. Breathe deeply, Frankie Girl, we are headed to Paris, the city of lights and love."

"Ahh, that feels so good," murmured Frankie. "I'm already imagining the city lights and sidewalk cafes and walking through the streets hand in hand with you. The path to love is definitely in Paris. But let's take the first step right here."

Todd smiled and pulled her into his arms. He kissed her gently as the energy of love began to flow through them both. *Mr. Bailer,* Frankie thought, *the path to love is where I want to be, forever.*

BOOK CLUB DISCUSSION STARTERS

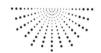

1. In Saturday Night at the Trailer Park Frankie Girl comes of age. How would you describe her journey so far? What was her before and after – the key points where she pivoted in her thoughts and feelings. What prompted her changes?

2. Sheriff Allen and Professor Todd Burton are both attracted to Frankie immediately. What characteristics does Frankie have that are so magnetic to these two men and to the other people who she crosses paths with – Tesh, Mrs. Balmer, Ms. Davis at the Community College.

3. Redemption is a key theme in the Frankie story. How would you describe its impact in her life? Has there been any redemption in your life or in anyone you know?

4. How would you describe Mr. Bailer and his beliefs? How is he able to convince Frankie to embrace 'the path to love?'

---

5. The book covers the heavy, dark subject of 'date nights' that Debbie endured. How could the situation Buck created have been handled differently? Could Frankie or Tesh have done anything to prevent or expose what was going on? What might have been the circumstances if they had acted? Have you ever been aware of a situation like this but didn't know what to do? Do you have thoughts or regrets about that situation in retrospect?

6. Frankie and Larry O have an unusual relationship – maybe not even a relationship, but an unexpected crossing in their lives. How would you describe Larry O, and what are your thoughts about the deal that Frankie initially struck with him regarding her father's banking problems?

7. Larry O seems to be taken with Debbie at times, but at other times he is cruel and mean to Debbie, according to Frankie. What do you think is Larry O's real intent with Debbie? Is there any sincerity in his "love" for Debbie?

8. Do you think Larry O should have gone to jail for arson and murder regarding the fire incident in the date night trailer?

9. There are several references to Frankie's deep, dark secret that she only shared with Mr. Bailer. She thought he would judge her harshly for it, but he didn't. What do you think her secret might be?

10. Tesh is a friend of the Taylor family and has a deep love for Frankie, in particular. She gives easily and endlessly for their welfare, even taking care of Rocky for several years. What advice would you give Tesh regarding the date night situation and the Taylor family in general?

11. Overall, which of the characters do you most identify with? If you could give a message to Frankie, what would you say?

ACKNOWLEDGEMENTS

To my father and mother for their beliefs and faith, a big Thanks. This story wouldn't exist if my father hadn't had his deep desire to bring souls to the kingdom.

To my siblings and their spouses, you've picked up where Mom and Dad left off in this 'long line of love.'

To my husband, Dwight, now you understand what I was doing at the computer until midnight! And thanks for your biggest endorsement ever in reading Book #1 and saying you can't wait to read the next one. I will cherish that forever.

To my kids, Gabe and Kate, I know I failed to answer some calls and I did miss some texts, but you know I love you to the moon and back. And you're both my favorites.

To my niece, Cali Radcliff, a bestselling author in her own right, who inspired me, pushed me, and kept me going forward with ideas, plot twists, and clarifying insights – your help is so much appreciated.

Behind every good book is a fabulous editor and I have Katherine Graham to thank for walking along side me on this journey with her guiding hand and insightful recommendations. Her early encouragement kept me going and gave me confidence that there was real merit in how I wrote Frankie's story.

To those whose paths I crossed while writing this book – thanks for answering the millions of questions I asked, smoothing out the tech issues I encountered, and inviting me into the author community. You are all friendly word soldiers on this sometimes-solitary journey. Much appreciated.

And to the Gideons International organization, thank you for fulfilling your mission of spreading the Good Word around the world. Reader, if you want to donate, click on this link: www.gideons.org/donate Tell them Frankie Girl sent you!

ABOUT THE AUTHOR

Writing in the genres of Modern Fiction, Family Drama, and Christian Fiction, Kae Wagner is a seasoned storyteller weaving love and redemption into page-turning tales. Her fast-paced, emotionally charged stories will both break your heart and fill your soul with hope.

Kae Wagner's characters face challenges that highlight the multifaceted nature of the human spirit, providing readers with profound insights into the enduring qualities of resilience and redemption, which are at the core of the human experience.

When not in fiction writing mode, she works with C-Suite Executives and Leaders as an executive coach, writing business books and creating leadership development courses.

When not immersed in words, she slips away for her guilty pleasure of riding quarter horses in the mountains of Wyoming.

To learn more about Kae Wagner's upcoming books and receive a gift of the Prologue to the Frankie Girl Series: *Little Scrap: The Fighter*, visit wwww.KaeWagner.com

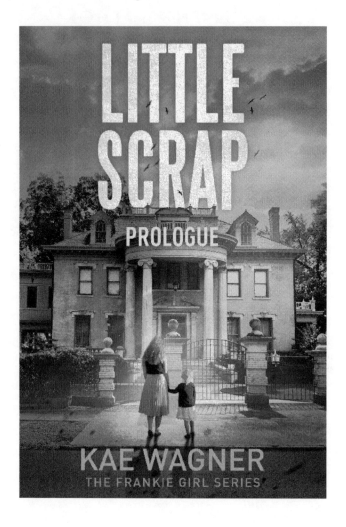

Made in the USA
Middletown, DE
22 August 2024

59035877R00170